LEVERAGE
THE ZOO JOB

KEITH R. A. DeCANDIDO

BERKLEY BOULEVARD BOOKS, NEW YORK

THE BERKLEY PUBLISHING GROUP
Published by the Penguin Group
Penguin Group (USA) Inc.
375 Hudson Street, New York, New York 10014, USA

USA / Canada / UK / Ireland / Australia / New Zealand / India / South Africa / China

Penguin Books Ltd., Registered Offices: 80 Strand, London WC2R 0RL, England
For more information about the Penguin Group, visit penguin.com

THE ZOO JOB

A Berkley Boulevard Book / published by arrangement with
Leverage Holdings, Inc. and Keith DeCandido

PUBLISHING HISTORY
Berkley Boulevard mass-market edition / March 2013

For information, address: The Berkley Publishing Group
a division of Penguin Group (USA) Inc.
375 Hudson Street, New York 10014

ISBN: 978-0-425-25384-7

PRINTED IN THE UNITED STATES OF AMERICA

10 9 8 7 6 5 4 3 2 1

Interior text design by Laura K. Corless.

ALWAYS LEARNING   PEARSON

ACKNOWLEDGMENTS

Primary thanks go to my amazing editor, Ginjer Buchanan, and my even more amazing agent, Lucienne Diver, who are both amazing (did I mention that?). Also to John Rogers (who goes way above and beyond what the average show runner does, to everyone's benefit), Chris Downey, and all the other fine folks at *Leverage*, who are amazing as well. (This is the part where the copy editor flags this page for repetitious word use.)

I want to make a special note of thanks also to *Leverage* staff writer Geoffrey Thorne, who was a good buddy before either of us ever had anything to do with *Leverage*, as we've both put in time in the *Star Trek* novel trenches. I also will never forget that one San Diego Comic-Con dinner where we sat around all night and gossiped like hell . . .

Of course, I must give thanks and praise to Timothy Hutton, Gina Bellman, Christian Kane, Beth Riesgraf, Aldis Hodge, Leigh Guyer, Madeleine Rogers, Goran Visnjic, Odessa Rae, Robert Blanche, Rick Overton, Gerald Downey,

ACKNOWLEDGMENTS

and the amazing Mark A. Sheppard, who have played various characters in this novel on television, giving me faces and voices with which to work.

Other helpful folks include former Bronx Zoo marketing maven (and treasured high school classmate) Rachel Drosopolous-Libretti, the people responsible for the *Leverage* wiki (leverage.wikia.com), M. Sieiro Garcia for aid with the Portuguese language, the kind folks at the Starbucks up the street, where a large chunk of this novel got written accompanied by too many Venti iced coffees to count, and Laura Anne Gilman, David Mack, Dale Mazur, and Tina Randleman, just for general niftiness.

Finally, tremendous thanks to Wrenn Simms, Jacob Sommer, and GraceAnne Andreassi DeCandido (aka The Mom) for massive amounts of editorial assistance.

AUTHOR'S NOTE

For them that are concerned about such things, *The Zoo Job* takes place during the late fourth season of *Leverage*, sometime after "The Queen's Gambit Job" and sometime before "The Radio Job."

The town of Brillinger and the nation of Malani are both fictional. Any similarities to actual central Massachusetts towns or western African nations living or dead are purely coincidental.

LAST WEEK

Zoë Kerrigan held up her cell phone, currently in picture-taking mode, finger poised over the camera icon, as she waited for the red panda to wake up.

It was her fifth trip to the Brillinger Zoo since she and Dad moved out to this central Massachusetts town, also called Brillinger, a couple of years ago. They'd lived in Boston all their lives, but after Dad's car accident, and after he'd had to testify in court against his former boss—and after they'd gotten all that money—they moved out here.

Zoë hadn't wanted to leave Boston, but Dad said he didn't feel safe there anymore, which was silly, since the bad guys who hurt them were now in jail. But Dad said it was best, so they moved.

She still mostly hated it out here, but she loved the zoo. For the first year, she hadn't even known about it. After she started high school, she spent an entire class day on a field trip to the Brillinger Zoo, and she got to see the giraffes and the bears and the lemurs (though they called them something else, but they looked like lemurs) and the red panda.

Unfortunately, the red panda was asleep that day. Mind you, it was *so totally cute* when it was asleep, but she wanted to see it awake and moving around and stuff.

She begged Dad to take her back, and eventually he gave in and they came to the zoo on a chilly Saturday afternoon.

Once again, the red panda was asleep. However, she convinced Dad to pay for the two of them to become Zoo Boosters, which gave them free admittance to the zoo anytime and a discount on merchandise.

The third time, the red panda was asleep, although on a different tree branch than before. Same thing for the fourth trip.

Right now, though, she was bound and determined. When they'd arrived at the zoo on this lovely spring morning, she made a beeline for the red panda. Bypassing the reptile enclosure, the bear preserve, and the lemurs-that-weren't-actually-called-lemurs, she walked up the paved hill to the wooden fence that separated the red panda from the people. She didn't bother reading the placard telling the history of the red panda, as she'd long since memorized it. Zoë was fully aware that this red panda was named Mei, which was Chinese for "beautiful," it came from China, mostly ate bamboo, and was more related to a raccoon than the traditional black-and-white panda.

Of course, Mei was asleep. As usual. Zoë took out her cell phone, put it into camera mode, and waited.

The second the red panda woke up, she was going to take

a picture. With her phone, which it had taken her a year to convince Dad to get her. He didn't give in until right before she started high school. The online forms he had to fill out included a mandatory field for the child's cell-phone number (in case of emergencies), so he couldn't even place her in the school until he got her the cell phone she'd been asking for since forever.

Speaking of Dad, he'd gone off to the bathroom. When he came back, he asked, "Hasn't he woken up yet?"

"Not yet."

"Honey, maybe we should go see something else."

"I want to see the red panda wake up!"

"We can go look at the giraffes, and maybe the aye-ayes."

She turned to stare at Dad. "The what?"

"The aye-ayes. Y'know the things that look like lemurs."

"Those *are* lemurs, Dad." She sighed loudly and turned back to look at the red panda. It still lay sleeping, one paw over its eyes, curled up on a tree branch and looking *incredibly* adorable.

But she'd seen this adorable five times now. She wanted to see the red panda be adorable while awake.

Dad took out his own cell phone and checked the display, then put it back. "It's already afternoon. Surprised there aren't more people here."

Zoë said nothing, but she was surprised, too. The most crowded she'd ever seen the zoo was when she came on the field trip—but then, she was with her class the entire time. Each time she'd come with Dad, it was emptier.

A woman came walking up the incline toward the red panda exhibit. She wore a denim blouse and those beige pants that had lots of pockets. The blouse pocket had an ID clipped to it that looked a lot like the badge Dad wore to work, but it had the zoo's name on it. It was a different color from the ones worn by the other zoo staff, though—gold instead of silver.

She was the same height as Zoë and had a big smile on her face. "Hi there! I hope you're having a good time."

"The red panda won't wake up."

Dad made a funny face at that. "You'll have to excuse my daughter, she's a bit—er, single-minded."

The woman laughed. "I understand. What's your name, sweetheart?"

"Zoë. Zoë Kerrigan."

The woman put out her hand. "How are you, Zoë. I'm Marney Brillinger—I'm the general manager of the zoo."

Zoë hadn't particularly wanted to talk to the woman until she said she was the zoo manager, at which point she returned the handshake. "Very pleased to meet you."

"The pleasure's all mine, Zoë. Have you been here before?"

"Mhm. And the red panda's always asleep!"

Dad added, "It's our fourth trip, and Mei here's been out like a light each time."

"Fifth," Zoë muttered. Dad wasn't there for the class trip, of course—he couldn't chaperone like Barry Willcott's dad and Laurie Kornetsky's mom because he had to work. Zoë didn't understand why Dad got the job—as a tax accountant at that little place on Main Street—when they had all that money from when he turned his bosses in, but Dad said that was going to pay for Zoë's college.

"Have you always been here around this time of day?" Marney asked.

Zoë nodded.

"Well, Zoë, that's the problem. See, red pandas are nocturnal. That means—"

"They sleep mostly at night, right?" Zoë remembered that *nocturnal* meant "night."

"Not quite." Marney smiled. "A nocturnal animal is one that's *awake* at night."

"Oh!" Zoë blinked. Now she just felt stupid for not knowing that.

"Tell you what," Marney said. "Why don't you go off and look at the rest of the zoo, and come back here around four o'clock or so? By then, I bet that Mei'll be wide-awake, and maybe you can see him eat something."

Zoë started to say, "Awesome!" but stopped herself. Barry Willcott always said "awesome!" and he sounded like a total dork. "That's great!" she said instead, and put her cell phone back in her purse.

"Thank you, Ms. Brillinger," Dad said to Marney. "I honestly thought her arm was going to fall off holding her phone up like that."

Zoë rolled her eyes. *"Dad . . ."* She put her hand in his and they started walking away from the slumbering red panda.

"That's quite all right, Mr. Kerrigan." Marney followed them as they headed back the way they came.

Looking at Dad, Zoë asked, "We gonna see the lemurs?"

Dad started to nod his head, but Marney said, "Actually, they're aye-ayes."

Before Zoë could correct her the same way she'd corrected Dad, Marney kept talking as they walked slowly down the tree-lined, paved path.

"They're just one type of lemur, and the only kind we

have here at the zoo, unfortunately. People keep asking why we don't have lemurs that look like King Julien in *Madagascar*."

Frowning, Zoë said, "I didn't like that movie. Dad made me watch it."

Marney looked at Dad. "That's odd—it's usually the other way around."

Dad shrugged. "I like the penguins. They kind of remind me of this group of people I met in Boston. If you don't mind my asking, Ms. Brillinger—"

"Call me Marney, please."

"Marney, then—I assume you're part of the same family that founded the town and the zoo?"

Nodding, Marney said, "Chester Brillinger came over on the *Mayflower* in 1620. He was a Stranger, not a Saint."

Dad frowned. "Beg pardon?"

Zoë smiled. "That means he wasn't one of the religious Pilgrims, he was one of the other people on the trip."

Nodding, Marney said, "That's right, Zoë. Very good. You learn that in school?"

"No," she said emphatically.

"My daughter's a history buff—this year." Dad grinned. "Last year she was a math geek."

"Hey, I still like math!"

Marney laughed, then continued. "Well, anyhow, Josiah Brillinger sailed for the crown and was given a land grant in return in 1745. He founded the town."

Zoë asked, "He was a privateer?"

"Yah. Then Ezekiel Brillinger built an estate north of town in 1831. He was a naturalist, so he collected a ton of plants and animals, which Thomas Brillinger turned into a zoo in 1897. That's why it's *his* name in big letters on the front gate. Ezekiel's name is in smaller letters, so fewer people point at his name and laugh."

Dad nodded. "Kids tend to make fun of things they've never seen before."

"Actually, it's the adults who tend to ask me why anybody would name their kid Ezekiel. The kids think it's cool."

Zoë looked over at Dad. "Isn't Ezekiel from the Bible?"

Again Dad nodded, smiling this time.

They arrived at the small building with the tiny sign that read LITTLE MADAGASCAR. Dad pushed the door open and Zoë let go of his hand and ran right up to the metal fence that separated the people from the animals. Well, that and the wire mesh. She took out her cell phone and started taking pictures of the three lemurs—or rather, aye-ayes. She was the only one in the room, aside from Dad and Marney.

"I, uh, can't help but notice how poor the attendance is," Dad said. "Partly because the general manager has time to come over and tell my daughter about the sleeping habits of red pandas and her complete family history back to the *Mayflower*. Mostly because you're practically the only other person I've seen since we came in."

Marney sighed. "It's been rough the last couple of years, with the economy and all, and these aye-ayes were our last new attraction—and we got them five years ago. It'll be okay, though. We've got two black rhinos on their way from Malani today. That's why I'm wandering around the zoo—I was going stir-crazy sitting in my office waiting for my guys to call from the docks in Boston. We're having the big opening next month."

One of the aye-ayes ran up a tree branch, then jumped

down and ran through a hollow log. To Zoë's surprise, it then ran back up the tree branch, jumped down again in the same spot, and ran through the same hollow log. It did this several times, and Zoë decided to start filming it with her phone.

She was startled by a song that started playing. It turned out to be Marney's own cell phone, playing some guitar riff that Zoë didn't recognize.

Marney put the phone to her ear, a huge grin on her face. "Talk to me, Bobby, have we achieved rhino?"

Zoë could actually hear the person on the other end, though his voice was tinny. "They're not here, Marn." He had a thick accent, and his nickname for Marney sounded more like *mahn* than *marn*.

The grin disappeared, and Marney now looked the way Dad did whenever he thought about Boston. "What do you mean they're not there, Bobby? Did the ship come in?"

"Oh, yeah," Bobby said, "the ship showed up, but there ain't no rhinos on it. Cap'n said they never got no rhinos in Malani. We're wicked screwed, is what I think."

For a moment Zoë only heard the rustling of the branches as the aye-ayes ran around the enclosure.

Bobby's little voice asked, "Marn, you there?"

"I'm—I—dammit! I don't understand, how can this have—I don't even—"

"Look, Marn, you gotta call your priest pal, 'cause this is crap right here."

"Oh, I'm gonna call him, believe me." Marney started walking out the door of Little Madagascar, phone glued to her ear.

"We gotta get back in the truck and hit the road, but this really blows, Marn. You need to—"

Zoë didn't hear the rest of what Bobby thought Marney needed to do, as she left Little Madagascar. Dad stared after her, looking worried.

But he shook it off in a minute, and he and Zoë wandered around the rest of the zoo. She enjoyed the giraffes and the bears—she got a great video of the brown bear swimming— and they had a late lunch at the Pink Flamingo Café. The café was empty except for the staff and a mother with a kid who Zoë figured was her son. The boy was eating soft-serve ice cream and the mother was playing with her phone.

For her part, Zoë had set her phone's alarm to go off at three forty-five so they'd be able to get back to the red panda in time. When it went off to the sound of her favorite Katy Perry song, she tugged on Dad's shirt to go see Mei.

The red panda was still asleep when they got there, but he looked like he was moving. Zoë whipped out her phone and started recording. One of Mei's eyes opened, and then the red panda opened and closed its mouth a few times, making a *tcha* noise each time, then it yawned.

It was quite possibly the cutest thing Zoë had ever seen in her life. And she recorded it all! She couldn't wait to put it online.

She and Dad walked toward the exit, hand in hand. "Thanks so much, Dad!"

"My pleasure, honey. Now c'mon, let's go . . ." Dad's voice trailed off, and he stopped walking.

Looking up, Zoë saw that Dad was looking at something. Following his eyes, she saw that he was looking at Marney, who was standing near the entrance, having an animated conversation on her phone.

"Yes, I *know* that you can't refund—" She cut herself off,

KEITH R. A. DeCANDIDO

listening to someone talk, but Zoë couldn't understand it this time. "Look, I just want to know what happened to— Hello? Dammit!"

After saying that last word, she put the phone back in her pocket.

"Is everything okay?" Dad asked her.

"What?" Marney turned angrily on them, then her face got nicer when she saw it was her and Dad. "Oh, I'm sorry, Mr.— uh . . ."

"Kerrigan. What's wrong? Is it the rhinos?"

She nodded. "They're gone. The person I got them from said he put them on the ship, but the captain says he never had them. He never even spoke to the person I got them from. This wasn't an official deal with the government, it was through a—a private buyer, so I don't really have much of a legal recourse. We're on the hook for hundreds of thousands of dollars, and no black rhinos to show for it. We're so screwed." She grimaced for a second then shook her head sadly. "I'm sorry, I really shouldn't be telling you all this. Everything will be fine, just—"

"Dad," Zoë whispered.

"What is it, honey?" Dad asked.

"We should tell her about—"

Dad interrupted quickly. "Zoë, I'm not sure that this is any of our business."

"But, Dad, he helps people! He helped us!"

Marney was frowning now, and turned to walk back into the zoo. "I'm sorry, but I should go."

Zoë looked firmly at her father. "C'mon, Dad!"

At that, Marney turned around. "Honestly, we'll be fine.

I'll figure something out. This zoo has survived for over a hundred years, it'll survive this, too."

Dad looked all weird for a second. Then he set his jaw the way he did when he decided he was going to do something—his jaw looked just like that when he decided he was going to fink on his old boss—and said, "Maybe you will, but if you don't, I know a man you need to talk to. You can find him at McRory's Pub in Boston."

"A guy who hangs out in a bar is supposed to help me?" Marney didn't sound convinced.

"He and his friends can," Zoë said emphatically. "Dad told me once that there are wolves in the world and they stop them. If it wasn't for them, Dad would be dead!"

Dad put a hand on Zoë's shoulder. "Zoë's exaggerating, but—well, this man helped me out when I was in a bad way. It was the kind of trouble that could've gotten us both hurt very badly. In the end, the people responsible paid for it, and we were able to start over here in Brillinger. Trust me when I tell you, Marney, this man will help you.

"His name is Nathan Ford."

|||||| **ONE** ||||||

NOW

Arthur Andrechuk, the CEO of AA Investments, wore a happy smile as he got out of his Lexus. After beeping the car into a locked state, he straightened his black necktie and approached the entrance to his building. Arthur always wore a tailored black suit with a white shirt and a black necktie, even on days that he himself had declared to be casual dress. It always reminded everyone who looked at him that he was in charge.

"Good morning, Mr. Andrechuk," the new security guard whose name Arthur didn't care enough to remember said. He was sitting behind the Formica security desk, a copy of the *Boston Globe* opened to the sports section.

"It is, in fact, a very good morning"—Arthur stared down at the man's nameplate—"McGann. It's a beautiful spring day here in Beantown. Do you know why I call Boston Beantown, McGann?"

"I'm sure I don't know, Mr. Andrechuk."

Arthur leaned over the desk and spoke in a mock-conspiratorial whisper. "It drives Bostonians *crazy*." He straightened and grabbed his ID, which was clipped to one of the belt loops on his suit pants. He removed it and ran it over the security gate's scanner. The red light turned into a green light, the metal bar levered aside, and he entered, replacing the clip on the loop. "The other thing that drives 'em crazy is wearing anything that says 'New York Yankees' on it, of course. I think, McGann, that I'm going to wear my Yankee cap to work tomorrow. Had that sucker since I was a kid. Got it at Cap Day. Well, okay, my dad got it at Cap Day and I stole it while he and Mom were divorcing, but, y'know, whatever works."

"Of course, Mr. Andrechuk." McGann returned to his newspaper.

Arthur went to the elevator bank and stared at McGann. Then he fished his phone out of his jacket pocket and dialed his assistant, even though he was going to see her within five minutes once the elevator took him to the top floor.

"Yes, Mr. Andrechuk?"

"Yvonne, I want you to look into the new security guy, McGann. I don't like him."

"He came very highly recommended."

The elevator dinged and the doors spread apart. As he entered, Arthur said, "I'm sure he did, but I think he's trying to hide a southern accent. You *know* how I feel about people from the South."

"Yes, Mr. Andrechuk."

He pushed the button for the thirteenth floor, and the elevator quietly started moving up. When he'd first bought the building, the top floor was the fourteenth. He'd changed that right away, seeing no reason to give in to superstitious nonsense. He'd seen that a lot in the older buildings in New York, but AA's headquarters were modern enough that he thought the architects wouldn't have succumbed to that ridiculousness.

Someone Arthur didn't recognize got on at two and got off at ten. She never made eye contact with Arthur, which was how he preferred it.

Upon his arrival at the thirteenth floor, Yvonne was, of course, waiting for him as the doors opened. He'd been impressed with her skill when she first started just appearing when he arrived like that, until he realized that her computer alerted her whenever his ID was pinged in the building.

"You've got the meeting with the people from Deutsche Bank at eleven, lunch with the woman from Consolidated, and the regular staff meeting's at three."

Arthur frowned as he walked toward his office. "Why isn't it at four?"

"Jenna has to pick up her son from school, so Fred reschedu—"

Shaking his head, Arthur opened the door to his office, with the etched glass that read ARTHUR ANDRECHUK, CHIEF EXECUTIVE OFFICER. "The staff meeting is *always* Monday at four. It's always *been* Monday at four, it always *will be* Monday at four. Put the meeting back at four, remind Jenna that attendance at the Monday-at-four staff meeting is mandatory, and tell Fred to get his ass in my office ASAP."

"Yes, Mr. Andrechuk." Yvonne followed him into his office. This used to annoy Arthur, but he soon learned that she did it only when she had more to say. "A.J. says that the office e-mail still isn't working."

"What's wrong with it?"

"Files aren't attaching."

Arthur sat down at his desk, which was neat and orderly as always. It was also made of mahogany, which violated multiple fire safety laws. He'd been fined a couple of times, but he didn't care. The boss should have a wooden desk, as far as he was concerned.

He turned on his computer and waited for it to boot up. "I thought A.J. fixed that."

Yvonne shook her head. "So did he. He had to call in tech support."

Eyes widening, Arthur repeated Yvonne's words. "*A.J.* had to call in tech support? Okay, mark this day down in the calendar. I may have to cancel his bonus, if Mr. High-and-Mighty Computer Genius can't fix an e-mail problem. Did he *have* to call in tech support?"

Shrugging, Yvonne said, "He said it was that or start sending files on paper through interdepartmental mail."

"Right, because what AA's all about is being retro." Arthur shook his head. "Fine, when's the tech guy getting here?"

"Sometime between nine and three."

Arthur snorted. "Like the damn cable company."

"And—" Yvonne hesitated, which was never good. "Ms. Menendez is on line one."

"Oh, for Christ's sake, what does she want *now*?" Arthur leaned back in his chair. Rosa Menendez was a CPA at a local accounting firm. "All right, I'll talk to her." He made a shooing motion with one hand while grabbing the phone with the other. Once Yvonne closed the door, he stabbed at the 1 button. "What *is* it, Rosa? You can't keep calling me here, we—"

"We got a *big* problem, Artie. The IRS is sending two auditors named Smith and Baker to see you *today*! I got pinged on it from my friend over there."

"Yeah, so?"

"Are you *serious*? Artie, we can't—"

"Did you certify that the pension accounts are all kosher?"

"Of *course* I did, but—"

"And did A.J. make sure the computer files are all in order? Oh, wait, you didn't take care of that, I did." He smiled, even though Rosa couldn't see it. "The whole point of the exercise, Rosa, is to siphon money off from the pensions in such a way that the IRS *won't* notice. It's probably just some random audit. Don't worry about it. In fact, this helps us. If the SEC looks into us and sees a clean bill of health from the IRS, we'll be golden. They won't expect anything."

"I don't know, Artie, I'm not sure I can—"

Arthur leaned forward in his chair, resting his elbows on his neat mahogany desk. "Rosa, I've paid you good money to keep certifying that the pension funds are okay, money that I know you've already spent because Pedro is still getting Gylenia for his multiple sclerosis, and you can't afford the four grand a month for it on your own. So you'd better think very carefully about how you finish that sentence."

Silence.

"Yeah, that's what I thought. Don't sweat the IRS, Rosa,

I'm ready for anything they'll find. Just keep doing what I've paid you to do. In a month, this will all be over, Pedro can take his Gylenia in San Lorenzo, and I'll be on a beach in the Bahamas."

The moment he hung up the phone, Yvonne opened the door. "Uh, Mr. Andrechuk? There are two people here from the IRS to see you. They don't have an appointment, but—"

Standing up, Arthur said, "That's quite all right, Yvonne, send them in." He walked around to the other side of his desk and put on his best smile.

The two IRS agents were wearing dark suits, which Arthur appreciated, and had deadly serious expressions on their faces. One was a lovely brunette, the other a tall black guy. Both held briefcases, and both showed their IDs, which Arthur studied closely. They looked legit—they were far from the first IRS employees he'd ever met. And the names— Smith and Baker—matched the ones Rosa had provided.

"Hello, I'm Arthur Andrechuk." He held out his hand.

The woman did not accept the handshake. "I'm S. J. Smith, this is my colleague Thomas Baker."

Baker nodded his head. "How do you do, Mr. Anderson?"

"That's Andrechuk."

"Of course, Mr. Anderchik."

Arthur gave up and turned back to Smith. "What can I do for the IRS today, Ms. Smith?"

"You can stay out of our way while we do a full audit. I'll need access to your computer system and all your client files."

"Of course!" Arthur said enthusiastically. "Let me take you down to our chief programmer's office. That's A.J.

Kiroda. He handles all our computer systems, and he can walk you through—"

Smith tartly said, "We don't need anyone to 'walk us through' anything, Mr. Andrechuk." She used air quotes, which just gave Arthur another reason to dislike her.

He led them to the elevator to take them down to A.J.'s office on seven.

After he pushed the down button, his COO, Manfred Shannon, came by. "Hey, Artie, you wanted to see me?"

"Not especially, but it's the only way to talk to you." He grabbed Fred's arm, shot a smile at Smith and Baker, said, "Excuse me just for one second, I need to consult with my COO," then yanked him back toward his own office.

"What's wrong, Artie?"

"What's wrong? Why did you reschedule the Monday-at-four meeting?"

"Jenna needs—"

Arthur held up both hands. "I could give a damn. Jenna's an analyst. I've got analysts pouring out of the dozens of universities they have in this town every year who can do just as good a job as her and take a fraction of the pay. I don't *need* Jenna, and will gleefully replace her with someone who *won't* try to disrupt our schedule with her idiotic child-care problems. I pay her well enough to afford a nanny, and her husband makes almost as much as she does. So she can suck it up and find someone else to drag her kid's ass home from school, and we're having our meeting at four, got me?"

"Um, well, I—"

"The answer to that question, Fred, in case you weren't sure? Is yes."

Fred swallowed. "Yes."

"Good. Now if you'll excuse me, I've got to go play nice with the IRS."

That got Fred to swallow again. "What do *they* want?"

"To justify their existence by interfering with mine. Don't worry about it, just take care of this."

"Okay."

Fred wandered back toward his own office while Arthur rejoined Smith and Baker at the elevator bank.

"Sorry about that. Business, you know."

The IRS people said nothing. Then the elevator arrived, and they went down to A.J.'s office—which was empty.

Grumbling, Arthur pulled his cell phone out of his jacket pocket and dialed A.J.'s cell.

"Yeah, boss?"

A.J. was the only person who called him boss. Arthur didn't really like it that much, but he also didn't like the idea of discouraging the practice.

"Why the hell aren't you in your office?"

"The tech support guy's there."

Arthur peered inside the office to make sure he hadn't missed anything, but no, there were just A.J.'s three desks, each with a computer station. "No, he isn't. And neither is anyone else."

"He probably went to the bathroom. I'll be right there."

Replacing his phone, Arthur looked over at the IRS people. "He'll be right here."

Moments later, a short Asian man wearing a flannel shirt came jogging down the hall, a bag of corn chips in his hand. "Sorry about that."

Arthur introduced the IRS people and told him to help them in any way he could.

Leading them in, A.J. said, "Okay, the tech support guy's using number one, so you two can use two and three."

"You're in good hands, here," Arthur said, putting his reassuring smile back on. "If you need me, I'll be in my office."

Baker said, "Thanks very much, Mr. Anderson."

"It's Andrech—" He sighed. "Never mind."

Leaving them to it, he took the elevator back to his office.

Yvonne looked up in surprise when the elevator chimed and he stepped out. "Mr. Andrechuk? What are you doing here?"

He looked sidewise at his assistant. "I work here. As a matter of fact, I happen to own the place. You might recall that *that* is my office."

"I know that, Mr. Andrechuk, but—" Yvonne hesitated. "I just got an alert that you entered the server room—and you haven't left yet."

"That's crazy, I haven't been in there in months."

Several thoughts went through Arthur's head at once. Only he, A.J., and Fred had access to the server room. Fred was up here in his office—he looked over to be sure, and there he was on the phone, probably with Jenna explaining the facts of life to her—and he'd just seen A.J. in his.

The server room had an ID scanner. Arthur's hand went down to the ID clipped to his pants.

Except it wasn't. He felt nothing, and looking down, he saw nothing. His ID was gone.

Somebody had stolen it and used it to get into the room.

The one room in the entire world where one could see *all* of AA's accounting records.

And the tech support guy was unaccounted for.

"Call McGann, tell him to get his southern ass to the server room."

"Yes, Mr. Andrechuk." Yvonne nodded while Arthur rang for the elevator, which took him back down to seven.

He passed A.J.'s office, where the two IRS people were hunched over one of the stations while A.J. watched. There was a small netbook set up next to the workstation, which Baker typed on occasionally. Still no sign of the tech support guy.

"Excuse me," he said softly, not wanting to give the IRS people anything to be suspicious of, "but I need to borrow Mr. Kiroda for a second. A.J.?"

As soon as A.J. cleared the doorway, Arthur grabbed his arm even harder than he'd grabbed Fred's.

"Ow! Artie, what's—"

"Someone broke into the server room."

"That's impossible."

"They stole my ID."

"How?"

Arthur blinked and stopped walking. "I don't know." He shook his head and continued moving. "Doesn't matter, they're in there now, and we have to—"

They arrived at the door, which was closed—but the green light on the ID scanner was still on, which didn't make sense. When the door closed all the way, the light went back to red until another approved ID was scanned.

Arthur peered more closely at the door—and saw a piece of cardboard wedged between the doorframe and the door, right where the latch was. Which meant the door had never registered as closed.

He yanked the door open, which proved his point—but nobody was there.

A.J. immediately went over to the workstation. It was a stand-up station with an adjustable keyboard. A.J. had to lever it downward so he could work comfortably, then started tapping on the keyboard.

"Looks like we're good. I'm not seeing any sign that anyone's used this puppy since I was in here yesterday."

That didn't make any sense. Why would someone steal his ID and then go into this room just to—

Then it hit him. "Yes someone did. The keyboard was adjusted to someone taller than you."

A.J. held up both hands, palms up. "I'm telling you, Artie, there's *no* sign that anyone tried to—"

"How can there be *no* sign, dumb-ass? He obviously *used* it! Even if he tried to get in and hit a firewall, wouldn't there be a sign of that?"

"Well, sure, but—"

"If he broke in here to play Minesweeper, you'd see it. So if you didn't, it means we had a pro in here who covered his tracks. Dammit!" He pointed at the workstation. "Figure it out, A.J., or it's more than just your ass."

He walked out, pushing the door open, and this time removing the cardboard. A.J. had his ID and could get out that way, and he didn't want anyone *else* wandering in.

Smith then stuck her brunette head out of A.J.'s office. "Mr. Andrechuk, may we see you a minute, please?"

"I'm sorry, Ms. Smith, really, but we've got a major security breach here, and I need to deal with it." Even as Arthur said that, he wondered where the hell McGann was. He'd told Yvonne to get him to the server room.

"Mr. Andrechuk, you have much big—"

Holding up a finger with one hand, Arthur retrieved his cell phone with the other and called the front desk. "Just one second."

Smith put her hands on her hips. "You don't have a second, Mr. Andrechuk, you—"

Arthur ignored her as the security desk went to voice mail. "Seriously?" He hit end, then called his assistant. "Yvonne, where the hell is McGann?"

"He said he was reporting right to you."

"Well, he's not here now, and I need—"

"Mr. Andrechuk!"

This Smith woman was getting on Arthur's nerves. "What!?"

"I need you to come in here and explain why we're reading your company's entire pension fund at one hundred and forty-nine dollars and seventy-two cents."

Arthur opened his mouth, then closed it. He'd told Rosa that he was ready for anything the IRS would find—but he never expected them to find the real amount in the pension fund.

"I also need you to explain this audio file that we were just e-mailed."

"Um—"

She motioned with a finger for him to come in, and then entered A.J.'s office.

Reluctantly, Arthur followed, if for no other reason than curiosity as to what that audio file was.

Looking at Baker, Smith said, "Play it."

Baker nodded and tapped his netbook's track pad.

Arthur then heard his own voice: *"The whole point of the exercise, Rosa, is to siphon money off from the pensions in such a way that the IRS won't notice. It's probably just some random audit. Don't worry about it. In fact, this helps us. If the SEC looks into us and sees a clean bill of health from the IRS, we'll be golden. They won't expect anything."* There was a pause, then: *"Rosa, I've paid you good money to keep certifying that the pension funds are okay, money that I know you've already spent because Pedro is still getting—"*

There was likely more to the recording, but Arthur didn't hear it because he was too busy running.

Not bothering with the elevator, he ran up the stairs to the top floor. His heart pounded like a trip-hammer, and not just from the exertion. Somehow, someway, A.J.'s programming had been messed up. He was *so close* . . .

By the time he reached ten, he was winded, and swore that he would, dammit, start *using* his gym membership.

When he burst onto the thirteenth floor, he stumbled toward his office, trying to catch his breath.

Yvonne rose, and Fred came running out of his own office.

"Mr. Andrechuk?"

"Artie, what happened?"

The elevator dinged open and Arthur turned in a panic, fearing it would be the IRS people.

But no, it was McGann. "Oh, thank Christ. Listen, McGann, I need you to get me out of here *now*. Yvonne, call A.J., tell him to wipe everything before—"

His next words were cut off by McGann's forearm slamming into his throat.

Arthur fell to the floor, his vision swimming from his head striking the tile. Arthur had always hated carpeting, and refused to put any on the thirteenth floor, a decision he was hazily regretting as spots danced before his eyes.

Vaguely, he heard McGann say, "'Bout time I got to hit him. Nate, I got him."

He also heard Fred say, "Looks like Jenna can pick up her kid after all . . ."

AN HOUR AGO

Nate Ford's voice sounded in Alec Hardison's ear. "All set, Hardison?"

Hardison was sitting in the rear compartment of Lucille, going over his code one last time. "Just doing a final check. Then all I have to do is show up to do tech support, put in the jump drive, and the program does the rest."

His incredibly brilliant program would piggyback onto the one Kiroda was using to siphon off AA's pension funds into Andrechuk's account. Only now, it would be siphoned off into one of Hardison's accounts. "The money'll be in my account by end-of-business, and then we'll be able to pay back all of AA's employees who don't even know they've been robbed yet." Hardison frowned. "That's not right."

"What isn't right?" Nate asked.

"They ain't been robbed. When you get robbed, somebody's standin' in front of you takin' your money."

"Yes, Hardison," Nate said patiently, "that's why we're thieves and not robbers."

"Yeah, but what do we call what's happenin' to these people? I mean, if they were victims of a robbery, they were robbed, but they're victims of a theft, so they were—what? Thefted?"

"Dammit, Hardison!" That, of course, was Eliot Spencer. "Will you shut up about verbs and get in here? I just had to listen to Andrechuk go on about 'Beantown.' Again. If we don't end this soon, I'm gonna have to hit him. He just got on the elevator."

Nate said, "Parker, go."

Hardison leaned forward and read over the last of the code. From Parker's comms, he heard the telltale ding of an elevator opening. That had to be her getting on the elevator on the second floor. With a knowing smile, he imagined the scene: Parker walking onto the elevator without making eye contact with Andrechuk, lifting the CEO's ID, without him noticing, and then getting off at ten. Just like they'd planned it. His girl knew her stuff.

Once Hardison was done checking his code—it was almost perfect, he just modified one line that would make things run more efficiently—he leaned back, stretching his arms and cracking his neck.

Then he noticed that the bug that Eliot had placed on Andrechuk's office phone went online.

As he listened to Andrechuk's conversation with his confederate, Hardison felt the blood drain from his face. "Nate, we got us a *big* problem. The IRS is coming."

"That's tomorrow, Hardison. Sophie and I will—"

"No, Nate, the *real* IRS. Andrechuk just got a heads-up from his pet CPA that two auditors are showing up." He alt-tabbed to another window and hacked into the IRS mainframe, doing a search on the two names that Rosa Menendez had mentioned. Sure enough: "I got a Simone J. Smith and a Thomas Allan Baker scheduled to do a random audit of AA *this morning.*"

"They're already here," Eliot said. "I just passed them through security."

Knowing full well that Nate would not listen to his advice, Hardison said, "We gotta abort. I can't do this with the IRS breathing down—"

"No, we just change the plan," Nate interrupted, saying exactly what Hardison knew he would say.

"Plan K, right? That's the one where you kiss all the other plans good-bye?"

"No, the plan's actually more or less the same, the only difference is what you do once you're in the server room. Instead of a program that reroutes the pension money, I want you to get rid of what Kiroda did to hide it."

At times, Hardison hated discussions over comms, because he really wanted to look Nate in the eye when he told him to go perform an anatomical impossibility upon himself. "Nate, I just spent the better part of a day writing this very elegant, very sophisticated program, and now you're telling me to trash it to—"

"Yes, Hardison, and do something that doesn't *need* to be elegant or complicated. Just strip away Kiroda's fakery."

" 'Just'? Really? You people ha—"

Eliot jumped in. "Hardison, I swear, if you start the 'you people have no idea what I do' speech . . ."

"All right, all right." Hardison sighed. He went over to his netbook, composed an e-mail to the two IRS auditors, whose addresses he'd gotten off the mainframe he'd hacked, and set it to send in twenty minutes. "I'm goin' in."

Hardison went in, got the Trademark Eliot Spencer Scowl (patent pending) from "McGann" at the security desk, and then met up with A.J. Kiroda.

It was almost a shame to trash this guy's program. Kiroda was good. Not as good as Hardison, of course, but maybe almost as good as Ka0s. The AA computer maven had done a beautiful job of creating a computerized illusion, cloaking reality in a dazzle of false information that would fool all but the most skilled of programmers. Unfortunately for him, Hardison *was* the most skilled of programmers.

In another life, Hardison might have called him "friend."

But Kiroda was helping the mark screw people out of their retirement money. What was worse, Hardison hadn't been able to find any sign that Kiroda had been paid extra for this; he was just doing what his boss told him to do, even though it screwed his fellow employees. At least Menendez had been doing it to help get meds her husband needed.

Once Hardison sat down to "fix the e-mail problem," Kiroda left him alone. Parker met Hardison at the server room door. She used Andrechuk's ID to get him in, then shoved a piece of cardboard in the doorjamb.

After readjusting the keyboard—Kiroda was very short—Hardison went in and did just as Nate asked, stripping out all the code that Kiroda used to mask his boss skimming from the pension fund. Parker then dragged him through an air vent to the outside.

He stood and coughed for several seconds once they were out. "Them things is *dusty*! I got allergies, and I need—need—" He coughed some more.

Parker slammed him on the back a little too hard, and Hardison stumbled forward. He looked up at her and said, "Really?"

Then he heard a very loud thump over the comms, followed by Eliot saying, "'Bout time I got to hit him. Nate, I got him."

"Good," Nate said. "Leave him for the IRS and the feds."

"How'd the feds get here so fast?"

"Someone called them," Nate said in his smug voice.

Hardison really hated Nate's smug voice. He bent over, hands on knees, coughing some more, making sure his back was angled so Parker couldn't hit him again.

Eliot met up with them outside. "C'mon, let's *go.*"

Holding up a finger, Hardison said, "Hang on. Dust—allergies—"

"Fine, then I'm drivin'."

Hardison pulled himself upright. "Oh, *hell* no. You are *not* driving Lucille!"

|||||| TWO ||||||

Every time Nate Ford entered John McRory's Pub, he expected it to be larger.

That was, of course, a consequence of his spending so much time in this bar as a youth. He was Jimmy Ford's son, and this bar was Jimmy Ford's office. His father's idea of day care was to sit young Nate down at the bar and show him how to play three-card monte.

When Nate grew up, he went to a seminary in California, as far away from Jimmy as possible both geographically and ethically. The seminary didn't take, but California did. He made Los Angeles his home for years, traveling extensively for his job at the insurance firm of IYS—though he didn't return to Boston until after his father had been incarcerated.

Now he'd made McRory's his own. As a teenager, he thumbed his nose at Jimmy Ford by moving three thousand miles away and studying to be a priest. As an adult, he continued to thumb his nose in other ways.

The bar hadn't really changed all that much since the days in the early part of the twentieth century when it catered to Irish immigrants: furnished in polished wood, with a selection of booze that tended toward the beers and Scotches and whiskeys. It catered to a neighborhood crowd, mostly white—at present. Alec Hardison was the only person of color in the place, sitting at the bar with Parker—they liked to enjoy each other's company: hence only one television, instead of multiple TVs tuned to NESN and all the ESPN stations.

Hardison owned the building above it, where Nate's apartment was located, and it and the bar combined to become the unofficial headquarters for their operation. The jobs often began and ended in the place, and Nate was, at the moment, handling the final stages of their latest. Jenna Stannis, the client, was sitting at one of the booths when he came in from the back. She was nursing an amber beer.

In direct contrast to the nervous grimace she was wearing when she came to McRory's two weeks ago, Jenna now met him with a relaxed smile. "Mr. Ford, I don't know how you did what you did, but thank you. There was a part of me that still didn't entirely believe that Arthur was ripping us all off, so when the IRS shut the place down and the FBI arrested him . . ." She shook her head and took a long gulp of her beer. "Oh, that feels good. Honestly, I've been afraid to drink, y'know?"

Nate did not particularly understand this feeling, but said nothing as he sat down.

Jenna went on: "I really didn't think anybody would be

able to get through A.J.'s program. My only regret is that I didn't see your guy take Arthur down. I'm just glad I got to see him led away in handcuffs."

Smiling, Nate said, "It was our pleasure, Jenna. It's gonna take a while for the SEC and the IRS and the FBI to plow through everything, but Arthur Andrechuk is definitely going down—and your pensions should all be restored." He reached into his jacket's inner pocket and pulled out an envelope. "But just in case—this is for you. It's the entirety of your pension to date. I know it's not the best time to be unemployed, so this should keep you going until you find another job."

The nervous grimace came back. "Mr. Ford, I—I can't take this!"

"Sure you can."

But even as he spoke, he noticed another person with a nervous grimace: a short, blond-haired woman who had just entered the bar and ordered a single-malt Scotch from Cora behind the bar. She was looking nervously around the bar, as if trying to find someone—and then her eyes fell on Nate and she quickly looked away.

Nate suspected that their newest client had just walked in the door. Especially since she matched the description in Zoë Kerrigan's e-mail of the previous day.

By the time he finished with Jenna, who left the bar with her relaxed smile even bigger than it had been when he handed her the pension money, the new client had ordered a second Scotch. Nate came over and sat down next to her and said without preamble, "You must be Marney Brillinger."

The woman almost choked on her Scotch. "How'd you—"

"I'm very good at what I do, Ms. Brillinger." Then the

slightest of smirks played on his lips. "Plus, I got an e-mail yesterday from Zoë Kerrigan."

Letting out a breath, Marney chuckled. "So you're *not* psychic. That's good—the way the Kerrigans talked you up, I was starting to wonder. You must be Nate Ford." She offered her hand, which he shook. She glanced behind her at the now-empty booth he'd been in. "I hope my staring didn't chase that woman away."

"It's okay. She just figured you were my next client."

Marney snorted. "*I'm* not even sure I'm your next client."

Cora came over and provided Nate with a shot glass filled with Irish whiskey. Nodding to the bartender in gratitude, he took a quick slug. "Usually when people get to the point where they come through that door, they're at their wit's end and have tried everything they could. Have you tried everything you could to save your zoo?"

Defensively, Marney asked, "How do you know the zoo needs saving?"

"Because I looked you up, and you've been working for that zoo—which has been in your family since it opened in the nineteenth century—since you were a teenager. Because Zoë mentioned that the zoo was in trouble, a fact backed up by the zoo's financials, which are pretty dire. And because your Web site lists an indefinite postponement of the opening of your black rhino exhibit, which you've been hyping for the last two months."

Marney let out another breath. "Yeah." She finished off her second Scotch and waved at Cora for a third. "You're right, the zoo's hemorrhaging money right now. Crappy economy, small zoo, off the usual beaten tourist paths . . . It's been a perfect storm of suck. Plus, we haven't had anything new in ages. My father was the general manager before me, and he really didn't do much with the business. I took over after he—he died . . ." She trailed off.

Cora brought her Scotch and she sipped it. "I'm sorry, I just—let's just say I've got some complicated feelings about my father, and leave it at that."

Nate tensed for just a moment and glanced over at the unoccupied stool at the end of the bar where his father used to hold court.

Marney went on. "Anyhow, after my father's heart attack, the first thing I had to do in my new position as general manager was bring the zoo into the twenty-first century: more up-to-date signage, some interactive displays, more merchandizing. Plus, we needed some new animals. We got some aye-ayes from Madagascar, and that gave us a membership and attendance bump for a year or two, but it's flattened out again.

"So three months ago, I started up a correspondence with a priest in Malani. He said he'd be able to sell us two black rhinos. We don't have any rhinos, and the black rhinos are endangered. He was giving us a male and a female that we might be able to breed—that might help us get into the Save Our Species program, and maybe some government money, as well. Worst case, we get some new animals in the mix."

Cora wandered by, looked at both drinks, and noticed that Nate had not, as yet, finished his Irish whiskey. That would be for later, after the client was done filling him in. "So what happened?" he asked.

"I sent him two hundred thousand dollars, he said the rhinos were put on a ship called the *Black Star* bound for

Boston. My guys went to Boston and met the *Black Star*, and no rhinos. Reverend Maimona assured me that he put them on the *Black Star*—but it turns out there are about fifty ships with that name."

"Somebody pulled a fast one?"

She shook her head. "Not the reverend. He actually gave me proof that he put the animals on the *Black Star*—photos and such. But it wasn't the same ship that pulled into Boston."

"He still could be part of the deception."

Marney didn't look comfortable with the idea that she'd been conned by a man of God, which struck Nate as charmingly naïve. "It doesn't matter. The point is, the only way spending two hundred grand on these animals was going to be worth it was if we actually, y'know, got them. And the money's just . . . *gone*."

Ford frowned. "Aren't you insured?"

"Yes, we are. By your former employer, actually." She smiled at Ford's double take. "I looked you up, too. You were an investigator for IYS up until about four years ago. Then you went completely off the grid. Except a couple years ago, when Matt Kerrigan realized that his employers at First Boston Independent pocketed the bailout money they got after the crash in '08 and were in bed with the Irish mob. After they tried to kill him, you took down the Irish mob, took down the president of First Boston, and got the Kerrigans a nice nest egg."

Nate just nodded. Given how much Zoë had told him in her e-mail about Marney, it wasn't surprising that she had been equally forthcoming to Marney with what she knew about Nate and his crew. After all, she *was* a teenage girl.

He did, however, take a sip of his whiskey before asking,

"So why not report the loss of the rhinos? You obviously have proof that you were the victim of a fraud."

"If I report it, we'll get the money back, but our premiums will go through the roof. No, actually, they're *already* through the roof—this will make them hit the stratosphere. My father wasn't always the best at following safety regulations, and one of our bears died when a support strut broke. It almost killed a visitor, too, and we had to settle with her family." She shuddered. "We can't really afford our policy now. If I report this . . ."

Nate nodded. "What does your board of directors say?"

She shrugged. "They're just writing it off as a loss. And there's one other problem."

"Reverend Maimona didn't obtain the rhinos legally?"

Marney squirmed a bit on the stool and sipped more Scotch, which was all the answer Nate needed. "I'm afraid I—well, I didn't ask a lot of questions. If I report this—to IYS or to Interpol or whoever—they *will* ask questions, and I'm not sure the zoo would come out unscathed."

Nate contemplated his whiskey for a moment. Marney had provided all the particulars, and now he had to ask the most important question of all: "What is it you want my team to do?"

Marney blew out a long breath, briefly puffing her cheeks. "Honestly? The only way the Brillinger Zoo survives after this is if you can find the rhinos. The exhibit opens, we get press and publicity, I apply for a government grant or three, and our animals don't get sold off to the highest bidder. The lucky ones would get bought by another zoo—but the *highest* bidder would probably be some rich asshole who likes exotic animals but doesn't actually know how to take care of them." A look of disgust formed on her face, and she washed it away with the rest of her Scotch.

"After the thing with the bear, we needed money quick. We had three polar bears—Huey, Dewey, and Louie—so my father decided to sell one of them. Some rich guy in Montana always wanted to have a polar bear for his estate, even though he had no clue how to take care of him, so he paid half a million for poor Louie. In less than six months, Louie was dead." She palmed a tear off her cheek. "He was only four— he should've lived another fifteen years at *least*, and that old bastard . . ."

While Nate was no kind of animal lover, that type of cruelty due to ignorance never failed to stick in his craw. Putting a comforting hand on Marney's shoulder, he said, "I'm sorry."

"I'm not letting that happen to the rest of them. Plus, who knows where those black rhinos are? There are less than five thousand left in the world, Mr. Ford. The year I was born, there were almost fifteen thousand. We can't afford to lose *any*. One subspecies of black rhino has already been declared extinct, and the other three aren't that far behind."

"All right, then."

Marney blinked. "I'm sorry?"

"We'll help you. We'll get you your rhinos, and we'll save your zoo."

"Just like that?"

Nate felt his lips curl upward a bit. "Just like that. We'll be in touch." Then he gulped down his whiskey in one shot and went over to talk to Hardison and Parker.

Marney watched as Ford walked to the other end of the bar. The bartender came over to take his glass away, and Marney asked her, "What just happened?"

"Nate said he'll help you. That means he'll help you."

"Okay." She shook her head. "I'm not even sure I *want* his help. I just came here to talk to him, to see what he offers. Now . . ."

Nodding, the bartender said, "That's Nate. If it means anything, he's never failed yet. He even saved this bar once. Him and his team, they're the best."

"Hope so." Marney sipped some more of her Scotch. "I just—I don't know what I'll do if the zoo goes under. I grew up in that zoo, and I always knew one day I was going to run it. It's practically synonymous with the town, with my family—with *me*. I don't *have* anything else." She shook her head and chuckled. "I guess I am okay with him taking the job. But I didn't even get to tell him how much it means to me to—"

Putting a hand on hers, the bartender stared right at Marney with her green eyes. Marney returned the gaze, realizing that this woman cared deeply for Nate Ford—and also thought very highly of him. It was half of the look that she usually wore on her face when she thought about her father—the caring-deeply part, since he never gave her reason to think highly of him. The bastard died before she could resolve her ambivalence.

"He knows," the bartender said. "That's why he took the case. He only helps people who genuinely need it."

"Looks like I do." Marney gulped down the last of her Scotch. "Time to hit the road."

"You're not driving, are you?" Cora asked.

Marney shook her head, an action she immediately regretted, as it made the room swirl. "No, no, no, I'll catch a train to Fitchburg, and I'll be sober by the time I get there to drive back to Brillinger from there." She thought back over what she'd just said. "Certainly more sober than I am now."

"You want me to call you a cab to take you to North Station?"

Opening her mouth to say she'd be fine taking the T, Marney thought about it for several seconds and then said, "Yes," rather than risk nodding and causing the room to twirl again.

As the bartender pulled out a cell phone, she walked over to what looked like an espresso machine. "I'll make you some coffee—on the house."

Retaking her bar stool, Marney said, "Uh, thanks?"

"You're Nate's client," Cora said, as if that explained everything.

And maybe it did.

Marney just hoped that Nathan Ford lived up to the hype. After all, the last time several people told her something was a sure thing, they were assuring her over and over that obtaining two black rhinos would absolutely save the zoo . . .

|||||| THREE ||||||

NOW

"Okay, Hardison, run it."

The woman who generally referred to herself as Sophie Devereaux watched as Hardison, in response to Nate's request, clicked the remote, and several images appeared on the giant screen that took up the bulk of the east wall of the lower level of Nate's two-level flat. Each new image appeared in sequence slightly off-kilter from the previous one, giving the two-dimensional impression of a three-dimensional stack of files. Sophie had always found it curious how computer programmers tried so hard to create the illusion of their paper analogues—using file-folder images to indicate directories, even calling them folders, while word processing programs tried at least on the surface to imitate the typing of letters onto a piece of paper. And here, Hardison was opening windows that were "stacked" like papers on a desk.

Some images, she easily recognized. For example, the home page of the Brillinger Zoo Web site was clearly labeled as such, and she knew a map of Africa when she saw one. Others Sophie knew were generally financial statements and records, though the images piled on too quickly for her to see whose financials they were. Hardison also called up a You-Tube page, but again the images came up too fast for Sophie to see what the subject of the video was. There were recent photos of, respectively, a blond-haired white woman, a black priest with a monk's fringe of hair but a bald crown, a dilapidated building, a ship in a port with the words BLACK STAR emblazoned on the hull, some wild animals, and a dark-skinned man in a military uniform. Sophie also spied a sepia-toned image of someone in late-nineteenth-century clothing that was sufficiently accurate that she supposed it was probably scanned from an actual century-and-a-quarter-old photograph, as opposed to a re-creation.

"Which one's the mark?" she asked.

Nate surprised her by saying, "None of them. We don't know who the mark is, because we don't know who stole the black rhinos."

That got Parker's attention. "How do you steal a black rhino? Much less two?"

"Very carefully, I would think," Nate said with the head tilt he often affected. "The point, though, is that the zoo needs those black rhinos. Hardison?"

Even as Sophie listened raptly to Hardison explaining the history of the zoo—the sepia-toned photo was the zoo's founder, Thomas Brillinger, an ancestor of the blonde, Marney Brillinger, who was the current general manager of the zoo and also the team's client—she watched the others' reactions.

Parker only half paid attention to what Hardison said, which was not unusual—the thief's eyes were focused on the part of the screen showing wild animals, prompting a grin. Fortunately, it was Parker's *happy* grin, which they'd been seeing more and more of lately. That was infinitely preferable to the grin she'd often worn in the early days after Nate gathered them all together in Chicago and they set up shop in Los Angeles. *That* grin tended to appear on Parker's face half a minute before something blew up. That grin was generally the precursor to utter chaos. That grin frightened the hell out of Sophie.

Over by the kitchen, Nate was looking around the room. His eyes locked with Sophie's, and she gave him a smile, prompting him to quickly look away, which, in turn, prompted Sophie to stifle a sigh of annoyance.

It was absurd, was what it was. Everyone on the team knew that Nate and Sophie were "friends with benefits." Sophie had never heard this term until Hardison used it, and it sounded distinctively American to her ears, at once euphemistic and derogatory in its yoking of romance with capitalism. Nate told her once that he'd always thought of this kind of relationship as an excuse to either avoid commitment or justify bad behavior. But it wasn't bad behavior—yet there he was, looking away guiltily as if he'd done something horribly wrong. The same man who regularly led them on jobs that involved repeated law breaking, which he did without blinking an eyelash.

Cursing the part of Nate that was still a bloody seminary

student, Sophie looked over at Eliot, who sat in the easy chair. (Hardison kept insisting on calling it "the comfy chair." Sophie wasn't sure what bothered her more, Hardison making *Monty Python* references or doing so with a truly atrocious attempt at a British accent.) Eliot was chewing on a sandwich that he'd arrived with in a brown paper bag. It was mortadella, sliced extra thin, from a *salumeria* he liked, with lettuce, mozzarella cheese, and balsamic vinaigrette.

Sophie noticed that Nate, after looking with an almost longing expression at Eliot's sandwich, then retreated to the kitchen. He immediately started checking the cabinets, only to find the seemingly endless supply of horrendous junk food and undrinkable orange libations that Hardison kept in Nate's duplex. It bitterly amused Sophie that Hardison had more food in Nate's flat than Nate himself did.

"On top of everything else," Hardison was saying as he clicked the remote to zoom in on one of the financials, which turned out to be a loan agreement, "they've taken out a buncha loans, which are gonna default if they can't pay in a year."

That got Nate to temporarily abandon his quest for food. "Why so soon a default?"

"Too big a risk, especially after the thing with the bear." Hardison clicked again, bringing the YouTube page to the fore. He started the video, which was shaky and pixelated, indicating that it was made with a cheap mobile phone; it showed people running about and screaming, and a bear visibly trapped under what looked like a large plank of wood.

Sophie winced, and she noticed Parker doing the same. Even Hardison got a queasy expression, prompting him to stop the video before it was completed.

Though it was obvious, Sophie felt the need to say out loud, "That's awful."

"Marney's father didn't do the best job of caretaking," Nate said drily.

Hardison nodded. "Yeah, but after he died of a heart attack a couple years ago, she got everything all back in order—barely. Problem is, zoo's hangin' by a thread. The black rhinos were gonna be the big thing, but they're gone."

"Now, what doesn't make sense here," Nate said, "is how blasé the board of directors is about this. They're having trouble making their insurance payments now, so reporting this to IYS—"

That brought Sophie up short. "IYS?"

Nate waved her off and said exactly what he shouldn't have said and yet exactly what Sophie knew he would say: "Doesn't matter."

"Doesn't it?"

Turning to stare at her, Nate said slowly, "No, it doesn't."

That was Nate's I-don't-want-to-talk-about-it voice. Sophie replied by saying, "All right," in her we-*will*-talk-about-this-later-whether-you-want-to-or-not voice.

She'd had a hell of a time getting Nate to recognize that voice.

Nate started pacing between the desk and the screen. "Marney's *not* reporting it because it'll hike their premiums even higher, and the zoo will probably go under."

Hardison clicked another of the financial reports to the fore of the screen. "Nate's right about everything he just said except the word 'probably.'"

Sophie asked, "So why is the board pushing to report it?"

"That is an excellent question. Some of its members have to be dirty. Hardison, what'd you find out?"

Everyone turned to give Hardison an expectant look. This was when he generally provided a list of often very entertaining secrets, lies, cover-ups, and other gossip.

As a result, everyone was brought up short when he just shrugged and said, "Nothing."

"Excuse me?" Nate asked, stunned.

"Nothing. Nada. Zip. Zilch. Ziparoonio. These guys are *animal lovers*, Nate. They're all regular people—"

"*Rich* regular people," Nate added testily.

But Hardison shook his head. "These folks are house-in-the-suburbs rich, not mansion-on-the-hill rich. And they're the kinda people who like animals and buy stock in zoos, so . . ."

For the first time Parker spoke. "That doesn't mean anything. Hitler was an animal lover."

Hardison shot her a look. "Yeah, but I don't think he went around killing people and being the evilest person in history because he was an animal lover. I think he was doing that 'cause he was *Adolf Hitler*."

"Actually," Sophie said, "Hitler was an excellent grifter, if you think about it. Postwar Germany was devastated, they'd been beaten in the war and then strangled by reparations to the rest of Europe. They were the easiest of marks, and he sold them all on falsehoods, playing on their fears for his own gain. It's the same thing every grifter does."

"Except for the part about being evil," Parker added.

"Right."

Eliot was staring at Sophie with the incredulous expression he usually reserved for Parker. "Are you seriously comparing Hitler to—well, us?"

"Of course not!" Sophie said, appalled at the very notion. "I mean, structurally, it's a similar thing, but structurally, we're similar to plenty of people. And we used to be—"

"Not Hitler!" Hardison was shaking his head. "Woman, you are *not*—"

Nate held up both hands. "Can we get back on track, please?"

"Fine by me." Eliot was still staring daggers at Sophie.

"There's another reason why Marney won't contact IYS. They have investigators. Now, their three best aren't there anymore."

Sophie gave him a playful smile. "If you do say so yourself."

Pointedly ignoring the dig, Nate said, "I quit, Sterling went to Interpol, and Owen Wallace got fired and is in an Oregon prison."

Sophie nodded, remembering Wallace as a good man who let his obsession over a missing Vincent van Gogh painting get the better of him. He was arrested after he fired a handgun in the middle of a roller-skating rink.

"Unfortunately," Nate continued, "since we forced Blackpoole out, IYS has been on an austerity kick—which means a hiring freeze. They didn't replace Sterling when he quit, they didn't replace Owen when he got fired, and they didn't replace two others who retired. So now they have eight people doing the work of twelve."

"And none of them as good as Sterling or Owen," Parker said.

Nate regarded Parker with annoyance.

"Or you," Parker added quickly. "I was going to say you. Really!"

With the ease of long practice, Sophie was able to keep herself from grinning, but it was a near thing.

Sighing, Nate turned back to the screen. "In any event, even without having any of their best people left, IYS might still find out that there were some—well, irregularities."

"What kind of irregularities?" Eliot asked.

Hardison clicked the remote, bringing forward the map of Africa, the dilapidated building, the priest, the man in uniform, and the picture of the *Black Star.*

Nate looked at Eliot. "She brokered the deal to get the black rhinos from Malani."

Eliot winced. Sophie knew that look on his face: Eliot had been to Malani before joining Nate's crew, and during that period in his life, he usually only visited countries in order to do unpleasant things in them.

"Lemme guess," Hardison said. "You were there when General Polonia took over?"

"No—before that." Eliot stared right at Nate. "I was there when Damien Moreau needed to run arms through Malani."

NINE YEARS AGO

As he got out of the rental car, Eliot Spencer looked very carefully at the two men pacing back and forth in front of Aloysius Mbenga's mansion in Pequeño Lago. They wore the uniforms of the Malani Royal Army, in service to King Lionel.

The driver had just brought him and Damien Moreau to

this edifice in Malani City's only real suburb. As he got out of the other side of the car, Moreau nodded at the driver, who kept the motor running, grabbed a copy of the *International Herald Tribune*, and started flipping through it.

Eliot lowered his head and ran a hand through his close-cropped air as he whispered to Moreau. "Those guys may be dressed like MRA, but they're trained by SF."

Without looking at Eliot, Moreau said, "You can tell they're U.S. Army Special Forces just by the way they pace?"

"It's a very distinctive pace."

Moreau nodded.

As they walked toward the entrance, one of the army guys stopped pacing and opened the huge wooden door. Eliot could see an earpiece, through which he had probably been informed by the gate guard that they were coming. The man said nothing, simply holding the door for them, then leading them through a lavish foyer into a living room with a leather couch, a matching easy chair, an end table on which sat an expensive marble sculpture, what looked like a Rembrandt on the wall over a massive fireplace, which was currently inactive, and several stone figurines on a mantelpiece.

A sideboard was behind the leather couch, and standing in front of it was Aloysius Mbenga, one of the richest men in Malani. He was pouring an amber liquid from a crystal decanter into a crystal glass. Mbenga's suit probably cost as much as the Rembrandt, and he wore a diamond-encrusted ring on his left pinkie. A diamond pin sat in his suit jacket's buttonhole as well. Given that he'd made his fortune off diamond mining, this wasn't very surprising.

The soldier remained standing at parade rest to the left of the doorway. As Moreau moved to stand facing Mbenga,

Eliot placed himself in a position between his employer and the soldier, close to the door.

"So, Mr. Moreau," Mbenga said, "I understand that you wish to sell arms in my country, and that you wish to use my men, my warehouses, and my shipping company."

" 'Use' is such a strong word."

"Hire, then?"

"Oh, no, it's very much the right word. Simply a strong one."

"And why would I agree to this?"

Moreau had stared at the sideboard several times, but was not offered a drink. He then started to walk around Mbenga. "If you agree to my terms, you will receive fifteen percent of all monies I make. The arms business is quite lucrative, and is about to get more so. You will do well."

"I do not require any more money, Mr. Moreau."

That prompted one of Moreau's smiles that made him look like a cat about to chow down on a mouse. "Yes, but if you do not agree to allow me to—to *hire* your services, I will be forced to show your wife the video footage of your many and varied trysts." He walked up to the sideboard and grabbed the decanter.

Eliot saw the soldier tense, but Mbenga held up a hand and he relaxed.

As he poured, Moreau said, "You really shouldn't use a wireless video camera to record your exploits."

"Do you wish to know why I record those 'exploits,' Mr. Moreau?" Mbenga broke into a huge grin, showing off a perfect set of white teeth. "So my wife may watch them. It is what she enjoys. I'm afraid that if you're going to blackmail me, you're going to have to work a bit harder."

Eliot had tremendous self-control. He needed it in his line

of work, because losing control meant people died—people who weren't supposed to die, anyhow. So it was very easy for him not to burst out laughing at Damien Moreau being out-maneuvered by a couple who turned out to be kinkier than he had apparently expected.

Mbenga snatched the drink out of Moreau's hand before he could take a sip and placed it back on the sideboard. "You don't have time to drink. You are leaving."

Moreau then glanced over at Eliot. "Spencer," was all he said.

Eliot whipped his fist out with an *uraken* strike to the soldier's solar plexus. As the soldier struggled for breath and reached for his weapon, Eliot did a quick right sweep, his ankle colliding with the soldier's Achilles' heel. He fell to the ground, and Eliot kicked him in the left temple.

"Your man there was trained by Special Forces. My man there took him down in three and a half seconds."

Eliot had counted it as three and a quarter, but he was willing to forgive Moreau for rounding off.

Moreau then leaned in to stage-whisper in Mbenga's ear. "If you refuse my offer, the next time your wife decides to enjoy one of your shows, Spencer will do something similar to her. And *she* does *not* have Special Forces training."

NOW

"Then what happened?"

Nate noticed that Parker had been sitting on the edge of her seat during Eliot's quick summary of his time in Malani in Damien Moreau's employ.

Eliot took a quick bite of his sandwich before replying to Parker's question. "Mbenga called Moreau's bluff. He had another tryst, we traced the wireless signal to the location where the wife was watching. I went in, put a finger to her temple, and said 'blam.' Mbenga was in Moreau's pocket after that."

"Will that help us now?" Sophie asked. "I mean, the man obviously isn't in Moreau's pocket anymore."

Nate allowed himself a small smile of pride at that. Moreau—a money launderer, arms dealer, and one of the most notorious criminals in the world—was rotting in a prison cell in San Lorenzo, a country he'd all but owned until Nate showed up. Anyone previously in his pocket was now free to run loose.

"No, he's moved pockets—to General Polonia's."

Shaking his head, Hardison said, "That ain't good." He hit the remote, highlighting Malani in purple on the African map on the screen. The tiny nation was a strip of land wedged between Angola and Namibia on the western coast, just north of South Africa. The man in the military uniform also moved to the foreground. "The region was ruled by one of the Bantu kingdoms until the 1500s, when the Portuguese showed up and colonized the whole area. In 1974, there was a coup in Portugal, and a bunch of their colonies declared independence—Angola, Mozambique, East Timor, Malani. King Lionel was crowned as the new Bantu king in 1975, and he lasted until 2003, when there was another coup, this time on him."

"Led," Eliot added, "by troops armed with weapons supplied by Damien Moreau."

"Why am I not surprised?" Sophie muttered.

"There were free elections, they put a president into power, she lasted all of two months before the military took over." Hardison pointed at the general. "General Olorun Polonia's in charge now, and he's been keeping his iron fist pretty well polished ever since."

"And Aloysius Mbenga's his minister of finance," Eliot added.

Sophie was staring at the image of the general. "Is Olorun really his given name?"

Hardison blinked. "Uh—I guess so. Not sure, really. Why?"

"Olorun is the divine creator of all things in Yoruba mythology," Sophie said, "ruler of all the heavens. Either his parents thought *very* highly of him—or he took the name on purpose."

Eliot swallowed the last of his sandwich. "Either way, he's a bastard."

Parker asked, "Is he the one they bought the hippos from?"

"Rhinos," Hardison said, "black rhinos, and no. Ms. Brillinger did the deal with a priest named Michael Maimona." He brought the reverend's face to the fore. "He's not exactly legit, insofar as he's got his fingers in all kinds a' pies, but it all seems to be to finance his hospital." Another click, and the battered old building moved to the center. "This place isn't just a medical clinic; it's an orphanage and a homeless shelter. The clinic's supply list doesn't match their official purchases list, so they're probably gettin' stuff off the black market."

"He ain't gettin' it from the government," Eliot said. "Polonia figures the sick should just die and be done with it.

53

Malani's got an overpopulation problem anyhow. People flee across the border to Namibia all the time."

Hardison clicked the *Black Star* forward. "Now, according to Ms. Brillinger, the Reverend Maimona put the black rhinos on the *Black Star*, and then another ship called the *Black Star* pulled into Boston last week." He shook his head. "I checked into it, but the shipping records are a mess. There's, like, a hundred *Black Star*s, and half of them are called something else now."

Nate frowned. "Don't ships have transponders that allow you to track them?"

"Yeah, and if I knew which of the hundreds of thousands of transponders floating around the Atlantic Ocean belonged to *either* of the *Black Star*s we're talkin' about, I'd be able to track 'em, but otherwise? It's like findin' a needle in a big pile of other needles."

Parker stared quizzically at Hardison. "Not like a needle in a haystack?"

"Needle in a haystack's easy—just bring a magnet."

Eliot stared witheringly at Hardison. "You take the poetry out of everything."

"Says the man who'd just punch the haystack."

Nate let the others engage in their usual banter while he thought through the best plan of attack. After that, he thought of seven or eight more plans of attack. Then he went with Plan D.

He walked over to the screen and cut off whatever point-less argument Hardison, Eliot, and Parker were indulging in. "All right. Sophie, you and Eliot are going to Malani."

Eliot stood up. "Nate, my contacts there are eight or nine years old, and mostly don't like me much."

"We need to find out what happened to the rhinos on that end, and whether the culprit is Reverend Maimona or the owners of the *Black Star* or some other third party. Worst case, there's a man over there living in a snake pit trying to keep kids from dying. If he's being screwed, I'd like to fix that."

To Nate's relief, but not to his surprise, Eliot said nothing in response.

"Meanwhile, Parker, Hardison, and I will look more closely into the Brillinger Zoo's board of directors. Animal lovers or not, *something*'s not right there."

He looked around at the others. Sophie had that faraway look she got when she was trying to figure out the best approach to her mark. Parker was fiddling with her fingernails. Eliot was like a coiled spring; now that they had a job, a plan, and a direction, he was ready to go into action. As for Hardison, he looked frustrated because, as usual, the rest of the team hadn't done a sufficient job of appreciating what he did.

What Hardison never understood was that Nate didn't care *how* everyone did what they did. He was no more concerned with the specifics of Hardison's computer work than he was with the details of Eliot's punches and kicks, or which lock picks Parker used, or the methodology Sophie used to create her characters—though that part he actually did understand, as he used many of the same techniques himself.

Nate nurtured the hope that Hardison would someday comprehend that lack of need for the leader to know the details.

After letting out a quick breath, and realizing that he desperately needed an Irish whiskey, Nate looked at his crew. "Let's go steal back some rhinos."

|||||| FOUR ||||||

NOW

The Reverend Michael Maimona looked out over the dozen or so sweaty people gathered in the chapel.

The word *chapel* was perhaps stretching it a bit. It was the only room in the clinic that could fit more than six people. The word also only really applied on Sunday mornings. On weekdays, the space served as a classroom, and every evening it was a dining hall. Dinner was the only meal the reverend could serve here. People generally provided their own breakfast, and lunch was a luxury they couldn't afford.

The ceiling fan overhead labored, moving the humid, stale air around. Reaching into the pocket of his linen slacks, Michael pulled out a stained handkerchief and dabbed his bald pate.

After a quick glance down at the Bible, he read aloud to his flock. " 'And a leper came to him, beseeching him, and kneeling said to him, "If you will, you can make me clean." Moved with pity, he stretched out his hand and touched him, and said to him, "I will. Be clean." And immediately, the leprosy left him, and he was made clean. And he sternly charged him, and sent him away at once, and said to him, "See that you say nothing to anyone, but go, show yourself to the priest, and offer for your cleansing what Moses commanded, for a proof to the people." But he went out and began to talk freely about it, and to spread the news, so that Jesus could no longer openly enter a town, but was out in the country. And people came to him from every quarter.' " He looked around at the bored-looking faces. "You'd think Jesus would have known better, yes?"

That got a chuckle out of everyone.

"When word got around that Jesus could heal people, they wouldn't leave him alone. Sickness, after all, is something to be avoided, yes? So everywhere he went, the sick came upon him. But for all that he admonished the leper not to spread the word, he did not turn the others away."

A young boy in the third row coughed, then looked up apologetically at Michael. The reverend just nodded and continued.

"But if you continue reading the Gospel of Mark, you'll see that Jesus continued to heal—but also continued to preach. Everywhere he went, he spread the gift of God by healing, but he also spread the word of God, healing the spirit as much as he was healing the body. Now, I would not presume to liken myself to the Lord or His son, but what we do here at the clinic is very much the same thing. Just as the people of Galilee came for the healing but stayed for the preaching, so I expect it of all of you." He grinned. "One could say that listening to me is the price you have to pay."

This prompted more chuckles.

The grin faded. "But the work we do here is as important

as what Jesus did two thousand years ago. People's bodies need healing, but so do their spirits. It is easy to look outside our walls and feel despair. To think that God has forsaken us. The people of Galilee likely felt the same way. We see war and strife all around, starvation and poverty. Like Jesus, we wish to fix it."

As Michael spoke, three men entered the chapel via the rear door. In contrast to everyone else in the room—who all wore cotton or linen shirts and slacks that were threadbare and worn and sweat-stained—these men were dressed in tailored suits. Two of them were much larger than the third, but the smaller one was definitely the one in charge. Michael would have known this even if he didn't recognize the man.

Ignoring the trio, who remained standing in the rear, he went on with his sermon.

"Now, one might say, Jesus failed, yes? True, he healed some people, but he was condemned to die and the Romans were still in power and people still suffered. But that misses the important part: he healed some people. Without Jesus, those people would have continued to suffer. And that is what matters. Just as what we do here matters, even if the rich and powerful continue to grind us down." He pointedly looked at the new arrivals as he said this. "Just saving one body, just saving one soul, makes it worth all the trouble."

Holding up the Bible, he said, "This is the word of the Lord."

A dozen people all mumbled, "Amen."

Michael's Sunday services were a blend of assorted Christian traditions, so the call-and-response was different from what it would be in other churches, having over time developed its own style. He was nominally Episcopalian, but he worked aspects of several other types of Christianity into his mass, as well as some of his own.

However, he lifted the ending straight from Catholicism, which he'd always thought the best benediction possible: "The mass is ended, go in peace."

The congregation got up and shuffled toward the side exits, all of them specifically avoiding the rear door. Even the people who didn't recognize the man in the suit knew that it was best to avoid anyone who was well dressed. Such people never had the best interests of the clinic's residents at heart.

One person—a young woman named Catia—came up to Michael. "Reverend, Amalia wished me to inform you that the shipment of insulin has been delayed again."

Michael sighed. They had several diabetics in their care, and their current supply of insulin was getting dangerously low. This was the third postponement of that shipment.

"Thank you, Catia."

The young woman then glanced back at the three men, still standing at the rear. "Will you be okay with them?"

"Of course," Michael said with a confidence he didn't entirely feel. Somehow he doubted that the cross around his neck would do much to prevent the two large men from pounding him into mulch if the shorter man ordered them to do so.

But people like this preyed on weakness. He would not show any to them.

Once Catia departed, the three men walked forward. "An impressive sermon, Reverend. I particularly liked the part about rich and powerful men grinding down the oppressed masses. Very poetic."

"What is it you want, Minister Mbenga?"

The Malani minister of finance's face widened as he let

loose with a gap-toothed smile. Michael had never understood why someone as wealthy as Aloysius Mbenga had never gotten the tooth replaced.

He also fantasized about Mbenga losing the tooth from being punched in the face by one of the many people on whom he'd stepped on his rise to near the top of the proverbial heap.

"What I want, Reverend, is to make you an offer. Your insulin shipment has been delayed three times now. I can assure you, those delays will continue. You should therefore use another source. Conveniently for you, I have one, which can provide you with three cases at noon tomorrow. All I ask is that one of my men inspect the packages before you distribute them to your patients."

Michael sighed. "Guns or narcotics?"

The gap-toothed smile again. "Does it matter? You will not receive insulin otherwise."

In fact, Michael had several other insulin sources, but none of them could deliver a supply as quickly as Monday afternoon.

"It is also possible," Mbenga casually added, "that I will be required to alert Interpol to your recent transaction with America. I'm sure they'll be quite interested in your theft and illegal shipment of two endangered black rhinoceroses."

A retort that the rhinos were not stolen died on Michael's lips. Interpol wouldn't see it that way. The fact that the rhinos did not arrive where they were supposed to was problematic, but that actually would make it harder for the illegal shipment charge to stick. The theft charge would be enough, though, to ruin him and force the clinic to close.

He couldn't let that happen.

"Very well, Minister. I'll expect the insulin at noon tomorrow."

"Oh, you will receive it, rest assured."

With that, Mbenga turned to leave, his two baobab-size bodyguards following him out.

Once he was gone, Michael made the slump-shouldered walk to his office. Amalia Sanger was standing outside it, finishing off a phone call. Amalia didn't have a formal job title—Michael often referred to her as his "Lord High Everything Else," after the character of Pooh-Bah from *The Mikado*. Amalia's utter lack of familiarity with the Gilbert and Sullivan operetta just made the nickname all the more appealing to Michael.

Regardless, the clinic would have long since collapsed under its own weight without her organizational skills.

As she pocketed her cell phone, she looked at Michael and immediately noticed the slump in his posture. "Well, that's not good. What happened?"

Michael explained as he entered his airless office. A small desk fan did an even less effective job of moving air around than the ceiling fan in the chapel. The papers on his desk were weighed down with rocks that served as paperweights. As he spoke, he flicked the switch on the back of his ancient PC. It whined as it went into its slow booting process, played out in green on black on the decades-old monitor.

Amalia shook her head. "Michael, we can't let the government in like that! It starts with this, and ends with—"

"Harold and Marcus and Amira not getting their insulin. We're dancing on the edge with them as it is. If we don't get another shipment by tomorrow—"

Holding up a hand, Amalia said, "Fine, fine." She made a face. "I warned you that dealing with that zoo would bite us on the ass."

"Dealing with that zoo gave us the money to secure a reliable supplier of both penicillin and adrenaline. I'd say it was money well spent."

"Yes, but you wouldn't have given in to Mbenga if it was just the threat of no insulin. You've got ins with every medical supplier on three continents. We would've gotten it eventually. No, it was the threat of Interpol that convinced you—wasn't it?"

Michael let out a long breath and ran his ragged handkerchief over his pate once again by way of avoiding having to answer the question.

"That's what I thought." Amalia folded her arms. "We're gonna get bit on the ass by this."

With a smile, Michael said, "My cheeks are quite well gnawed on already, Amalia. I wouldn't have lasted this long otherwise."

"Excuse me?" a new voice intruded.

Michael looked up and past Amalia to see a man standing in the doorway to his office, hair neatly tied back in a ponytail. He wore a suit that was more off-the-rack than the ones worn by Mbenga and his bodyguards, and a pair of Ray-Bans that probably helped with the sun outside but were just an affectation in the poorly lit clinic.

Amalia cried out, "Who let you in here?" at the same time that Michael softly asked, "May I help you?"

The man looked back and forth between them. "Which question should I answer first?"

"Mine," Amalia said before Michael could speak.

"The door was open, ma'am. My name's John Smith, and I'm here on behalf of Doctors Without Borders." Smith was American, and had a faint Boston accent—which Michael

63

mainly could recognize after spending several months talking over the phone with various employees of the Brillinger Zoo.

"No, you're not," Amalia said with a scowl. "First of all, John Smith? Really? Nobody's actually named John Smith."

"Actually, ma'am," Smith said, "there are seventeen John Smiths listed in the Boston white pages alone."

That got a sardonic smile out of Amalia. "But you're not one of them, right? 'Cause you're CIA. And the reason I know you're CIA is because you called it Doctors Without Borders. Anybody who actually worked for them would call it Médecins Sans Frontières. That, and you're, like, the fifteenth CIA agent I've met since King Lionel was overthrown. I recognize the type."

Smith looked past Amalia at Michael. "Reverend, you're gonna be giving polio inoculations next week. You're gonna need help. I have a doctor who's up from South Africa, and she's more than willing to volunteer."

"Really?" Michael asked, raising a quizzical eyebrow at Smith. "Out of the goodness of her heart?"

"That's what Doc—" Smith cocked his head to the side for a second, then looked at Amalia. "That's what Médecins Sans Frontières does. She's worked at clinics all up and down Africa, and she's fully qualified."

Amalia was giving Smith the dirtiest look in her arsenal— Michael still had nightmares from the last time he was on the receiving end of one of those. "What do you get in return?"

"The satisfaction of a job well done, ma'am."

"Who is this doctor?" Michael asked.

Transferring her gaze of doom onto Michael, Amalia said, "Michael, you can't be seriously considering—"

"Having a qualified doctor assist during the inoculations,

which is traditionally a time when we're overrun with people and during which you are constantly complaining about how understaffed we are?"

Amalia said nothing, though Michael could tell she had plenty *to* say. She just didn't want to verbalize it in front of Smith.

Michael repeated his question to Smith: "I ask again, who is this doctor?"

Reaching into the inner pocket of his jacket, Smith pulled out a jump drive. "Her name's Dr. Bernadine Onslow, and I've got all her information right here."

Michael felt a spontaneous laugh explode from his mouth. "I'm afraid, Mr. Smith, that all I may do with that is clean my ears." He pointed at the computer, currently blinking a DOS prompt at him. "Our computer isn't sophisticated enough to handle a three-and-a-half-inch disk, much less your jump drive. If you bring a paper file on your doctor, I will look it over and consider having her join us."

Smith nodded. "All right, then, I'll have it for you tomorrow morning. But, Reverend? I don't think there's anything to 'consider,' do you? After all, it'd be a damn shame if Interpol found out about those black rhinos."

With that, he turned on his heel and departed.

Amalia opened her mouth to speak, but Michael cut her off. "Do *not* say it, Amalia. We needed the money."

"And now we're being extorted by the CIA *and* General Polonia's government. This will end *badly*, Michael."

The reverend blew out a breath. "I should have taken my own advice."

Amalia frowned. "What do you mean?"

"I ended the service by requesting that everyone go in peace. It seems I failed rather spectacularly at that."

TWO DAYS AGO

"John Smith? Really? Nobody's actually named John Smith."

Without even looking at Eliot, Hardison clicked on his remote.

Looking over at the screen in Nate's apartment, Eliot saw a white-pages Web site that listed people named John Smith in Boston, Massachusetts. There were seventeen entries.

"All right, fine," Eliot said reluctantly. He hated admitting that Hardison was right while actually in Hardison's presence. "It's still gonna sound fake."

"That's the idea," Sophie said. "We need them to think you are CIA, and since you can't exactly come out and say that you're with the CIA, we have to push them toward it."

Parker was at the kitchen table, munching on a bowlful of dry cereal. "Why can't you say you're with the CIA?"

By now Eliot really thought he should no longer have been surprised at things Parker didn't know. And yet she always managed to do it. "Nobody with the Company says they're with the Company. Best way to find a fake spook is to find one that says he's a spook."

Sophie shook her head and stood up from the table. "What concerns me is the duration of this job. What if I'm still there when they inoculations start? I don't actually know how to do that."

Hardison shook his head. "That's not for another week and a half."

"Yes, but if we're done by then, they'll be shorthanded."

"You do realize," Hardison said, "we're talkin' 'bout someone who probably extorted two hundred grand from a zoo, right?"

"Besides," Eliot added, "that's the beauty of the cover. They think we're CIA, they won't ask questions—or even be all that surprised—if we pull out all of a sudden. And I can show you how to use the syringe."

"Eliot, that's a far cry from being able to—"

"You're not supposed to do it perfectly." Eliot walked over to Sophie. "CIA's been using clinics like Maimona's for covert ops for a couple years now. They give inoculations, they 'screw up,' and blood gets on the needle. Then they test the DNA in the blood, and compare it against terrorists they're looking for. It's how they found bin Laden."

Hardison gave Eliot his wide-eyed look. "Seriously? That actually happened?"

"*Happens.*" Eliot shook his head. "That's what *happens* out here in the real world."

"Whatever, man." Hardison handed him a jump drive. "Plug this sucker into their computer. It's got Sophie's dossier—Dr. Bernadine Onslow's whole history right there. Meanwhile, it'll grab all their files."

"Can't you just hack in?" Sophie asked.

Hardison shook his head. "No wireless network, and I haven't been able to find a strong enough connection to let me in. They're probably using old tech. I may find a way in eventually, but this way's easier, faster, and safer."

NOW

Eliot subvocalized as he wandered down the halls of the clinic. "So much for easier, faster, and safer, Hardison."

Hardison was yawning as he spoke over Eliot's earbud. "Yeah, I heard. It's Duberman all over again."

"You awake, or what?" Eliot asked angrily. He was cranky partly because Hardison was half asleep, partly because he was also thinking about the 1980s-era PC he'd found at Dubertech, and it bugged him when he and Hardison were on the same wavelength.

"Gimme a break, man, it's six A.M. here. On a Sunday morning, that's when I usually go to *bed*."

Eliot sometimes forgot that most people needed more than three hours of sleep a night. "I'm walkin' past a ton of file cabinets here. Looks like we'll have to do this the old-fashioned way."

"Great." Hardison yawned again.

"It's fine," Sophie said. "I'll go by with Eliot tomorrow, and once they accept me, I'll check the files by hand."

"By hand. Right," Hardison muttered. "Between this and Nate's surveillance, we're partyin' like it's 1969."

"Get over it, Hardison," Eliot said as he exited the clinic into the bright West African sun. "These people can barely afford lightbulbs."

"What's your read on Reverend Maimona, Eliot?" Sophie asked.

"Not sure. He's got dirt on his hands—but not blood. And I get the vibe that he really does want to help people. But I can't tell if he screwed our client over or if he's just another victim."

"Well, I'll meet him tomorrow," Sophie said, and then put on her Afrikaans accent, "as Dr. Onslow, and then we shall know."

|||||| FIVE ||||||

Parker was starting to think that Nate was punishing her for something.

She had no idea what, of course. That would require knowing how Nate's brain worked, and Parker didn't particularly want to go there. Nate's brain was a scary place, full of vipers and monsters and alcohol and things.

But Nate was also the smartest person Parker knew, after Hardison. And Parker knew *a lot* of smart people. Her mentor, Archie Leach, was incredibly smart, and then there was that French gendarme who almost caught her that one time in Nice, and of course there was Jim Sterling—Parker preferred not to think about Sterling if at all possible, as his brain was worse than Nate's—but even with all those people, Nate was almost the smartest.

So all in all, Parker figured that he had good reason for

sticking her on this stupid surveillance work. But she well and truly hated it. Surveillance was *boring*. Sure, there were moments when you had to be careful that nobody saw you, but Parker had been breaking into high-security museums before she was old enough to vote. Not that she ever voted. She wasn't even sure *how* to vote. It probably wasn't all that complicated, after all, lots of people did it, and most of them weren't as smart as Nate, or Sterling, or Archie, or that cop in Nice, or Hardison.

The point was, it was ridiculously easy for Parker to avoid being seen while she spied on people. Parker *hated* easy. There wasn't any kind of challenge to it.

Plus it just seemed so *pointless*. Hardison himself had said it best two days ago: "Nate, I can track their digital footprint all over everywhere without havin' to get up from"—he had put on a British accent—"the *comfy chair*!" Back to his normal voice: "Why we gotta go all over creation, when—"

"Because we need to know *who* these people are," Nate had interrupted, "not just what they do when they're sitting at their computer and where they take their cell phones."

There were six people on the Brillinger Zoo board of directors. Nate assigned two each to Parker and Hardison, and took the other two for himself.

The first one on Parker's list was Steven Fischer. He lived in a house in Wilbraham. According to Hardison, he was a widower, and according to Parker, after following him around for a day, he was the single most boring human being who ever lived. And Parker knew even more boring people than she knew smart people. There was her good friend Peggy, who was very sweet, but very very dull. Of course, her boringness was what made her of interest to Parker. She liked the idea of having friends, even if that friend talked *way* too much about cats and catering. Then there was Archie's daughter, whom Parker had never formally met, but on whom she spied a few times after she and Archie reunited for that Wakefield Agriculture job. She was stupendously boring. Then there were all those other gendarmes in Nice, who were not only boring, but *stupid*. Parker was able to run rings around them, which made it easier to get away from the smart one.

And, of course, Steven Fischer, who had them all beat for boring.

"Parker, how's it going?"

Never was Parker more grateful to hear Nate's voice in her head.

"Yesterday, Steven Fischer got up at eight o'clock, read the news on his laptop while eating a piece of dry toast and drinking pineapple juice, walked on his exercise thingie for fifteen minutes, watched some stupid morning talk show, called his daughter and talked for half an hour, called his granddaughter and talked for half an hour, ate lunch, which consisted of a protein shake and *another* glass of pineapple juice, called his broker, walked to the church that's a mile away, played bingo for *three hours*, walked back home, microwaved a frozen dinner and ate it while watching television, then went to bed at eleven."

"Parker—"

"Today, you know what he did? *The exact same thing!*"

Hardison came on the earbud. "Nate, I've checked this guy's digital footprint, and it's a rut. He really does do the same thing every day. Only time he's ever varied the routine is Saturday nights, 'cause his church don't do bingo then, and whenever there's a board meeting for the zoo, when he drives to Brillinger. It's a dead end."

"He drives in a 1985 Buick LeSabre." Parker added this for no reason except that she'd broken into the garage at one point last night because she was bored. It had to be contagious. And there was, perhaps, no greater comment on Fischer's boringness than the fact that the most interesting thing about him was that he drove an old workhorse of a car.

"All right, fine," Nate said. "It's been two days, that's enough. Move on to MacAvoy."

"Yay!" Parker swung down off the tree branch she was sitting on and landed in Fischer's front yard.

"Parker," Nate said slowly, "were you just in a tree?"

"Fischer has a very nice oak in his front yard. I could see *everything*, it was *great*!" It was true. The branch she'd been on was right between the two floors of the two-story house. Hardison had said that Fischer and his late wife had raised their kids in that house, but it was really too big for him by himself. He only used the kitchen, living room, and one bedroom—and she could see all three from that branch.

Her jumping down and crying "Yay!" was the first actual noise she'd made since she started spying on Fischer, and since it was midevening, he was currently in the living room watching some television show or other about detectives or lawyers or something, his plastic frozen-dinner container abandoned next to him on the couch. Now he ran to the window and stared right at Parker.

Shaking his fist, he cried, "Get off my lawn!"

Grinning widely, Parker did as he requested. She ran toward the car Hardison had rented for her under her Alice White identity. The vehicle was parked around the corner.

"Did he just say what I think he just said?" Hardison asked.

"Want me to go back and ask?"

Nate and Hardison both said, *"No!"* in perfect unison.

When she got to the car—a beige 2004 Toyota Corolla, which was as boring a car as Fischer was a person—she noticed a white piece of paper and an orange envelope stuck under the windshield. "Hardison, I got a parking ticket."

"Didn't I tell you to look at the signs to make sure it was legal?"

Parker hesitated. "You—probably did, yeah." She took the ticket and envelope off the windshield and tossed them to the ground. "You'll take care of it, right?"

"You're just lucky they didn't tow your ass—and *yeah*, I'll take care of it. Y'know, the signs are *right there* on the street, in English and everything."

As she pulled into traffic and blazed down the suburban road at fifty miles an hour, she realized that sometimes Hardison could be just as boring as Fischer.

||||||| SIX |||||||

Sophie followed Eliot into the clinic and was immediately struck by how open it looked. The impression was entirely illusory, as the building had many narrow corridors that led into tiny rooms, but there were no doors. Looking more closely, she saw that some of the doorways had broken and bent hinges—but the rest were in perfect shape. Sophie suspected that some of the doors had been removed forcibly, and the Reverend Maimona had just decided to take the rest off.

Ceiling fans wobbled above, mostly serving to draw people's attention to their own perspiration, but not doing much to provide relief, at least on the face of it. Given how close to the bone the running of such a place as this had to be, that they were willing to spend the money to keep the fans going revealed just how necessary they were.

As she dabbed some of the perspiration off her own forehead, Sophie seriously considered donating enough money to buy air-conditioning units for the building.

The walls of the clinic were the light beige that white walls inevitably turned after years of never being cleaned. Sophie saw several children chasing each other through the hallways, an older woman fruitlessly pursuing them, urging them in Portuguese to slow down.

As the older woman passed by Sophie and Eliot, she looked at them with fear and suspicion. The woman herself was in a threadbare housedress that looked like she had first worn it twenty-five years and fifteen pounds ago. Even so, she was far better dressed than the children she chased, who wore only shorts that had once been slacks, the legs of which had been sloppily cut off.

The path to the Reverend Maimona's office included passing by the many file cabinets Eliot had mentioned on his way out yesterday. They lined an entire wall of the corridor for about fifty meters. Each drawer's contents were indicated by words in Portuguese on labels that were still white, unlike the walls, so they'd been applied recently. It looked as if the Portuguese words were typed on a manual typewriter. At three equidistant points atop the cabinets were wire-frame baskets, piled haphazardly with overstuffed file folders. Each basket was labeled with the word *REPUDIAR*—these were files that needed to be put back away and hadn't been yet.

A woman stood at the doorway to the reverend's office, radiating hostility. She was leaning against a wooden desk that was piled with papers and what Sophie assumed to be the very manual typewriter that had made all the labels on the file cabinets and baskets. She suspected that, if Hardison were here, he'd have burst a blood vessel by now.

The hostile woman simply had to be Amalia, the reverend's assistant. She had all the suspicion—but none of the fear—that the old woman had shown earlier. The dress she wore was a polyester knockoff of a designer dress, which must have been agony to wear in this heat.

"Welcome back, Agent Smith." Amalia spoke in as unwelcoming a tone as was possible. She straightened up from leaning on the desk, causing the desk to shift on uneven legs.

"I told you, ma'am," Eliot said, "I'm not an agent of anything."

"Of course." Amalia turned to Sophie and offered a hand. The smile was still insincere, but she put more effort in disguising the fact for Sophie. "You must be Dr. Onslow. I'm Amalia Sanger."

Adding an Afrikaans accent to her usual speech pattern, Sophie said, "My pleasure, Ms. Sanger." She switched the small briefcase from under her right arm to under her left so she could return the handshake. "What is it you do here?"

Before Amalia could answer, a voice spoke from inside the office. "She is the Lord High Everything Else."

A figure matching that of the pictures Hardison had shown the team of the Reverend Maimona came out from the office, bearing a small smile.

Sophie turned slightly. "Ah, *The Mikado*. I saw a magnificent performance of it in London during a vacation there." This was actually true, except for the vacation part. Sophie almost hadn't attended the performance after she was rejected for the role of Katisha—rejected even as the understudy, or a place in the chorus, or indeed any position that placed her anywhere near the theater prior to opening.

"You are quite lucky," Maimona said, his smile widening.

Amalia threw up her hands. "Does everyone know this play but me?"

"In any case," the reverend said, "unlike Pooh-Bah, Amalia has worked for her title. She does whatever is necessary to keep us open, yes? As do we all—few of us in this clinic have single tasks."

Maimona wore a brown linen shirt and matching linen pants. The top two buttons of his shirt were unbuttoned, revealing a gold necklace with a cross dangling at the end of it. His clothes were well worn and sweat-stained, but looked like they had been pressed prior to his putting them on. Idly, Sophie wondered if the reverend had done the ironing himself or if that was part of what Amalia did to keep the clinic open. She was obviously the one most concerned with keeping up appearances.

"You must be the Reverend Maimona," Sophie said, offering her hand.

"The cross around my neck always gives it away."

Unlike Amalia, whose hands were callused only at the fingertips—no doubt from using the manual typewriter—Maimona's hands were completely callused. This was a man who'd done plenty of hard work.

Three of the fingers of the hand he shook with also felt uneven. They'd obviously been broken, possibly more than once—or just once and reset badly. There was also a tightness in his handshake that indicated a stiff shoulder. Possibly he'd been shot there—Sophie had once had a similar hitch in her own handshake after Nate shot her in the right shoulder in Paris about a decade or so earlier. (In his defense, she'd shot him first when he broke in on her stealing several paintings.) It had taken her years of exercises to get rid of that tell. Maimona had less reason to work to hide the fact that he'd been shot.

"Please come in, Dr. Onslow," the reverend said, indicating his office with one hand. He then cut between Sophie and Eliot. "Thank you, Mr. Smith, that will be all."

Eliot got that smoldering look he got in his eyes when somebody pissed him off. While still keeping his face pointing at the reverend, he flicked his eyes briefly at Sophie.

She nodded almost imperceptibly. Eliot then nodded at Maimona somewhat more perceptibly. "I'll be outside if you need me, Dr. Onslow."

"I should be fine, Mr. Smith," Sophie said in an only partially reassuring tone.

Eliot left, followed quickly by Amalia. As Sophie moved into the reverend's office, she heard footsteps approach and a voice speak in Portuguese: "Amalia, I cannot find the Assis file."

"Did you check under *A*?" Sophie heard a mischievous tone in Amalia's voice that hadn't been there when she was dealing with Eliot.

Tightly, the man said, "Yes, of course I did."

"It's probably in one of the baskets."

"Those huge baskets atop the file cabinets? When were they last refiled, when Lionel was king?"

The two voices faded as they moved away from the office, no doubt to search for the errant file. Sophie took a seat in the guest chair that faced the desk, placing the briefcase in her lap.

As Maimona walked around to his side of the desk, she

KEITH R. A. DeCANDIDO

noted the piles of papers, maps, pamphlets, flyers, and more, all weighed down with rocks, as well as the ancient computer that took up half the desk.

Sophie removed from the briefcase a manila folder that was filled with eight-and-a-half-by-eleven sheets of paper—printouts of everything Hardison had put on the jump drive—and handed it across the desk.

"Here is my full dossier, Reverend. I hope you appreciate how much this cost. The Internet café in Malani City charged three marks per page!" The Malani mark was the equivalent of a pound in the UK, or one and a half U.S. dollars. Sophie could afford the money, of course, but it was still a fairly outrageous price to have to pay.

Maimona flipped through the pages. "I'm sure Mr. Smith's employers can spare the cash."

"Actually, he made me pay for it myself." Sophie added a touch of bitterness to her tone.

"Somehow, that does not surprise me." He looked up from the papers. "You seem to be quite qualified, Dr. Onslow. So tell me—why are you here?"

"I've been with Médecins Sans Frontières for—goodness, almost six years now. Seems like only yesterday I joined."

"Time does fly," the reverend said with a sad head shake. "It seems also like only yesterday that I started this clinic. But it was, in fact, eight years ago."

"Right after the coup?"

The reverend nodded. "The fighting was—was awful. There were many refugees, and many more sick and wounded. This building had been a school under King Lionel, and President Madeira was going to have it changed to a community center. When General Polonia started his revolution, he made it into a barracks, then abandoned it when he took power." Maimona shook his head. "The land was originally owned by the Portuguese government, and when they pulled out in 1975, it was given to the Church, which opened the original school. After Polonia . . ." He shrugged. "Nobody ever made a formal claim on it after that."

"So, strictly speaking, it's yours?"

"After a fashion." He smiled. "But we're here to speak of you."

"What do you wish to know?"

"Why here? Why now?"

"Until I joined the organization, I lived in South Africa my entire life." Sophie folded her hands primly in her lap. "I'm quite familiar with the turbulence of this region, especially once King Lionel was overthrown. It was places like this clinic that inspired me. When I learned that you were doing inoculations, I thought it would be a fine opportunity."

"That is very—very noble of you, Dr. Onslow."

"Thank you."

"And also quite absurd." Maimona steepled his fingers. "Let us be honest, yes? That is why I did not invite Mr. Smith to this meeting. You're here because the Americans wish you to be here for whatever reason."

Internally, Sophie smiled in triumph. It was always a trick to play a character well enough to be almost convincing, but not quite. It would have been child's play for her to sell the reverend on her devotion to providing medicine for the people of Malani, but much harder to find that slightly off note of someone reciting a platitude to try to sound authentic without really meaning it.

And it worked, since he saw right through the platitude.

"I'm here to help you with the inoculations, Reverend. That is all that I am able to say."

Reverend Maimona snorted and shook his head. "Ah, yes, plausible deniability. They should print *that* on U.S. currency, it is far more apt than *e pluribus unum* or 'in God we trust.'"

"I do know that Mr. Smith has very good reasons for wanting me here. Ones that will make the world a better place."

"Really?" The reverend leaned back in his chair. "Better for whom, precisely? Surely not the people of Malani."

"I'd say getting rid of terrorists in the area is a very good—" She put a hand to her mouth. "I'm sorry, I shouldn't have said anything."

Maimona shook his head and chuckled. "You needn't apologize. I am not a child, yes? I am aware that the Americans are interested solely in their so-called war on terror—as if a concept can be warred upon. As for getting rid of terrorists, I have lived in western Africa my entire life, Doctor, and I can assure you that the greatest terrorist I have ever seen is sitting in the palace right now. Is he your target?"

Sophie nervously shook her head in order to convey regret that she'd accidentally made a slip of the tongue. "I'm sorry, I've said more than I should, already."

The reverend simply nodded.

After a brief pause, she leaned forward. "Reverend, I'm here to work. Regardless of what you think of me or Mr. Smith, I'm here. I'm willing to do any task, no matter how menial."

The setup was perfect for the reverend to ask his new doctor to refile the material in the wire-frame baskets, thus providing Sophie with an excellent opportunity to go through the clinic's files. He had already said that everyone did a little of everything to keep the place going, so this was a man who would think nothing of giving an M.D. so mundane a task, and the need for the filing to be done had just been reinforced by the conversation outside.

But before the reverend could say anything, Amalia poked her head through the open doorway and spoke in a tight, annoyed voice. "Michael, the shipment has arrived."

"Excellent." The reverend stood up. "Come, Dr. Onslow, you may help me inspect this shipment of insulin, yes? It's a new supplier, and I'm not sure what to expect. Your expertise would be most useful."

"Of course," Sophie said enthusiastically, masking her disappointment. Still, based on the conversation Amalia had had a few minutes ago, the filing wasn't likely to get done anytime soon—worst case, she could volunteer to do it later on.

The reverend led the way back down the corridor, accompanied by Amalia. The three of them were soon exiting the clinic. Several roads converged in front of the clinic, though calling them roads was perhaps giving them too much credit. They were very well-worn dirt paths, rendered somewhat flat by the constant pressing down of tires. The clinic had been built on top of a hill, and each road that moved away from it went down into jungle growth.

Like much of this region of Africa, Malani basically had two seasons: rain and summer. The former kept the trees alive, and the latter was doing its best to kill Sophie as she stepped outside and felt the bright midday sun pound down on her. She was regretting bothering with the linen jacket that she was wearing over her sundress. Reaching into that jacket's pocket, she pulled out a large pair of sunglasses.

Two vehicles were parked outside the clinic. One was a lorry—it looked like an old army surplus vehicle—the entire lower half of which was covered in dirt, as were the bottom quarter of the side windows and the parts of the windshield that weren't covered by the wipers. The lorry was surrounded by ten men. Six were in various types of civilian clothes—most of them looking like hand-me-downs—and each carried the same type of rifle. The other four wore black T-shirts and black cargo pants and were carrying different types of rifles. Behind the lorry was parked a black Escalade with tinted windows that looked like it was fresh off the lot. It, too, had dirt all over the tires, but only there and on bits of the rims.

Eliot's voice sounded in Sophie's ear. "I don't like this. Insulin shipments shouldn't come with two sets of armed guards. One set makes sense, but there's two separate groups here. The guys in black are carrying H&K MP5s. That's standard issue for the Malani Army. The others are carrying AK-47 knockoffs that are all over the black market. I'm guessing the AKs are the ones guarding the insulin and the MP5s are here to take their cut."

Sophie nodded to herself. Eliot had confirmed what she suspected from looking at them. She regarded her companions. "Why is the military here to guard a shipment?"

"An excellent question," the reverend said sullenly.

One of the men in black walked over to them. "Reverend,

we are here to inspect the shipment, and make sure that this medicine meets government standards. Once we are satisfied, you may take custody of it."

Sophie watched as the soldiers removed the boxes of insulin from the lorry and placed them on the ground. The boxes were insulated to keep the insulin cold.

She noticed that one box was noticeably heavier than the others. The soldier who unloaded it was not a small man, but had a bit of trouble with it, and needed assistance to carry it.

Without even inspecting the box further, the first soldier came over to the reverend and pointed at that box. "We will need to confiscate that box. The others pass inspection."

The two soldiers carried the box to the Escalade and placed it in the boot. It was done with less care than you would expect for a box that was supposed to be filled with glass vials containing insulin. The men in black all piled into the car, then, and drove off.

"That was—odd," Sophie said to both the reverend and Eliot.

The latter replied first. "I'm on it." Sophie could hear him starting their rental car through her earbud. Her initial annoyance at his departing with their only vehicle was tamped down by the fact that she wanted to stick around the clinic anyhow.

As for Maimona, he simply stared after the Escalade as it drove off.

But Amalia did reply to what Sophie said: "We'll be happy to explain what just happened, Dr. Onslow—as soon as you tell us what, precisely, you and Mr. Smith are up to."

Placing a hand on Amalia's shoulder, the reverend gently

said, "Enough, Amalia. Dr. Onslow, if you'd be so kind as to check the vials, please." Then he attempted a smile, though it didn't make it to his eyes. "Then perhaps I could interest you in doing some filing."

Sophie returned the smile. "I'd be delighted."

||||||| SEVEN |||||||

Reverend Maimona's clinic was located outside Malani City, at the intersection of several roads. It was a hub, truly, that interconnected Malani City with four other small towns, with the clinic servicing people from all five municipalities.

Driving the Focus that he and Sophie had rented—and Eliot had made yet another mental note to strangle Hardison, this time for sticking them with so low performance and low clearance a car to drive through the uneven roads of Malani—Eliot followed the Escalade down the long road that went through the jungle, circling around Malani City toward Pequeño Lago. The road that had been cut through the jungle changed widths on a regular basis, though it had yet to be significantly wider than the Escalade.

Eliot wondered which fat cat was getting the contraband in the insulin case. Malani certainly had no shortage of them;

the diamond mines had been very profitable for a very long time.

Not wanting to look like he was following the Escalade, he tailgated the vehicle for a while, performing a bit of what his old buddy Shelley used to call "vehicular sodomy." When the road finally widened enough to allow him to pass, he shifted to the left and went around the large SUV.

Gunning the accelerator—for whatever small increase in speed that "gunning" a Focus could accomplish—Eliot zoomed ahead until he was out of sight of the Escalade and on a particularly narrow stretch. Then he slammed on the brakes, skidding the car into position so it was completely blocking the road. Then he popped the hood, got out of the car, and lifted it, putting the bar in place to keep it open.

Screwing a look of confusion on his face, Eliot stared at the engine block intently.

The Escalade pulled into view a minute later, and slowed to a halt about four feet from the Focus.

The lead soldier—the same one who'd told Maimona that he was confiscating one of the boxes—stepped out of the shotgun side of the Escalade. The MP5 was strapped to his shoulder.

"You need to move that vehicle now."

Eliot turned to the man and spoke in a higher-pitched tone than normal. "Would if I could. Why you think I spent so much time trying to get past *your* slow ass?" He pointed at the perfectly functioning engine block. "The damn thing just seized up on me. I don't suppose you know anything about cars?"

The man snarled and turned toward the Escalade. Eliot's

Portuguese was a bit rusty, but he was pretty sure that he instructed one of the two soldiers in the backseat to come out.

Thug One came out of the back, with Thug Two getting out the other side, pulling a cigarette out of a pack that was tucked into the sleeve of his T-shirt. The driver stayed behind the wheel.

Giving Eliot a derisive look, Thug One stepped up to the hood. Eliot moved out of his way, putting himself between Thug One and the leader.

Four guys, Eliot figured he could take them in half a minute.

As soon as Thug One peered in to look at the engine, Eliot knocked the metal stand aside. The hood came crashing down on the back of the man's neck while Eliot simultaneously delivered a spear hand to the leader's throat, just below the Adam's apple.

Five seconds, and one was already down, with another in bad shape.

The leader made a *hkkkkk!* noise and stumbled backward. Thug Two was in the middle of lighting up, and he dropped both Zippo and cigarette while fumbling for his MP5. In the two seconds required for him to do both of these things, Eliot took one step and delivered a roundhouse kick to his face, his polished shoe colliding with Thug Two's nose. Blood spurted from the proboscis, and Thug Two screamed and put his hands to his face.

Eliot allowed himself a brief smile. No matter how much training you had, if a sensitive part of your anatomy got hurt, you put your hands to it. This left Thug Two's belly free and clear for Eliot to deliver an uppercut to his solar plexus, which doubled the man over, adding an inability to breathe to his broken nose.

Nine seconds, two down.

Eliot Spencer had first studied martial arts as a boy, and he remembered the first teacher he ever had—a second-degree black belt named *Senpai* Clifford—who was explaining how you said different parts of the body in Japanese. The solar plexus, he'd said, was called *suigetu*, which he said literally translated into English as "the moon in the water." And then *Senpai* Clifford told the story of a monkey who went up to a lake and saw the reflection of the moon in that lake. He grabbed for the moon, but his paw in the water ruined the reflection and made the moon disappear. After the water calmed, the moon returned, and he grabbed for it again—only for it to disappear again.

That, *Senpai* Clifford explained, was why *suigetu* was the word for solar plexus—because if you're hit there, you can no more catch your breath than the monkey can catch the moon on the water.

Eliot suspected that Thug Two felt very much like that monkey right about now.

The driver, seeing what was happening, fumbled with the door to get out, but Eliot was right there and he slammed it shut right on the man's head.

By this time, the leader had regained his professionalism, but he'd also stumbled back a few steps, which put him on the other side of the Escalade from Eliot. He raised his MP5 and came around, but Eliot was ready for him, grabbing the muzzle and pushing it aside just as the leader squeezed the trigger.

A dozen or so rounds flew into the jungle as Eliot palm-heeled the leader in the left temple.

The driver tried to open the door again, and this time Eliot back-kicked the door shut, knocking the driver back into the passenger seat.

Before the leader could recover from his disorientation, Eliot elbowed his face, grabbed him by the back of his T-shirt, and slammed his head down onto the hood of the Escalade.

Sixteen seconds. Three down.

The driver tried once again to get out of the Escalade, and Eliot once again slammed the door, this time with his hands. Opening the door, he then reached in, grabbed the driver, and pulled him out of the SUV, turned him around, wrapped his arm around the man's entire head, and waited for him to fall unconscious.

Twenty-three seconds. Thug Two was still on the ground trying to breathe and keep all his blood from pouring out of his nose. Thug One was lying still under the hood of the Focus, and the driver was doing likewise on the ground in front of the Escalade.

Eliot felt no pride in accomplishing his task. The thirty-second time frame was merely a goal, something to test his efficiency. He never felt any kind of pride in performing an act of violence. While he was the first to admit that it was sometimes fun—like when he coldcocked that self-centered jackass Andrechuk back in Boston—it was never pleasurable. Violence was a last resort, not a first one, and the number of times he'd had to use it was an incredibly depressing commentary on the world in general and the work he did with Nate Ford and the rest of the team in particular.

Reaching into the still-open driver's-side door of the Escalade, he unlocked the back door and then walked around to inspect the mystery box. It had a fairly simple, if secure, latch to keep it shut. Eliot unhooked it and raised the lid, feeling the cool air of the refrigerated box on his hands and face. Condensation burst out of the box and dissipated. Inside was a row of vials with a clear liquid in each, but the vials were less than half the height of the box, so there had to be another layer of them below it. There were handholds on either side of the container, so Eliot grabbed them and gently lifted the container out of the box.

Setting it next to the box, he looked down to see, not another layer of insulin, but the pieces of what looked suspiciously like a Russian-built rocket-propelled grenade launcher.

Putting a hand to his ear, he said, "Sophie, these guys are running weapons through the clinic." He hesitated. "Well, *a* weapon, anyhow. This looks like the pieces of an RPG-32 buried under a pile of insulin."

Sophie just said a quiet, "Mhm," which meant she couldn't talk safely.

"Not sure why they're just moving one RPG—unless it's a test run, seeing if the clinic's a safe way to run them under the radar." He put the insulin back in the box and relatched it. "But then, we can just ask Maimona when I bring this box back to the clinic."

Hefting the box, he brought it around to the back of the Focus and placed it in front of the trunk. Removing the key chain from his pants pocket, he clicked the trunk open and placed the box inside.

After closing the trunk, he went over to the Escalade—kicking Thug Two in the solar plexus just to be on the safe side—and popped the hood. Lifting it up—it had a hinge that allowed it to stay up without a metal rod—he reached for the fuse box on the driver's side, popped the lid, and yanked out the large brown fuse.

Replacing the lid of the fuse box, he then closed the hood and pocketed the fuse. The Escalade was now the world's most expensive roadblock.

Moving to the front of the Focus, Eliot yanked Thug One out by his legs. The man fell to the road with a *fwump* while the hood clicked back into the locked position.

With the Escalade blocking the road, Eliot had to continue straight to Pequeño Lago. But taking the scenic route would give Sophie more time to check the files and learn more about Maimona's clinic.

"I'll be back in about two hours, Sophie. Good luck."

||||| **EIGHT** |||||

NOW

Nate Ford sat in the dingy bar in Jaffrey, New Hampshire, nursing a drink.

He did not nurse it because he was attempting to remain sober at ten in the morning; he nursed it because it was a particularly dreadful brand of Canadian whiskey that Nate had never heard of—and just yesterday, he would have claimed to have known all of them. The notion of actually partaking of more than the one sip he'd managed to choke down filled him with a nameless dread.

Nate had come to this southwestern New Hampshire town because it was the home of Belinda Morgan, one of the Brillinger Zoo's board members. This bar on U.S. Route 202 seemed to be where she spent the lion's share of her time.

After spending a quarter of an hour in the place, Nate had to confess to having no clue why Morgan liked meeting people here. It was dark and dank, had an awful selection of liquor, and had an open floor plan that led to the worst kind of acoustics for having discreet meetings. If the place was full, it wouldn't matter, but it was ten in the morning, and Morgan and the two people she was meeting with were half the bar's current occupancy. Nate didn't even need to plant a bug to hear what the three of them were saying.

Not that they were saying anything of great interest. Morgan was active in her church, the two people she was meeting with were trustees of same, and they were discussing the upcoming calendar. The conversation was lively and wholesome, and escaped being the dullest thing in the world only by virtue of Parker having already found that with Steven Fischer.

It would have driven Nate to drink if this bar served anything drinkable.

"Nate, are you there?" It was Sophie.

Touching his ear, Nate subvocalized so the rest of the bar wouldn't hear him. "I'm here."

She and Eliot had filled him in before and during his journey to Jaffrey. Nate had told Eliot to hold off on returning to the clinic awhile longer, until Sophie could get more intel from the files.

"I'm taking a break from filing. The system is—unique?"

Nate chuckled. "In what way?"

"I've had to guess where to file half these folders. However, I have managed to establish a few things. Reverend Maimona did sell the black rhinos to the Brillinger Zoo. I took photos with my phone of the letters they sent back and forth."

Hardison barged in on the conversation. "Wait, what? Letters? As in on paper?"

"Typed on a manual typewriter, no less." Sophie's voice was dripping with mischievousness.

"Don't burst a blood vessel, Hardison," Nate said with a small smile.

"I can't work under these conditions, Nate. How do I hack a manual typewriter?"

"The *point* is," Sophie said quickly, back to business, "that the black rhinos were a gift from a grateful client who had received an emergency appendectomy at the clinic. He offered two black rhinos for the clinic to use as they would, in a letter dated six months ago. The reverend sent a letter back asking if the gift was entirely legal." Sophie's tone changed a bit to what Nate recognized as her dry-wit voice. "The client's reply was less than specific in that regard, but said that the reverend's saving his life was worth any price."

Before Nate could reply, Hardison said, "An *appendectomy* saved his life?"

"Medical care in Malani is abysmal under the best of circumstances," Sophie said.

"The best," Nate added, "would've probably been under the Portuguese or King Lionel. I doubt General Polonia gives much of a damn about the health care of anyone past his ministers and his soldiers. So if someone lets a bad appendix get too far, it could burst and kill them."

"*Damn,*" Hardison muttered. "So Appendix Guy gave them the rhinos?"

Sophie said, "Yes. The deal was brokered for the zoo by someone named Declan McAllister in Vermont."

Nate frowned. "Hardison, that name ring a bell?"

"Not that I can think of." Hardison's fingers tapping on some keys could be heard in the background. "He doesn't work for the zoo, and he isn't an immediate family member or known business associate of anyone who works there. I'll dig around."

Nate had only been listening to Morgan's conversation with half an ear while he talked with his crew, but the word *zoo* caught his attention when one of her companions said, "Hey, I got an e-mail from the zoo—the black rhino exhibit's been canceled? I was really looking forward to that."

Morgan held up both her hands. "Don't get me started on that nonsense. McAllister put Marney onto those rhinos, and I *knew* it would go badly. Everybody else thinks McAllister walks on water, but I think he's a snake in the grass, I'll tell you *that* for free."

"Hardison," Nate muttered as Morgan continued to bitch and moan about McAllister, "whoever this guy is, the board knows him. He may have had dealings with the zoo before."

"I'm diggin' into it, Nate," Hardison repeated defensively.

"So what happened?" Morgan's other companion asked.

"Marney paid a hundred grand each for the rhinos, and the rhinos never showed up."

The companion nodded. "But the insurance is taking care of it, right?"

Morgan shook her head. "Marney won't file a claim, and the board can't do it without the general manager's approval. Anyhow, enough of that. Tell me about the new guy in your office."

Nate frowned. That didn't sound right. "Hardison, can you call up the Brillinger Zoo's insurance policy with IYS?"

"Yeah, gimme a sec." A few keystrokes later. "Got it."

"Okay, I need you to look at—"

"Nate, I'm gonna stop you right there. I can follow pretty much every programming language out there, I can make a two-hundred-year-old diary out of some really nasty ingredients, I can even make sense out of the instruction booklets that come with IKEA furniture, but I can*not* make heads or tails of this nonsense right here."

Pulling his phone out of his pocket, Nate started, "Hardison—"

"Seriously, man, what *language* is this written in?"

"Hardison—"

"I have seen some—"

"Hardison!" At Nate's barking the hacker's name, the few other occupants of the bar turned to look at him. Luckily, he was holding his cell phone, so he just continued in a normal speaking voice so that they would think he was using a Bluetooth device hidden by his hair. "Just send it to my phone, okay?"

"A'ight, but I can't promise it won't make the phone explode from all the gibberish."

"If it hasn't exploded from all the cat photos Parker sends around to everyone, or those ridiculous motivational posters you send—"

"*De*-motivational posters: they're jokes. And hell, I didn't even *get* those until I met you. I figured you'd appreciate it, since you know all that corporate stuff."

"Just—send it, please?"

"Done."

Looking down at the display on his phone, Nate saw that he had new e-mail to the nate@leverage.org account Hardison had created when the team had first started. Calling it up, he downloaded the attachment and started reading through it.

At one point, he heard Parker let loose with the giggle she always uttered whenever she jumped off a roof, which led him to believe that her surveillance of Sal Tartucci was going well. Either that or she was just jumping off a roof for fun. With Parker, he was never entirely sure.

The policy had dozens of riders that had been added on at various points, including one that stipulated that all insurance claims had to be made via the general manager, and that no other entity connected to the Brillinger Zoo could make a claim on this policy without the express permission in writing of the general manager of the zoo.

"Uh, Nate?"

Nate looked up from his phone. "Yes, Parker?"

"What was the name of the guy you wanted Hardison to find out more about again?"

"Declan McAllister."

"That's what I thought you said."

ONE HOUR AGO

Parker found that her second board member, Sal Tartucci, managed to be considerably less boring than Steven Fischer, but he wasn't any more interesting.

Tartucci led a much more active and random life. And

unlike Fischer, he wasn't a widower or retired. He lived in a large house in Brookfield with his wife and three kids, and worked in an office in Worcester, where he served as the chief operating officer for a small money-management firm called Elm Capital.

Hardison had hacked his e-mail and online calendar, but unfortunately the latter was blank and the former included about sixteen exhortations from his assistant to fill out his online calendar already and stop using the blotter calendar on his desk.

Elm only had a dozen employees, and their offices took up only half the floor of this building in Worcester's industrial park. The rest of the floor was taken up by a medical testing center, where doctors sent patients to get blood tests. Since it was designed for clients who came in off the street, the testing center left their door open. So Parker just went in, sat down, and got a clear view of the comings and goings without anybody noticing or caring that she was sitting on one of the uncomfortable couches in the waiting area for a couple of hours.

Parker occupied herself between openings of the door to Elm—signified by a loud clack—by reading up on *Time*'s coverage of the 2008 presidential election, since that was the most recent magazine on the coffee table in front of the couch. She had no idea who was president now—or, indeed, ever, though she was pretty sure that it was Abraham Lincoln who won World War II—so she wondered if it was the old white guy or the young black guy.

Another clack, and this time Tartucci was the one leaving the office, cell phone at his ear. "Yeah, I know the Little League game's tonight. I told you I'm gonna be there. The meeting won't last longer than six. We just gotta figure out what to do with AA's portfolio now that they've been shut down. Beth's leavin' early anyhow, her cat has to go to the vet. Yeah. Yeah, I'm off to that stupid lunch meeting in Newton. Love you, too!"

Parker got up and left and joined Tartucci at the elevator bank. He was making another phone call.

"Yeah, listen, I can't take the tickets for the Sox game. Well, for starters, they're playin' the Royals. Like I wanna watch *that*. Also, my boy's been after me to take him to the TD Center. Yeah, he likes hockey. How the hell should I know?" A ding, and then: "Elevator's here. Take care."

Tartucci and Parker joined the other four people in the elevator and went down the three flights.

While Tartucci headed toward the parking garage—he was probably driving to Newton for his meeting—Parker went out the main entrance toward a fast-food joint across the street and ordered some food to go. She then brought it back across the street. The guard at the desk didn't even look up from his e-reader tablet as she walked by. Several doctors had offices in the building, plus there was the medical testing place. All of them regularly accepted walk-ins, so each office took care of its own security—there was none for the building. Parker made a mental note to come back to this place and rob them blind.

She rode the elevator back up to three, this time approaching the door to Elm. She could easily have lifted Tartucci's ID and used that to get in, but Elm was too small a company to risk that. The very same clear view from the medical testing facility that allowed her to know when Tartucci left his office also made hacking the lock impractical. Which was too bad, as it was a pretty standard Simms-Mazur Mark III card reader—she could get past it in her sleep, but it would require taking the faceplate off, and someone would *probably* notice that.

With the usual thief avenues closed, she went with something Sophie would do: grifting her way in.

She rang the intercom buzzer next to the door. The speaker crackled with staticky noise for a second.

"Food delivery!" she shouted.

The door emitted a low buzz and made that clacking sound again, allowing Parker to pull it open.

Looking around, she saw a bullpen area. These people didn't even have cubicles—just desks all arranged in a big open space. Against the back wall were three offices, all with nameplates Velcro'd to the wall next to them and small windows with blinds showing the offices' insides. The one on the far left belonged to the chief executive officer—unsurprisingly, since it was in the corner, thus getting two windows instead of one. Parker could see him through the blinds (which were down, but open) typing away on his laptop. On the far right was an office occupied by a woman in a suit who was talking animatedly on the phone; this was the chief financial officer, who kept her blinds up.

The nameplate for the middle office read SALVATORE TARTUCCI, CHIEF OPERATING OFFICER. This office was closed and presumably locked, with the blinds down.

Parker glanced over at the CEO's and CFO's offices: they had rear windows with metal latches that held them locked in place when the windows were down.

Parker smiled.

She approached the reception desk, where a round-faced

KEITH R. A. DeCANDIDO

woman wearing a headset was talking. "I'm sorry, but Mr.
Tartucci is out of the office, I can send you to his voice mail.
No, I'm sorry, we can't give out his cell number. Thank you."
The receptionist pushed a button on the phone unit on her
desk and then looked at Parker. "Can I help you?"

"I got a food order here for Jones?"

The receptionist frowned and started looking nervous.
"Karen Jones doesn't work here anymore."

"Isn't this Dr. Jones's office? I was told to come to the
fourth floor . . ."

Now the receptionist was relieved. "You're on the third
floor, dear. You want to go up one."

Parker made herself go wide-eyed the way she usually did
whenever Eliot was explaining something. "Oh! Okay!
Thanks!"

She turned around, exited the office—the door could be
opened by anybody from the inside—tossed the bag of food
into a garbage can by the elevator, and took the stairs down
to where she'd parked the Chevrolet Aveo she'd rented.

Popping the Aveo's trunk, she pulled out her harness,
climbing wire, and her birthday present from Apollo, the
thief she'd met a couple of years ago. She stuffed them into a
backpack, then went back to the building. The guard *still*
hadn't looked up from his tablet.

When she boarded the elevator, she pushed the button for
the top floor. Other people got in and went to other floors,
and some got on at intermediate floors—but no one else was
going up to twenty as she was. After the last person got off
at eighteen, Parker put on a pair of gloves and smiled.

Early this morning, she'd gotten Hardison to provide her
with the schematics of the building, which she'd quickly

memorized. This building was adjacent to another building, with an alley between them. Pedestrians often used the alley as a shortcut from one building to the other, so Parker didn't want to risk being seen by approaching the third-floor window from the ground. That left making a descent from the roof.

Besides, seventeen-story falls were *way* more fun than three-story climbs.

Not that there wasn't *some* climbing. After she got the maintenance hatch open with ridiculous ease—it was an old building—and jumped up to grab the sides of the open hatch, she climbed onto the top of the elevator, then started clambering up the elevator cable.

The gloves protected her hands from the thick metal cable, but grease and grime soon covered her white blouse and slacks, which she belatedly realized she'd forgotten to change out of. Sophie was going to kill her for ruining such nice clothes.

Suddenly Sophie's voice sounded over her earbud. "Nate, are you there?"

Nate's voice came next: "I'm here."

Parker breathed a sigh of relief. Sophie was there to talk to Nate. Maybe she wouldn't even find out about the blouse and slacks being destroyed. Even though Sophie herself had picked them out for Parker when they went shopping that time at Newbury Street.

Maybe Parker just wouldn't tell her.

She focused on climbing the cable to the roof while Sophie filled Nate in on her and Hardison's end of the job. Apparently it had something to do with file cabinets, manual typewriters, Hardison bursting a blood vessel, an appendix, and someone named Declan McAllister. Parker didn't worry about it too much as she reached the top of the shaft and unscrewed the vent cover.

Once she climbed through the vent and found herself on the roof, she switched to a different pair of gloves, ones that were both lighter and cleaner. It wouldn't do to lose her grip on the climbing wire because her gloves were covered in gunk.

She shrugged out of her backpack and pulled out the harness inside it. After securing it to her torso, she hooked her special carbon-steel wire to it, then unspooled the wire up to a hundred and eighty feet, sticking a marker on the wire at that point. Placing the marker on the roof's cornice, she unspooled the wire from there to an air exhaust pipe, then wrapped the wire around the pipe several times before hooking it tightly to itself.

After tugging on it several times to make sure it wouldn't budge, she turned toward the roof's edge.

Then she smiled again.

"Hee hee *heeeeee*!"

The wind rushed past Parker's face as she plummeted, her heart racing with excitement as she saw the pavement growing closer and closer and closer. Parker liked to smile, but the only time she ever grinned was when she was in free fall. There was no rush remotely like it.

Well, except for all the other times she grinned and all the other rushes. Like the first time she broke into the Louvre. Or the time she discovered that the safe she was breaking into had actual cash instead of artifacts that she'd have to turn around and sell for cash, thus saving her a step. Or whenever she mastered something Archie taught her. Or when she was around Hardison. Or when she stole those shoes in the Philippines.

Aside from those rushes, though, this was the best.

Then she came to a sudden, violent stop as the wire hit its full length. The harness absorbed the impact of the jolt, so Parker only felt a slight tug.

Still hanging upside down, Parker pulled out Apollo's birthday present. The other thief had been hired by a grifter named Starke to do a job that ended up conflicting with one of Nate's jobs. But everything had worked out okay in the end, and Parker and Apollo—who was a *great* thief—had stayed in touch. For her birthday, he'd gotten her a magnetic "repeller," which was the size and shape of a TV remote and could push metal at short distances. Apollo said he had named it "Leslie" after a former lover whom he now found repellent.

Apollo's birthday was coming up. She needed to convince Hardison to build another one of his safecracking robots so she could give it to him as a present. He'd *love* it.

Placing Leslie at the window to Tartucci's empty office, Parker pushed the button. The gadget hummed, and then the metal window latch started to slowly inch forward. After a few seconds, the latch had moved completely around and out of its socket, thus freeing the window to be opened.

She was *definitely* going to rob this building blind at some point . . .

Parker jumped into the office, unhooking the climbing wire from her harness, and looked down at Tartucci's desk, shoving aside two manila folders, a laptop, a memo pad, and a mug filled with half a cup of coffee to reveal the blotter, which was also a calendar.

Today had LUNCH MTG IN NEWTON scrawled on it, which

matched what Tartucci had said on the phone, and there was also a mention of a meeting last week with someone named Andrechuk, which was the same name as the guy the team had just taken down—but then something else caught her eye.

"Uh, Nate?"

"Yes, Parker?" Nate said in reply.

"What was the name of the guy you wanted Hardison to find out more about again?"

"Declan McAllister."

"That's what I thought you said. I'm in Tartucci's office, and he's spending the weekend with 'Declan McA' in Vermont. He's leaving after work Friday."

Hardison's voice came on then. "All right, Nate, I've got a Declan McAllister who lives in Vermont. He's got a massive estate near Weston, but it's in the middle of nowhere. Turns out he and Tartucci went to grammar school together at some private academy in the Berkshires. And he—oh, man."

Parker frowned. "What is it, Hardison?"

"He's got permits to keep wildlife on his property."

"There's our connection," Nate said. "Parker, finish up there, and then you need to head up to Vermont."

Parker smiled. "Let's go steal a rhino?"

Nate let out a quick breath. "Just surveillance for now, Parker. Just because he has permits doesn't mean anything. Yet."

"Okay." Parker reached into the pocket of her grease-stained slacks and pulled out a jump drive, which she stuck into Tartucci's computer. He had not only left his computer on (with a screen saver composed of a slide show of pictures of his wife and kids), but hadn't even password-protected it. While Hardison's drive copied everything off the computer, Parker stuck a bug under the desk. Then she looked at the stuff lying on the desk, which included a letter thanking him for his donation to PETA, as well as the office electrical bill.

Once the download was complete, she collected the jump drive, put everything on the desk back where she found it, and climbed back out the window, hooking the wire back onto the harness. After closing the window, she put Leslie on reverse and pulled the latch toward her, locking it up again.

Parker just hoped that, by the time Tartucci drove back from Newton, the smell of grease in his office would have dissipated . . .

‖‖‖‖ NINE ‖‖‖‖

NOW

Terence Bisime tried to ignore the pains that shot through his calves as he operated the crane, slowly lowering the container onto the truck so Jacob could drive it to wherever it was being driven to, just like he'd done every workday for almost thirty years at the now-ironically-named King Lionel Port in Malani City.

A chirp came from the cell phone sitting in the drink holder on the dashboard in front of him, followed by a tinny voice over the phone's small speaker. "That's the last load, Terence."

Terence put the crane into standby mode and then grabbed the phone. "What happened to the truck that was bringing, um—whatever it was for the *Atlas*?"

Another chirp. "The *Atlas* radioed that they won't be in until Saturday. Some kind of storm in the cape."

That prompted a sigh from Terence. Meeting the truck, taking the container off the truck, and placing it on the *Atlas* would've been an additional half hour of overtime. The *Atlas* was apparently unwilling to pay the storage fee, so they were going straight from truck to ship. It cost extra, but not as much as storing the container overnight would have. Everyone, it seemed, was cutting corners these days.

After he parked the crane and climbed down out of it, Terence saw a very well-dressed, extremely attractive woman walking ahead of Pedro, who looked harried as he tried to keep up with her. Looking down, Terence saw that the raven-haired woman was wearing high heels—and still was able to outpace Pedro. Terence had never liked Pedro—he was Portuguese, and Terence was of a generation that still remembered the Portuguese as colonizers—so this amused him.

"Look, Dr. Ainley, I appreciate your concern, but—"

Speaking with a very clipped British accent—definitely upper class, not the Cockney Terence was used to hearing on British ships that came through the port—the Ainley woman said, "It's no use giving me your personal assurances, sir, as they are meaningless. You are not the person who will be operating the crane that places my elephants on the vessel, and therefore your insistence that everything will be fine holds absolutely no meaning. I wish to speak to the crane operator."

Now Terence stopped walking and folded his arms, regarding this tableau with a raised eyebrow. "You wish to speak to a crane operator, ma'am?"

Pedro waved him off. "Not now, Terence. Dr. Ainley, if you'd please—"

But Ainley brushed Pedro aside and looked right at Terence. "Are you such a man, Terence?"

That lovely voice saying his given name brought a rare smile to Terence's lips. "I am, yes. Terence Bisime, at your service."

With a dismissive wave at Pedro, but still fixing Terence with her lovely gaze, Ainley said, "Thank you, Mr. Macao, that will be all."

"Dr. Ainley, I think—"

"Mr. Macao, what I am interested in is procuring the services of this port to transport wild animals. Do you know what I am most assuredly *not* interested in?"

Pedro just swallowed and looked even more like an emu than usual.

Answering her own question, Ainley said, "What you *think*. Now go away, please, I wish to speak to someone who actually knows what he's talking about."

At that, Pedro turned and slunk off.

"Dr. Ainley, I must thank you," Terence said.

"And why is that, Terence? And please, do call me Antonia."

"For the first time in forty years, I am grateful to have lost half an hour of overtime. It permitted me to view that lovely exchange between you and Pedro."

"You don't like Mr. Macao?"

"He is Portuguese." Realizing that by itself that was insufficient explanation to a foreigner, Terence quickly added, "I'm sorry. He's likable enough, I suppose. But I'm of the generation that remembers when this land was a colony of Portugal. One of the few left, sadly."

Antonia Ainley's smile was so bright it almost warmed Terence as much as the sun did. "You're sad that your country is not still a colony?"

"Oh, no. Say what you will about King Lionel, President Madeira, or General Polonia—and I could say plenty about them, though I would say none of it in front of a woman of your breeding—"

Antonia inclined her head in response to these words.

"—they are, all of them, quite the improvement upon being ruled by Europeans from thousands of kilometers away."

"Fair enough. Well, I hope you'll indulge *this* European and answer a few of my questions?"

Terence started gingerly ambling toward the main office. He wanted to change out of his coveralls and go home, but with his calves in the shape they were in, it would take quite a while just to make it to the office. Whatever questions Antonia wanted to ask, surely he could answer them on the necessarily slow walk. "May I ask, Doctor—Antonia—what do I receive in return for this great intelligence?"

She laughed musically, walking alongside him as opposed to ahead of him, as she had done with Pedro, even though Terence walked at a quarter of the other man's pace. "I don't suppose telling you that, by providing me with a glowing report of your port's efficiency, you will secure more work for your employers is much of an incentive?"

Terence smirked. "No. I get paid regardless. And poorly, at that. People pay this port a great deal of money to use it in a manner that would keep it from being noticed, but those extra fees rarely make it down as far as the crane operator."

"I see. Well, I'm afraid I can offer you little other than the pleasure of my company." Making a show of looking down at his left hand, where he still wore his wedding ring, she added, "But you're married, so I doubt that's much of an incentive."

"Ah, no." Terence shook his head sadly. "My Vernetha died ten years ago. But I have never looked at another woman in all that time." He looked over at Antonia's beautiful face. "At least not until today. My children, my grandchildren, my coworkers—they all urge me to start seeing women again, that Vernetha would not wish me to be alone. There is a woman at our church, Nada, who has expressed interest. But I feel I am betraying my wife."

Antonia slipped her arm into his. It felt surprisingly comfortable and natural there. "I promise not to allow you to betray Vernetha, Terence. You see, I work for the London Zoo. We are acquiring a pair of elephants, and I wish to make sure they arrive safely. We've had some incidents in the past, in Angola, in Madagascar, and in Namibia, and I don't wish to repeat them here."

Terence nodded. "What is it you wish to know from me?"

"Have you handled wild animals before?"

"Of course."

"You're sure? I mean, all the containers you load look alike, don't they?"

With pride, Terence said, "Dr. Ainley, I recall every container that I have ever loaded in the forty years I have been on the job. What was in it, where I put it, and where it wound up."

"Really?"

The pride left his voice in short order. "No, not really—but I did up until my Vernetha died. After that, I only truly paid attention to those containers that had special instructions."

Antonia smiled up at him. "Like, say, wild animals?"

For the second time today, and in many months, Terence smiled. "Yes. Just last week, there were two black rhinos that were en route to Portland, Maine, in the United States."

"Interesting. And how did you handle them?"

For the rest of the walk to the office, Terence gave Dr. Ainley the minutest detail of how he handled the two black rhinos. He had no idea who negotiated the purchase—that was above his pay grade—but he knew that they came in on a truck rented by the Maimona Clinic, that it went on one of the dozen or so vessels called the *Black Star*, and that it was bound for Portland.

Antonia interrupted his description of how he had to wait for someone on the ground to verify that the airholes of the containers were not blocked. "How many other ships called *Black Star* were there?"

"On that day, there were three. One was bound for Colombo, Sri Lanka, the other for Boston Harbor, also in the U.S."

By this time, they had reached the office. Antonia removed her arm from Terence's, put a hand on his biceps, and said, "Thank you, Terence. You've been a tremendous help."

"So will your zoo be using this port?" Once, a decade ago, he would have said "our" port, but ever since General Polonia had taken over the country, he no longer felt like he was a part of the endeavor of running the port. He was just going through the motions until he died.

Giving him a hooded, seductive look, Antonia said, "I'll let you know."

Taking Antonia's hand, he kissed it genteelly, the way

he'd seen men do in old movies. "Thank you, Antonia, for the pleasure of your company."

"The pleasure was entirely mine, Terence. And you should get those legs looked at."

With that, she turned and walked off.

His sore calves didn't allow Terence to have a spring in his step as he walked through the back door of the office, which led to the locker room. Still, it was the first time in a long while that he ended his workday in a good mood, and that certainly had to count for something.

Perhaps he would see a doctor about his legs, as his daughter had been pleading with him to do. And perhaps he would ask Nada to have dinner with him this weekend.

HALF AN HOUR AGO

Sophie was grateful that her days as a thief and grifter, as well as her years of working with Nate Ford, had given her plenty of excess cash. It was the only thing that kept her from balking at the price of a cab ride to King Lionel Port from the Empire Hotel, where she and Eliot—or, rather, Bernadine Onslow and John Smith—were staying in Malani City. For the ridiculous sum of six marks per minute, she had to endure an un-air-conditioned ride on bumpy, pothole-filled roads in a fifteen-year-old sedan with minimal shock absorbers.

One of the clinic workers—a nice young man named Tomás—had given her a lift to the hotel from the clinic after the workday was done, as Eliot hadn't yet returned. Eliot had said he had a "personal errand" to run. Sophie assumed it was something connected to his work in Malani with Damien Moreau almost a decade ago.

Pointedly not offering to tip the driver—at those rates, the cabbies here bloody well didn't need tips, and at the skill level of this one's driving, he had hardly earned one—she paid her fare and went into the port office.

While giving her "Dr. Ainley" spiel to the port master, a tiresome little man named Pedro Macao, she slipped one of Hardison's jump drives into an unoccupied computer terminal.

Macao had to take a phone call, so Sophie asked to use the loo. After he pointed her in the right direction, she went into the one-person ladies' and plugged the jump drive into her phone.

"Got it," Hardison said into her earbud a few moments later. "Okay, this ain't right."

"What is it, Hardison?"

"There's no way these are the right shipping records. There's, like, maybe three ships a day going out *at best*. Ain't no way this port can stay afloat—um, so to speak."

"It's a corrupt regime, Hardison," Eliot said.

Sophie straightened. "Eliot, where've you been?"

"Busy," Eliot replied in his best don't-ask voice. Because his absence hadn't had any kind of effect on the job, and because of all of the team members, he was one most able to take care of himself, Sophie was willing to let it lie. For now.

Eliot continued: "You're not gonna find anything useful on a computer in that port."

"He's right about that," Hardison said. "The pictures Maimona sent to the zoo had four ships in the port along with the *Black Star*. One a' them was called the *Blue Meanie*."

"Seriously?" Eliot asked.

"Would I make that up?" Hardison asked defensively.

Eliot snorted. "No, if you made it up, it'd be *War of the Worlds* or *Professor What*, or whatever, not the Beatles."

"It's *World of Warcraft* and *Doctor Who*. Man, don't you even *listen* to me when I—"

"Not if I can help it," Eliot said.

"Boys, please?" Sophie said gently but firmly.

Hardison let out a dramatic sigh. "*Anyhow*, according to what I'm lookin' at right now, there was *one* ship in King Lionel Port that day—the *Blue Meanie*. None a' the others in the picture are in the records."

Sophie nodded. "A place like this, with no government oversight worth mentioning, they'd take most of their business on a cash basis with no paper trail—or an electronic one. It's a handy way to avoid tariffs."

"So how do we prove that the rhinos even came through there?" Eliot asked.

With a feral smile, Sophie said, "Leave that to me."

Thirty minutes later, she had her proof, in the form of the very charming old crane operator named Terence. The first trick Sophie learned as a grifter was to take advantage of her looks. Average men would almost always open up to a beautiful woman who paid attention to them, by virtue of the rarity of such an occurrence. With only a modicum of extra effort, she probably could have gotten Terence to betray his dead wife.

Not, she suspected, that the late Vernetha would have minded. She probably would have been proud of her husband.

As she walked toward the port's parking lot, Sophie said, "When in doubt, check in with the people who actually work for a living. They always see what nobody wishes them to see, because no one notices they're there."

"Nice work," Eliot said. "I'll be there in five minutes."

Five minutes later, Eliot pulled up in the Focus they'd rented. Climbing into the passenger seat, Sophie asked, "So where were you?"

"I told you I was busy."

Sophie knew this, of course, but she wanted to see Eliot face-to-face when he answered the question. Eliot had an excellent poker face when he needed it, but of late he'd tended to drop his guard around the rest of the team, thus becoming much easier for Sophie to read. Had he been angry at her repetition of the question, his eyes would have blazed and he would have scrunched up his face.

He did neither of those things. Instead, he looked up and away, glancing sidelong at her as he put the car in gear.

That was Eliot's guilty look. The last time she'd seen it on his face was when Parker asked him what horrible acts he'd committed when he worked for Moreau.

She wondered what he'd done this time. But he was no more likely to be forthcoming now than he was a year ago.

At least not yet.

They traveled back to the hotel in companionable silence. When they got to the hotel and parked, they went to Sophie's room first to go over what they knew with Nate and the others.

But as they approached the door, Eliot stopped her and pointed.

Frowning, she looked at the toothpick that she'd left in the door. It was right where she'd put it.

No—it was about half an inch below where she'd put it.

She stared at Eliot, who motioned her to move to the side of the door, then mimicked the action of putting the key card into the slot.

Nodding in response, Sophie inserted the key card, heard the slight click, and watched the light blink red before turning green.

Eliot then burst into the room at full speed, only to find it in complete darkness—except, Sophie noticed, for three red dots that had appeared on his chest. Eliot noticed the dots as well, and froze in place.

Then she heard an annoyingly familiar, British-accented voice. "About time you two arrived."

Sophie sighed heavily. This was all they needed.

A short, balding, round-faced man with a self-satisfied smirk screwed to his face sat on the easy chair, illuminated by the light provided by the corridor.

Jim Sterling looked right at her and said, "Hello, Sophie."

||||| TEN |||||

NOW

Hardison stood on the ladder, wearing a blue NSTAR shirt, a white NSTAR helmet, blue jeans, and brown work boots, pretending to fiddle with a junction box on the Harvard campus. Nearby, on one of the many tree-lined roads that snaked through the grounds of the ancient university, was parked the white NSTAR truck that Sophie's friend had procured for them. All Sophie had given Hardison was a name, a number, and instructions to say, "Sophie needs an NSTAR truck," and lo, she said, an NSTAR truck would appear. Which was exactly what happened.

It was one of several reasons why Hardison respected the crap out of Sophie. All his friends could do was coordinate an attack against a mess of dark elves. None of them could make an NSTAR truck magically appear.

The helmet and shirt, of course, were Hardison's own

work. He'd created dozens of official-looking jackets, coveralls, helmets, hats, uniforms, and other articles of clothing for each of the five team members for just such occasions as this.

But having the truck really sold it.

Hardison's current object of surveillance was really named Bartholomew Everett Allerton IV. Prior to moving to New England, Hardison would not have believed that anyone had a name like that outside of old *M*A*S*H* episodes, but residency in the land of blue bloods and *Mayflower* descendants had cured him of this illusion. He wasn't sure what amazed him more, that Allerton had survived to adulthood with the first name Bartholomew, or that he was the fourth man in a row to do so.

What especially impressed Hardison was that those few who called this guy by his first name actually called him "Bartholomew." Not "Bart," not "B.E.," but the full first name. Of course, most people called him "Mr. Allerton." He served as the vice president of financial affairs for Harvard, and as a result was referred to formally by just about everyone at his job, since it was in his power to wipe out financial aid packages, reduce salaries, manipulate endowments, and generally ruin the lives of anyone attending or working at the university.

Not that he did so. From all Hardison had seen, he was a quiet, friendly guy who went to work every day, took a walk on the campus during his lunch hour, and then went home to his luxury Cambridge apartment. He lived there with his husband, whom he'd married in June 2004, not long after Massachusetts made same-sex marriage legal.

It was just about lunchtime, so Hardison knew that Allerton would be taking his walk. Sure enough, a short, bald-ing, pudgy man in a rumpled brown suit and large glasses exited the Cronkite Center onto the quad. Two coeds were walking a large golden retriever across the grass, and at the sight of them, Allerton suddenly tensed up. The dog was try-ing to run at full speed, but one of the coeds maintained a tight grip on his leash, which was attached to a choke collar.

Standing stock-still and pointing an accusatory finger at the dog, Allerton cried out, "What is *that thing* doing here? There shouldn't be *any animals* on campus!"

"Excuse you?" said one of the coeds. "There's no rules against walking Lucas here. We take him through the quad every—"

Sweat beaded on Allerton's high forehead. "Just get him *out* of here, *right now*! I *hate* animals."

Lucas was currently sniffing the grass. When he was done sniffing, he peed on it.

"*God*, that's *disgusting*! I want to see your IDs *right now*!"

As the coeds started arguing, Hardison heard Parker's voice through his earbud. "Okay, I'm about ten miles from McAllister's estate."

Hardison blinked. "Already? Damn, girl, how fast were you *goin'*?"

"Thirty over the speed limit, apparently."

Not liking the sound of that, Hardison asked, "What does 'apparently' mean, exactly?"

"Nothing to worry about."

Shaking his head, Hardison wondered how soon a notice for an unpaid speeding ticket would arrive at the mail drop he used for Alice White, the identity for Parker under which she'd rented the car.

"Seriously, Hardison," Parker said, "there's nothing to worry about."

TWENTY-TWO MINUTES AGO

Trooper Michael Mazzarano sat in his cruiser, guzzling his fifteenth cup of crappy coffee this shift, hating his job.

Oh, he liked the job *generally*. Being state police *in general* was awesome. He got to carry a gun, he got to help maintain law and order in the great state of Massachusetts, and anytime he wanted to get laid, all he had to do was walk into Jacobson's Bar while in uniform and he had his choice of women.

As long as they didn't cry. Mike could never deal with women who cried.

Still, for all that *that* part of the job was totally awesome, he hated the actual work he had to do, which consisted of sitting in the damn cruiser and nailing people who drove recklessly on the road.

Who defined *recklessly* anyhow? Mike himself was never comfortable if he was going under eighty miles an hour—unless he was driving Mom's Buick, which didn't go over seventy without rattling. But in his own Benz? Or in the Ferrari he was going to buy someday? He had to be going at least eighty to be comfy, and better still up around ninety.

And he'd never hit anybody or anything in ten years of driving. So why should he punish drivers for doing the same thing?

Besides, it was dumb. The department didn't want to stop reckless drivers, they wanted to build up ticket revenue for the state—which really ended up meaning higher premiums collected by the insurance companies. Plus, if their unit didn't give as many tickets as the other units around the state, Sergeant Klissewicz yelled at them. Mike hated being yelled at by Klissewicz because he turned purple and started spitting and it was really gross.

It was all about statistics. When he joined the state cops, Mike thought the job would be about justice and solving crimes. Instead it was "did you give enough tickets this month" and "why did Sergeant D'Amato's unit give more tickets, especially when you had the holiday weekend" and all this other crap.

He hated it.

Two weeks ago, he got to talking with Detective Patrick Bonanno, hoping to see if there was some way to get a gold shield. Bonanno was walking with a cane, recovering from multiple gunshot wounds, and said, "I wouldn't do it, Mazzarano. When you're a detective, you piss off everyone you talk to."

That just got Mike to grin. "I give out speeding tickets. I already do that."

"Good point. Maybe you should try out."

Bonanno was respected and had recently been promoted. Mike could do worse for a rabbi. Not that he'd actually committed to helping him, but it was a step.

Right now he was sitting on I-91 near the Vermont border. The speed limit was sixty-five miles an hour this far north, and Mike just didn't see the point in giving out tickets to anyone unless they were at least twenty over. Most of the people who zoomed past his spot on the side of the road were going between sixty and eighty.

Then the Chevy Aveo zoomed by at ludicrous speeds. Checking the radar gun, he saw that it was going ninety-five.

Hitting the siren and putting his coffee into the cup holder, he accelerated onto the highway and floored it. He had to get to the Aveo before it went over the border. He could still give the ticket if he nabbed her in Vermont, but the VT staties got all pissy when Massachusetts troopers did that, and when they got pissy, they bitched to Klissewicz, which resulted in another yelling fit. Not worth it.

The Aveo slowed going up a hill, which enabled Mike to catch up to her and tailgate, siren blaring. This close, he could see that the driver was a blonde, which surprised him. It was usually guys who went this fast.

She'd been in the right lane, and then got into the left when he tailgated—and kept going. With a snarl, Mike pulled in behind her in the left lane, at which point she got back in the right. So he got in behind her *again*.

Finally, she got the hint and slowed down. This had happened to Mike three times before, and each time it was a teenager who'd never been caught speeding, and thought that they should get out of the cop car's way, not pull over for them.

The Aveo pulled onto the shoulder off the right lane and eventually came to a full stop. Mike did likewise with his cruiser, and then grabbed the blower. "Remain inside the vehicle, please," he said, his voice projected by the outer speakers to the Aveo.

Thankfully, the blonde didn't try to get out of the car.

Mike ran the license plate, only to discover that it was a rental from a place in Boston. It wasn't one of the chains, just some rent-a-wreck place he'd never heard of, and they only updated the state police on their rentals every Friday. The Aveo appeared in the system as unrented, which meant she'd only picked it up in the last few days.

Climbing out of the car, he put his hat on and walked slowly over to the car.

The blonde pushed the button to lower her window.

"License and regist—"

And then the woman burst into tears.

"I'm so sorry! I didn't mean to go so fast, but my boyfriend just broke up with me and my son's in jail *again* and I just wanted to drive up to Vermont and get away from it all, y'know, and it was just awful, and—"

Mike could feel his sphincter clench. "Please, ma'am," he begged, "stop crying. It'll be okay, if you can just give me your license and registration, and everything'll be—"

"—and then my mother went into rehab *again*, just because my father kept beating her up and then I had to blow up the house and—"

"Look, ma'am, you were going thirty over the speed limit, I have to—"

Tears streamed down her cheeks as she just kept going. "—the dog has diabetes and the cat has leukemia and I wanted to take my son to the zoo, but I can't because he ran away and—"

Now Mike was starting to feel seriously nauseated. Clutching his belly and wishing to *hell* this woman would stop crying, he held up a hand. "Look, it's fine, just go, and stay under the speed limit, okay?"

"Okay." She nodded quickly, and immediately hit the accelerator and drove off.

Snarling, Mike stumbled back to the car, hoping the stomachache would stop now that the crying woman was gone. He just *hated* it when women cried.

He collapsed into the driver's seat of the cruiser, not even bothering to close the door. He reached for his coffee, then tossed it aside. The idea of drinking any more suddenly made him feel ill.

Then he stared after the Aveo, only just now realizing that the blonde's shirt had been covered in black grease. And had she said something about blowing up her house?

NOW

Hardison started walking back to the truck. "Nate? Parker's almost there." He'd been expecting her to take another hour or so.

"Yeah, I heard." The background of Nate's comms sounded like wind, so Hardison guessed that he was back outside.

"I'm headin' to the truck to figure out how to get us in there. Beats the hell outta followin' Allerton around. Most exciting thing he's done is yell at two girls for bringin' a dog on campus." As he went to the borrowed NSTAR truck, he filled Nate in on Allerton's adventure with Lucas the dog and his two humans.

"No, no, that fits," Nate said.

"Fits *what*?"

A pause. "Not sure yet, but this is why I wanted to do a little old-fashioned surveillance."

"So it wasn't just to make me crazy?" Hardison couldn't resist saying.

"No, Hardison, it wasn't just to make you crazy. That was just a nice side effect."

Hardison shook his head at Nate's snark as he climbed into the NSTAR truck. Sometimes, the man just *begged* to have his credit rating trashed and get a butt load of porno spam in his in-box.

Nate continued. "The digital stuff is useful, yes, but it's only from the surveillance that we know that Allerton doesn't even like animals, that Morgan doesn't care much about the zoo, that the zoo has little to no impact on Fischer's daily routine, which never changes, and so on. We just assumed that these people were all animal lovers, but after watching them for a couple of days, that doesn't seem to be the case. Now, I've seen boards of directors that take a very active role, and I've seen boards that could give a rat's ass."

At this point, Hardison had his netbook up and running, using his own private secure portable wireless node to get online and call up a map of the area around McAllister's estate. "I'm guessin' we've decided these people are the don't-give-a-crap variety?"

"It's looking that way—but the board had to have done *something* that caused Marney to add a rider to their insurance policy that only she could approve an insurance claim. And it's the friend of a board member that set up the black rhino purchase. I've got a call in to one of my old colleagues at IYS."

"Uh, Nate?"

"What?"

"Well, we've met three of your old colleagues at IYS. One was the guy who got your kid killed. One was a nutjob who tried to steal a van Gogh. And the other one's *Sterling*."

"Not everyone there's crazy, Hardison."

"Coulda fooled me." He shook his head. "Fine, whatever. Parker, you there?"

"Yup. Just looking for a way in."

"All right." Hardison alt-tabbed over to the information he'd already gathered on McAllister. "I'm only findin' records for a few animals on his estate—an emu, a capuchin monkey, and two turtles—but he's got a heavy-duty e-fence around the whole place that packs enough of a wallop to knock out three elephants. I'm thinkin' he's tryin' to keep in a lot more than one frisky emu."

"Black-market animals?" Nate said.

"Mhm. Or stolen from ships called the *Black Star*."

"Seems a good bet."

Parker asked, "So how do I get in?"

"Most of the estate borders on Pond Lane, which is the street the estate's on, and Lake Drive." Hardison shook his head. "Up all night comin' up with *them* names. Anyhow, we also got us a state park on one side that's got a hiking trail. That may be the way in."

"What kind of e-fence is it?" Parker asked.

Hardison quickly found the purchase order for the electric fence, as well as its security history. "It's a Storm-Richards 61. He got it right around when he got the permits, along with a mess of smaller ones. The big one's got seventeen projectors all around the property."

"How does it work, Hardison?" Nate asked.

"Two ways. If you're wearing a collar, and you try to cross the fence, you get a *nasty* jolt. That's what he uses for the animals."

Nate asked, "What if you're not wearing a collar?"

"A much less nasty jolt—kinda like after you walk on a rug and touch a wall."

"I *hate* that," Parker muttered.

Hardison smiled. "But more importantly, it alerts the security system that someone's hit it. And part of the trigger's mechanical, so I can't hack it remotely."

Nate's breathing got a little louder, which meant he was thinking. "How many people on security?"

"Based on the security firm's payment records, just one guy, but still—"

"No, perfect. You don't want to hack it remotely, you want to take it out on-site, so the security guy goes to look at it, and Parker sneaks past him."

"So," Parker said, "I should take out a projector?"

Shaking his head, Hardison said, "A projector ain't gonna cut it. There's redundancies. He only needs twelve for the size perimeter he's got. In fact, the original purchase order's for twelve, but he got five more when . . ." And then he broke into a grin. ". . . when a bird set up a nest at the projector on the other side of the fence by the hiking trail. And there was another incident with a raccoon knocking the projector out of whack."

"That's our way in," Nate said. "Parker, can you mimic an animal attack on two projectors?"

"Yup." Parker's smile was actually audible—at least to Hardison, who smiled himself. "What are the two farthest from the main house?"

Alt-tabbing over to the map, Hardison said, "Right on the hiking trail. It's number eleven and seventeen."

"Why are eleven and seventeen next to each other?" Parker asked almost accusingly. "Twelve should be next to eleven."

"He put seventeen between eleven and twelve after he had to shore up the fence against nestin'." Hardison refrained from adding comments about OCD, knowing that he'd just regret it later when he and Parker were next in the same room. "I'm sendin' the map to your phone now."

"Okay." A pause. "I think I'm gonna need a change of clothes."

||||| ELEVEN |||||

"Hello, Sophie. Or would you rather I called you Jenny?" Sterling smirked. "That was, after all, the name you used when first we met."

Eliot had never actually seen Sterling smile. He had a variety of smirks, which Eliot had been tempted to categorize, but ultimately they all boiled down to "the smirk that makes me want to punch him in the face many times," so he didn't bother.

He only didn't punch him in the face many times right now because of the three red dots on his chest. Typically, Sterling didn't enter a situation that he wasn't in control of, and his method of dealing with the fact that Eliot wanted to punch him in the face many times was to train not one, but three snipers on him.

Sterling, of course, kept talking. "Or perhaps I should call you Rebecca. But that's the name of a dead woman, isn't it? The footage of you getting shot is very entertaining."

Eliot noted that Sophie didn't react at all to Sterling's provocation, and good for her. The job that had taken Damien Moreau down in San Lorenzo required that the team get involved in that nation's presidential election: Moreau's puppet president, Ribera, against a schoolteacher named Vittori. Sophie had posed as Vittori's fiancée, Rebecca Ibañez, and she was "shot" on international television as part of the grift.

Sophie finally spoke. "I'm glad you enjoyed it."

"Oh, I did." Sterling rose from the couch and started toward the doorway and the two of them. Under any other circumstances, Eliot would have stepped between the Interpol agent and his teammate, but he was rooted in place as long as those snipers were there.

Sterling walked right up to Sophie and smirked again. "On really bad days, I'll call up the video of you falling dramatically into President-Elect Vittori's arms. Gives me a nice warm and fuzzy feeling."

Rolling her eyes, Sophie asked, "What do you *want*, Sterling?"

"What I *want*," Sterling replied as he reached over to turn the hotel room's lights on, "is to capture a ring of international smugglers whose members include high-ranking members of General Polonia's government, as well as people in the U.S., Iraq, and India."

"And what has this to do with us?"

Sterling returned to the couch, then hesitated. "Where are my manners? Have a seat, won't you? *Not* you," he added with a sharp look at Eliot, "unless you promise to behave."

Through clenched teeth—he wasn't sure how itchy the

snipers' trigger fingers were, so he didn't want to risk moving any more than necessary—Eliot said, "Let's say I don't."

Sophie decided to go ahead and sit down on the easy chair that was positioned perpendicular to the sofa, which Eliot couldn't blame her for. The more civilized this conversation was, the more likely they were to emerge from it . . . well, not okay, because Sterling was involved, but as close to okay as was possible.

Sterling sat back down on the couch, folding his hands on his lap. "There are three choices available to you, Spencer. One, you stand very, very still until we're finished. Two, you move, three thirty-caliber rifle rounds rip through your chest, and I deliver your bloody corpse to the Butcher of Kiev as an early Christmas present and collect that price on your head. Three, you agree not to harm me in any manner—beyond, of course, your caustic wit, limited though it may be—and I call off the dogs and the three of us have a nice chat. Or six of us, assuming the rest of your little gang is listening in."

Eliot heard Nate's voice in his ear. "Eliot, it's your call, but right now option three's our best bet. His smugglers are probably our smugglers, and you're gonna be tripping over him either way."

Nate's deference to Eliot's own judgment was something of a compliment—he was usually enough of a control freak to want to maneuver all the chess pieces for himself, even from thousands of miles away—but it was also the right thing to do.

"Fine."

The damned smirk again. "I appreciate the brevity of your answer, but you're going to have to be a great deal more specific than that."

137

"I'll take door number three."

"Smart choice." Sterling reached up with one hand and snapped his fingers.

The three red dots disappeared.

Eliot then folded his arms, but didn't move from where he was standing. Sophie worked better in comfort. Eliot worked better when he stood between their enemy and the room's best exit.

And no doubt about it, Sterling was the enemy. Eliot had disliked him from jump, back when they went to help out Aimee and her father after the stable fire, and Sterling had mostly gotten in their way. The former insurance investigator had done nothing since to make Eliot any happier to be in his presence—not when he forced them to blow up their headquarters in Los Angeles, not when he tried to take control of the team after Nate and Maggie were kidnapped in Kiev, not when he went after the team in Boston, and especially not when he poisoned Eliot's coffee in Dubai and locked him in an electrical closet, an action for which Eliot fully intended to make Sterling pay sooner rather than later.

Of course, Sterling *knew* that, which was why he had three snipers backing him up tonight.

"There's a smuggling ring," Sterling said, once he realized that Eliot wasn't going to sit down, "running through Malani, which I've been trying to bring down for several months now. I actually have your team to thank for that."

"How's that, exactly?" Sophie asked.

"The infrastructure for this particular operation was already set up by Damien Moreau. General Polonia took it over once your lot brought Moreau down, but he doesn't have anything like Moreau's skills at keeping things from getting messy. I've managed to shut down all the smugglers' pipelines through Africa, but none of the people I've arrested have been willing to flip on their compatriots within the general's government."

Eliot nodded. Things were starting to make a bit of sense. "That's why they're using the clinic now."

Sterling smirked, of course. "Yes. All the pipelines they inherited from Moreau are compromised, so they had to create a new one. After setting up a deal for some black rhinos that would have the international animal rights community, the World Health Organization, *and* Interpol dropping on the clinic like a bag of bricks, they have one over our dear Reverend Maimona."

"You're Interpol, Sterling," Sophie said quietly. "Why haven't you done your impersonation of that bag of bricks?"

"I may be a bastard, but I'm not a *total* bastard. I bring down the clinic, Malani's already-appalling number of dead children increases tenfold. No, I need to find another way, and then the pair of you fall into my lap."

"What are you proposing?" Sophie was, Eliot noted, using her most neutral voice. She knew better than to try any grifter's tricks on Sterling, who'd seen it all before, and twice since Tuesday, but she wasn't going to give him anything either.

"Simple. I need proof that contraband's being run through the clinic. I have no idea what you need, but I'm sure that you'd be willing to help me do this. You've obviously targeted the clinic for whatever particular game you're running. I'll help you with it if you'll help me in closing this case."

"What makes you think we even need your help?" Eliot asked.

That brought the smirk back. "All right, cards on the table—you're after what happened to the black rhinos."

Neither Sophie nor Eliot responded in any way to this.

"Of course, you won't confirm or deny it, which means I'm probably right, since if I was wrong, you'd be gloating about it. But I'm not wrong—I know that the black rhinos were supposed to go to the Brillinger Zoo in Massachusetts, I know they didn't make it, I know that the zoo's in financial trouble, I know they *haven't* made a claim with Nate's and my esteemed former employers, and I know that the general manager of the zoo day-tripped into Boston via commuter rail and the T, getting off at the stop closest to McRory's. So let's dispense with the nonsense and get down to it." Sterling leaned forward. "You help me, and I'll provide proof that the Reverend Maimona acted in good faith with the Brillinger Zoo. Nothing that'll exactly stand up in court, but I'm sure enough to satisfy you that the reverend was a dupe."

Sophie raised an eyebrow. "If that's true, we don't *need* proof, and we can just leave."

"Well, hardly." Sterling leaned back and rested an arm on the back of the couch.

Eliot shook his head. "We try to leave, you'll stop us."

"Oh, much more than that. I don't particularly *want* to ruin the clinic, but I'll do it if I have to. And I'll make sure that the reverend assumes that the two criminals pretending to be John Smith and Bernadine Onslow are the ones responsible."

"Fine," Sophie said, folding her arms in her lap, "as long as we understand each other." She looked at Eliot.

With a sigh, Eliot said, "They're running weapons. Did a test this afternoon with the pieces of a Russian-built RPG being smuggled in with some insulin, which was 'confiscated' by Polonia's troops. I confiscated it right back."

Sterling nodded. "That fits. They've been supplying weapons to militia groups in the States, insurgents in the Middle East and Asia . . ." Then he shook his head. "Unfortunately, Spencer here 'confiscating' one weapon hidden in a medical shipment isn't anything I can actually use."

"Yeah, well, I wasn't exactly trying to close a case. That's *your* job."

Standing up, Sophie said, "Sterling, I'll offer you a deal. Let Eliot and me run this. We'll provide you with the proof you need to make arrests and shut down the ring for good."

"And how do I know you'll do that?" Sterling asked.

"You're blackmailing us." Sophie spoke as if she was admonishing a not-too-bright four-year-old.

Yet another smirk. "Yes, I am, aren't I? All right. We'll do it your way, for now—but if I don't have results in two days, we do it *my* way."

With that, Sterling got up and left the hotel room.

As Eliot quickly moved to the window, Sophie said, "Nate, what do you think?"

Looking out the window, Eliot saw two snipers on the roof across the way, and another on the roof next to that one, all packing up their rifles. A second later, they were gone. He supposed he shouldn't have been surprised that Sterling had hired pros. He always had in the past, from Quinn and Geary to, well, Nate's team.

In response to Sophie's question, Nate said, "I think that Sterling's desperate. He only came to us last time because his daughter was involved, and he couldn't get her back through Interpol, so he needed us."

"This time," Sophie said, "he's likely tried everything he can do as an Interpol agent, and it hasn't worked."

"My guess is he's getting pressure from his bosses to put this case down or move on to the next thing." Through the earbuds, Eliot heard Nate let out a breath. "Sterling's always been willing to play the long game, so if he's given you a deadline, it means he has one also."

Sophie gave a determined nod. "Then it will need to be something we can accomplish in two days. And I have just the right woman for the job."

After she explained the outline of the grift she had in mind, Nate signed off. Only after Nate was offline did she let out a long breath, a rare show of emotion that had Eliot instantly worried.

Just as she usually did, Sophie picked up on Eliot picking up on her sigh, and she smiled. "Oh, don't worry, Eliot. I'm not an emotional wreck or anything ridiculous like that."

Eliot wasn't entirely convinced. "So why the sigh?"

"Sterling."

Sophie put a lot of feeling into those two syllables, and Eliot could totally get behind it. "Yeah, I owe him big-time for what happened in Dubai."

"He *was* rescuing his—"

"I *know* he was rescuing his daughter!" Eliot started pacing across the hotel room carpet. "That don't excuse what he did!"

"True. And that's exactly what worries me." She hugged herself, as if she were cold. "Whenever I stole a bit of art that IYS had insured, I was always much happier when Nate was the one chasing me instead of Sterling."

"Well, yeah." Eliot shot her a very Sterling-like smirk. "You didn't have the hots for Sterling."

"It wasn't because of that!"

Eliot just stared at her.

"Entirely," she added weakly. "When Nate goes after you, he still thinks of you as a *person*. With Sterling, it was all about the goal of retrieving the art. Nothing else mattered, nothing else got in his way."

"Don't worry," Eliot said. "I ain't lettin' my guard down with him for a second."

"I know you won't." Sophie shook her head. "I just hope it's enough."

While he would never admit this out loud, Eliot hoped it was enough, too. Every time they'd encountered Sterling, at best, he got exactly what he wanted. At worst, he improved his position, often at the expense of the team. Eliot would be more than happy for Sterling to arrest Mbenga, of course, but that was more because he wanted to see Mbenga finally be put away than out of any desire to see Sterling pad his arrest record.

Eliot was bound and determined not to let Sterling get anything beyond that immediate goal of destroying Mbenga this time.

|||||| TWELVE ||||||

NOW

The mistake that Jack Randall had made was trusting his brother-in-law.

"I wouldn't have married him if I didn't think he was trustworthy," his sister had said.

"He's a good guy, he knows his ass from his elbow," his father had said. Dad had a tendency to judge people solely on their perceived ability to differentiate those two body parts.

So when Bobby, the brother-in-law in question, came to him with an investment opportunity that was "guaranteed," Jack heeded the advice of his sister and father and went along with it. After all, Bobby was trustworthy and he knew his ass from his elbow. What could possibly go wrong?

Thirty thousand dollars later, Jack was screwed. Bobby had gotten the whole family to go in on the deal—then it all fell apart, and he got his ass *and* his elbow the hell outta

Dodge. His sister had hired a private investigator, but had had no luck in finding her soon-to-be-ex-husband. Everyone in the family got completely hosed.

Especially Jack, who was still too young to qualify for Social Security, but too old to have much in the way of job prospects.

But he was still a beefy guy. Blowing out his knee in college all those years ago had ruined his football career, but he'd worked as a bouncer, security guard, and even done a stint as muscle for the Irish mob in Boston (though he generally didn't include that on his résumé). Figuring he'd find security work at a museum or an office building, instead he lucked into a rich guy in Vermont named McAllister who had his own private wildlife preserve.

It was easy work, mostly involving keeping an eye on security feeds from around the estate, making sure none of the wild animals got loose from their fancy electronic fences, and keeping an eye on the perimeter e-fence and making sure it didn't break down, allowing the animals to roam free. McAllister had a veritable *Wizard of Oz* of animals—he actually had lions and tigers and bears—that mostly wandered around their designated area, ate, slept, and drank.

Which meant Jack could get lots of reading done. Currently, he was going through the entire Nero Wolfe series by Rex Stout. He'd just finished *Murder by the Book* and was in the process of downloading *Triple Jeopardy* to his e-reader when the alarm went off.

Frowning, he leaned forward in the comfortable chair that McAllister had provided in the sunroom of his mansion, which served as security HQ for the estate. He looked over the massive screen that showed all the security feeds, but the animals were, as usual, doing the exact same things they were doing yesterday, and the day before that, and the day before *that*.

Then he realized that the alarm was for the perimeter fence. Both eleven and seventeen were down.

Jack sighed, really hoping this wasn't another damn raccoon.

When he first got the job, he asked why McAllister didn't have two people working at the same time. The boss's answer was, "You're here to keep an eye on the animals, not ask stupid questions."

But it wasn't a stupid question, and this demonstrated why. Two nodes down meant a hole in the fence, which he'd need to go out and check himself. Better to have two people, so one could keep an eye on the rest of the estate while the other did triage on the perimeter.

Not to mention the fact that he was half convinced that one of the animals was going to burst free when he was taking a leak.

He went out through the sunroom's door to where McAllister kept four electrically powered golf carts. After hopping into one, he started it up and took it through the estate.

Jack was actually somewhat grateful for the break in routine. He spent all day in the sunroom, mostly following along as Nero Wolfe, Archie Goodwin, and the gang solved the latest murder in New York City, so it was nice to get the opportunity to drive one of the golf carts over the hilly grasslands and trees. The carts had built-in, specially modified GPS devices that indicated where the electric fences were so that Jack could avoid them as he rambled through the estate.

It freaked him out a little driving this close to a tiger or an emu, and feeling like it could charge and attack at any time. Intellectually, he knew the animals couldn't do this—they'd be hit with a nasty electric shock to the collar they all wore if they tried—but it still *felt* like they could.

Right after he passed the tiger, he suddenly realized that he had no recollection of whether or not he'd closed the door behind him when he left the sunroom.

At one point, something made a noise in one of the oak trees, and Jack instinctively hunched over, reaching for his Taser, and cried out, "Jesus H!"

Jack was an excellent shot, but he hated carrying because the mere presence of a firearm tended to escalate matters. A Taser, though, was a damn handy thing to have when you were facing an animal intent on chowing down on your throat . . .

However, looking up, he just saw one of the capuchin monkeys leaping down out of the tree, then back up.

Finally, he arrived at node seventeen of the perimeter fence.

Or, rather, what was left of it. Just like that time right after he started the job, it looked like a raccoon or a fox or a ferret or *some* damn thing had gotten zapped by the fence and taken out its annoyance on the node. That was when Mc-Allister realized that he needed a few extra nodes for redundancy.

This, unfortunately, didn't help when two of the nodes were taken out. Jack tossed the remains of number seventeen into the back of the golf cart and then drove it down the fence line to number eleven.

Jack shook his head. Sure enough, it was another nest: six eggs being watched over by the world's most agitated eastern bluebird. This was the third time this had happened. Jack had no idea why starlings thought proximity to an electrical field was a good place to put a nest, but there it was. Maybe it kept the eggs warm.

At least number eleven had just been knocked off-kilter, so once he set it back in place, it clicked back on, and all was right with the world. Seventeen was dead, but eleven and twelve would take up the slack until they could get another replacement.

Jack climbed back into the golf cart and drove it back to the house, maneuvering around the animals. After he parked by the sunroom, he went into the house, relieved to see that he had, in fact, closed the door. Once he was inside, he checked all the security footage from the past twenty minutes to be sure that nobody had snuck into the temporary hole in the perimeter. Nobody had, and the animals were just putzing around like usual. Then he called up a window on the computer so he could write a memo to McAllister about the latest animal attack on his security.

AN HOUR AND A HALF AGO

Parker had thought that moving the bird's nest would be the easy part.

The first thing she did before heading to the hiking trail was to find a thrift shop in Weston where she could get a change of clothes. She had started to steal the clothes when Hardison gently said, "Uh, Parker?"

"What?"

"That's a thrift shop in a small town in Vermont that's

barely makin' it as it is. Remember, we only steal from people—"

"—who deserve it, right, right." Parker shook her head. Old habits died hard.

Then a thought occurred to her while she was flipping through one of the thrift store's racks in search of a medium black T-shirt. "Hardison, did you hack into McAllister's security system?"

The woman on the other side of the rack shot her a look. "Excuse me?"

"I wasn't talking to you," Parker said, even as Hardison replied.

"Yeah, and I'm setting it up so that they get yesterday's images of animals runnin' around instead of you breakin' in."

Parker nodded, but that wasn't what she needed to know. She found a T-shirt, then walked away from the rack and the woman with the accusing gaze. "Can you dig up a picture of the damage the raccoon did that one time?"

"I think so, yeah." A pause, then: "Okay, sendin' it to your phone."

She was now standing in front of a wall that had a bunch of knives on it. Her phone beeped, indicating a new e-mail, and Parker called it up, then got the attachment. "What's the size of these node things?"

Hardison said, "About five inches wide, a foot long, three inches tall. Why?"

Parker didn't reply, but stared at the picture, tried to figure out the exact size of the claw marks on the device's outer edge, then found a knife that had a blade of roughly the same size. "Just trying to make it look good."

"Make *what* look good?"

"My raccoon impersonation. I figure I'll damage one with a knife that'll look like raccoon marks, then stick a bird's nest by the other one, and I'm in."

She paid for the knife, black T-shirt, black jeans, black leather gloves, and brown hiking boots with Alice White's credit card. Hardison had set up a payment system for that card that was untraceable by the banks, drawing from Parker's own accounts.

A gas station next to the thrift store had a bathroom that Parker changed clothes in, tossing the grease-covered clothes into the trunk of the rental car, and hoping she could get them cleaned before Sophie got back from Africa. Then she hopped in and followed the directions Hardison had provided to the hiking trail's parking lot.

Forty-five minutes later, she finally made it to the eleventh node of the e-fence.

Looking up, she tried and failed to find a bird's nest.

It was time to climb a tree.

Parker had always loved to climb things. In fact, the first thing she ever climbed was a maple tree behind one of the foster homes she had lived in. It was a small house in the Bronx, and there were four trees in the backyard: a maple, an oak, a weeping willow, and a mimosa. The maple was the only one that was climbable, but it was the *perfect* climbing tree: plenty of handholds, places to sit, and more. She remembered the first time she got high enough to see over the roof of the house. To the north, she could discern the local church that her foster parents kept trying to get her to go to. To the south was a big apartment building. To the east was a bunch more houses with small yards, some of which also had trees, but they weren't as nice as hers. And to the west was the elevated train. That very same train was the one she took the first time she ran away from that home and went down to Manhattan to pick people's pockets.

And one of those pockets belonged to Archie, who began to train her.

She was put into a different foster home after running away that time, and the next one didn't have trees in back.

The maple tree in Vermont wasn't anywhere near as good a climbing tree as that one in the Bronx had been. The branches were poorly arranged, for one thing—a couple of times she practically had to hug the tree to get up high enough, as the branches were too far apart for even her strong legs to navigate.

One of the branches snapped under her weight at one point, forcing her to grab another one and dangle for a second before swinging herself upward.

Mostly, this served to remind her why she preferred to climb around in buildings and elevator shafts—much less shoddy construction than trees.

Finally, she got to a decent vantage point. The only view *this* tree gave her was of more trees, none of which seemed to have any nests.

With a sigh, she looked down to find the right branch for a foothold—and saw a bird's nest on the ground!

At least, it looked like one. There was a divot in the ground, and it was filled with branches, bits of grass, and six eggs. Standing next to it was a bird with blue wings. Parker knew very little about birds, but figured it was probably a bluebird since it was, well, blue. Mostly.

Parker leaped down from the tree with a happy yelp. The

divot that held the nest was on the other side of the hiking trail from the e-fence, but how hard could it be to move it?

Within a few minutes, she realized the fallacy of that position. She had assumed that the nest was portable, but after thinking about it for a second—a second's more thought than she'd previously ever given to bird's nests—she discovered that that made no sense. Nests weren't supposed to move, they were supposed to support. Structural integrity wasn't high on the list of characteristics that birds went for.

Parker discovered this after her attempt to pick up the nest with her gloved hands resulted in a bunch of scattered branches, an egg rolling toward the hiking trail, and a bluebird kicking up a fuss.

"Dammit," Parker muttered as she ran to retrieve the egg, gently carrying it back to the now-less-nestlike divot.

Luckily, the bluebird was small and limited in its ability to cause Parker harm beyond chirping pissily.

Running back across the hiking trail, Parker went over to the area just next to the e-fence device and started digging a small hole, using the knife she'd bought to loosen the dirt.

Once the hole was about the same size as the divot on which the nest rested, she started collecting branches and grass and such, arranging it in a similar way to how the nest on the other side of the trail was arranged. Satisfied that she had a nice nest, and making sure it was *right* up against the e-fence controller, she then carefully brought all six eggs over, much to the consternation of the bird, who was throwing a fit.

Leaving the mother bird to rearrange the nest to her own specifications—surely knocking the controller out of whack in the process—Parker then hiked down the trail to the next node.

Using the picture on her phone for reference, she simulated the four claw marks of a raccoon, spacing them the way they were spaced on the previous raccoon attack.

This time, though, sparks started flying from the controller, and Parker squeaked and jumped back.

Hardison's voice came over the earbud immediately. "Parker?"

"I'm fine," she said quickly.

"Well, whatever you did worked, 'cause number seventeen just went down. And there goes number eleven."

Parker grinned. "Knew Mama Bird would come through for me."

"Okay, where you are's still hot from the next node down, so you need to go about forty feet up the trail—that's where the hole in the fence is."

"Got it." Putting her knife inside her hiking boot, she ran up the trail.

She jogged until Hardison said, "Now," at which point she turned left and ran through the thick tree line onto McAllister's property.

At this point, she was relying on Hardison to be her eyes.

"All right," Hardison said. "I've got the security feed that the guard *can't* see. He's gettin' into a golf cart—he'll be there in, like, six minutes."

"Right." Parker continued to run through the trees, eventually coming through to a clearing—

—where she found herself face-to-face with an emu. She stopped running, and also stopped breathing.

"Uh, Hardison?"

"It's all right, just don't move forward. Sorry, still trying to find all the smaller e-fences for the animals. A'ight."

Hardison took a deep breath. "Back up about four steps then turn left and go about thirty feet, then turn right. That emu's right on the edge of its enclosure."

Parker got her breathing back under control and did as Hardison instructed. The emu looked way too much like a horse, except not really, and anyhow, she was totally over her fear of horses, except she wasn't, entirely. Exactly. She'd been around horses that were okay, but she'd also never entirely forgotten that horse that killed the clown right in front of her.

Stupid horse.

She tried not to think about it too much. And tried very hard not to look at the emu that looked way too much like a horse.

Doing as Hardison told her to do had become second nature to her, and most of the time she was okay with that. She was part of a team now, and this way was definitely better.

It was, however, a lot more confusing, too, and she wasn't always sure she liked it. Particularly on days like today when she worked by herself.

But she wasn't by herself. Nate was kibitzing, like he always did, and Hardison was helping her through everything. They were there with her.

She found herself remembering what Hardison had told her once: "I got you, girl." Which he said right before he packed her bag with a parachute, just in case she'd need to make a quick exit off the roof of the second tallest building in the world.

"All right," he said. "Keep going until you catch sight of the bears."

"Bears, plural?" Parker asked as she jogged away from the emu.

"It's fine, they're behind the e-fence."

"Hope so." She didn't like the idea of being mauled by a bear.

However, the bears turned out to be asleep on a big rock.

"All right, Parker. I need you to head for that tree just north of you."

Parker blinked for a second. She generally had an idea of the direction of the compass points, as it was the only way to keep track of where she was when she was crawling around a building's ductwork, but she hadn't seriously oriented herself yet to this place.

However, it only took her a second to realize Hardison meant to her right. Turning, she saw a big tree.

It wasn't until she was climbing it that she thought to ask, "Why?"

"Golf cart on approach."

"I don't—"

Then she did hear it: a very quiet hum, just before a white cart came into view, being driven by a middle-aged man in an ill-fitting suit.

"Stupid quiet golf carts," she subvocalized so only Hardison could hear her on the earbud.

Then she felt something fall on her back. Somehow, she managed not to scream—no sense in alerting Mr. Golf Cart that she was in the tree he was about to drive under—but she did flail her arms and almost lose her footing on the branch.

Grabbing another branch, she managed to steady herself, hoping that whatever fell on her would be all that Golf Cart would notice.

He cried out "Jesus H!" but the golf cart didn't stop. Looking down, Parker saw that it was some kind of monkey, like the type they used to have for organ grinders. It was little, with long arms, white fur on its head, and brown fur on the rest of it.

"You okay, Parker?"

The cart was now going off into the distance, so Parker felt comfortable whispering. "I'm fine."

The monkey chose that moment to climb back up the tree. It scrabbled up and sat right next to Parker on the branch.

And then it just stared at her.

"Hardison?"

"Yeah?"

"There's a monkey here."

"Where here?"

"In the tree. It's *staring* at me."

"What's it look like?"

"A little monkey! White fur on the head, brown fur everywhere else. A little over a foot long, not counting the tail."

"Okay, hang on." A pause. Parker could hear the clicking of Hardison's fingers over his keyboard. The monkey kept staring at her with what Parker was starting to realize were very adorable dark eyes. "That's what I thought. You got yourself one of the few animals McAllister has a record of. That's a capuchin monkey. But—" A few more keystrokes. "That's weird."

"Hardison, I'm sitting in a tree being stared at by a monkey. *What's weird?*"

"You're not inside one of the e-fences. Does the monkey have a collar?"

Parker peered closely at the monkey's neck, but did not see a collar. There had been one on the emu and both bears. "Nope."

"Huh. That's weird. All right, well, you're clear now, so keep going toward the house. The security guy's gonna need at least ten minutes to check everything out."

Jumping down from the tree, Parker landed softly, then got to her feet.

The monkey jumped down and landed next to her.

With a sigh, she started to jog in the direction of the estate.

To her annoyance, the monkey continued right alongside her.

She stopped running, and the monkey stopped, too.

Pointing at the oak tree they'd both just climbed down, Parker said, "Go back!"

The monkey just stared at her.

"Parker?" Hardison asked.

"It's the monkey, it won't—" She groaned. "Never mind."

Deciding to simply ignore the monkey, she kept jogging toward the estate, Hardison directing her around the other e-fences on the grounds—which were, Parker noted, incredibly green.

She didn't like that much green.

That damned, stupid, if rather cute monkey kept pace with her the whole way, right up until she came in sight of the huge mansion. Parts of it looked like a typical old-fashioned mansion that there were lots of in small New England towns, but there were add-ons, and they'd been done fairly sloppily, without much regard to aesthetics. Which Parker actually liked, because that kind of carelessness with architecture usually also meant carelessness with security.

Hardison spoke in her earbud. "All right, the security on the house itself is—"

"Irrelevant." Parker grinned. The door to the sunroom was ajar. "I can just walk in. Mr. Golf Cart forgot to close the door behind him."

"O-o-okay."

"First rule of being a thief, Hardison. No amount of training, preparation, equipment, or smarts can beat the mark being a total moron."

"Amen to that."

Parker slid through the space left between the door and the frame, being careful not to disturb anything.

The first thing she noticed was the computer desk. There was an e-reader abandoned on the desk chair, a nearly empty mug of coffee next to the keyboard, and a wide-screen monitor showing all the security feeds. One of the latter included a view of the capuchin monkey—still by her side—in a tree, but none included the golf cart.

"What if he notices that he's not on the footage he's looking at?"

"He hasn't yet," Hardison said. "First rule of being a thief, remember?"

With a chuckle, Parker said, "Right. Where do I go now?"

"McAllister's got good computer security. The network's hardwired, with the only wireless signals going to a few tablets. I could probably break in given enough time, but you should have one of my jump drives."

Parker nodded. "Where's the security guy?"

A pause. "Still looking at the mess you made."

"Good. Where's McAllister's office?"

The capuchin monkey then ran ahead of Parker and through the north door just as Hardison said, "Take the north door and head down the hallway to the staircase."

"Uh, okay."

Walking quickly through that doorway, Parker saw that the monkey was standing at the foot of the very staircase Hardison had directed her to. As soon as she came close, the monkey ran up the stairs.

As Parker followed him up, Hardison said, "Turn left when you get upstairs and it's the last door on the right."

When Parker was three quarters of the way up the stairs, the monkey dashed to the left. Upon arriving at the landing, she turned to see the monkey standing in front of the last door on the right.

Grinning, Parker said, "Okay, *that's* cool."

"What's cool?" Hardison asked.

"Um—nothing." She didn't feel like getting into an argument about the monkey. The one thing Parker didn't like about working with a team was the disagreeing and the arguing that often came with it. She'd gotten enough of that in the foster homes.

Pushing open the large wooden door, Parker stepped into a small room with a huge picture window providing a view of the grounds, including a lion (currently asleep) and an ostrich (currently drinking from a small pond). The window took up the entire east wall, with the door to the hallway on the west wall. A mahogany desk was parallel to the north wall, a leather chair between the desk and the wall, and a bookcase filled with leather-bound volumes sat against the south wall.

She described it all to Hardison. "The books haven't been touched by anything but dust in ages. I'm betting they don't even have words in them—just someone who wants leatherbound books on the shelf to make himself look smart."

"Yeah." Hardison didn't sound interested, but then he didn't care much about books. Neither did Parker, really, unless they were really valuable books—which was why she nailed these as sham antiques right off. "There a computer on the desk?"

"Mhm." Parker sat in the leather chair, which was way too low for her, but she didn't adjust it, as that was the sort of thing that let people know that someone had been in the room. It was one of the first things that Archie taught her: to put things back the way you found them. Better still, not to move them at all, but that wasn't always an option.

The monkey jumped onto the desk, and just sat there, staring at Parker.

Parker grabbed the mouse and moved it back and forth, and a password screen came up. "Computer's on, but it's asking for a password."

"Don't worry about that," Hardison said. "Long as it's on, my jump drive'll work its magic."

"Okay." Parker reached into her backpack and took out Hardison's jump drive, sliding it into one of the USB ports, and also took out a listening device and put it under McAllister's desk. The jump drive's yellow light went on and stayed on. Parker stared at it. "How long will it take?"

"It'll be done when the light goes off. How long depends on how much is on the computer. Longer it takes, the more we got, and the better off we are."

"Fine." Parker sighed. The monkey chose that moment to climb up onto her right shoulder, his long tail wrapping around to her left shoulder. "Awwww."

"Awww what?" Hardison asked.

"Uh, nothing," Parker said quickly, then started shuffling

the papers on McAllister's desk. "McAllister's got some, uh, some papers on the desk."

"What kind?"

"Receipts and invoices and packing lists," Parker said, shrugging.

"For what?" Hardison asked.

Blowing out an annoyed breath, Parker grabbed the papers and flipped through them one by one. "Let's see—some of this is food. I'm guessing for the animals, 'cause otherwise, yuck. Some gardening things—sod, tools, weed killer, stuff like that. There's a bill for a pickup from a fertilizer company. Why would—" Then it hit her. "Ew."

Luckily, that was when the yellow light on the jump drive went off.

"Okay, done. Now, how do we get out of here?"

"We?"

Parker blinked and winced. "I . . . how do *I* get out of here? Sorry, it's like you're here with me, y'know?" She gave the monkey—whom she was thinking about naming "Alec"—an apologetic look.

"I'm always with you, baby girl, you know that." Parker could hear Hardison's doofy grin—which she had to admit to liking. He put his serious voice back on after that, though. "A'ight, I'm gonna lead you through the front yard and out the main gate—follow my instructions *exactly*, otherwise you're gonna set off the eye beams."

Parker frowned. "Why didn't I just come in that way?"

"Because the route I'm about to give you takes you right under the sunroom window, in plain sight of the security guard—who's now seven minutes from being back on post, so time to move."

"Got it." Parker nodded, got up from the chair, made sure it was back in the position she'd left it, then did likewise with the papers. "Tell me where to go."

"Just follow me, baby girl, and I'll bring you home."

Patting the monkey—Alec—who had settled on her shoulder, Parker proceeded to follow Hardison's instructions to get her out of the estate. From there it was a bit of a hike to the lot where she'd left her car. Luckily, she'd bought hiking boots . . .

||||| THIRTEEN |||||

Nate Ford was somehow not surprised to find himself back, for the first time in five years, on the wide steps that led to the Boston Museum. The last time was when he—with the unwitting help of the four thieves who would later make up his team, and also with the witting help of the museum's security chief, Theodore Coswell—uncovered the scam being run by the museum's owner, Edgar Gladstone.

Now Gladstone was serving time in a minimum security prison—a bit that would be up soon, if Nate recalled correctly, thanks to Gladstone's giving up his confederates—and Coswell had moved on to work for some security firm or other.

But IYS was still the Boston Museum's insurance carrier, and the museum was starting up a new exhibit of Pre-

Raphaelite art. According to IYS's records, on which Hardison kept regular tabs at Nate's request, Elizabeth Turre was going to check over the exhibit security, make sure everything was up to IYS's standards. The security protocols that Sterling had put in place were not all still intact, but a lot of them were, and—much as it galled Nate to admit it, especially after Sterling got the drop on Sophie and Eliot in Malani—they were good ones.

Elizabeth wasn't the best investigator IYS had, but she was probably the most dogged. What she lacked in imagination and instinct she more than made up for in thoroughness. Nate knew full well that he had the gift of observation; Elizabeth didn't have it in the least, but she knew this about herself, and made up for it.

Nate and Elizabeth had traded voice-mail messages the night before, and this afternoon they were meeting for lunch at the museum. Right now he was sitting on the steps, along with dozens of other lunch goers, workers, tourists, and more.

"Hello, Nathan!" came a pleasant, if scratchy, voice from behind Nate. Rising to his feet, he found himself reminded of another of Elizabeth's most effective tools as an investigator: she looked like someone's grandma.

Barely scraping five feet tall, Elizabeth had gone prematurely silver at age thirty. Rather than dye it, she let it go, and accentuated the look by wearing cardigans, simple dresses, and glasses that rested on her nose or dangled from a chain around her neck. Elizabeth actually had 20/20 vision, but the glasses tended to relax people into thinking her harmless.

By the time they learned otherwise, it was often too late.

Elizabeth held out her arms, and Nate leaned over to embrace his former colleague. "It's good to see you, Elizabeth."

"Stop lying, Nathan. You never gave a damn about me one way or the other, and you're only talking to me now because you need something from me. Now come on, I only have about twenty minutes, so I'll buy you a lovely dirty-water hot dog."

The pair of them went down the stairs toward one of the hot-dog vendors. Trying to sound casual, Nate asked, "What, I can't just look up an old friend who happens to be in town?"

Elizabeth stared up at him from over her glasses, seeing right through him. "Nathan, you moved to Boston right after you brought Ian down. Since then, I've made thirteen trips to the Boston area, and seven more to New England in general. Not one of those times have you 'looked me up'—though to be fair, two of those times were when you were in prison."

Nate didn't know whether to be impressed or frightened. At this point, they were on line at the hot-dog stand behind three tourists from Eastern Europe, only one of whom spoke English, and she spoke it better than the Pakistani hot-dog vendor, who was having trouble parsing her accent. "How did you—"

With a small smile, Elizabeth said, "That would be telling." Then she uttered her musical laugh. "Oh, who am I kidding? James used to keep tabs on you, and then, when he bolted for Interpol, the rest of us kind of banded together to keep doing so. You're a legend in IYS, Nathan. You took down Ian, you took down Owen, you drove James away—"

"Sterling drove himself away," Nate said emphatically. He refused to take credit for anything his former friend had done.

"—plus, God, Nathan . . ." Elizabeth shook her head. "You're living the dream."

Nate stared at Elizabeth as if she had grown another head. By this time, the tourists had gotten their hot dogs, pretzels, and sodas, and he and Elizabeth were up next.

"Two hot dogs, both with mustard and sauerkraut, plus a Diet Coke." Then she added, "And whatever he's having."

For a moment Nate again stared at Elizabeth, wondering where, exactly, she was going to put two hot dogs, while simultaneously wondering what she needed a diet soda for when she barely weighed a hundred pounds soaking wet. Then he looked over at the Pakistani vendor and said, "One dog, mustard only, and a bottle of water."

The vendor nodded, pulled three buns out of torn shrink-wrap with latex-gloved hands, then opened a lid at the front of his stand. Steam floated out as in succession he speared three hot dogs floating in water of dubious cleanliness and placed them in the buns. After grabbing a squeeze bottle of mustard, he squirted some of the brown substance on all three, then opened another lid on the front of his stand, pulling out some sauerkraut to place on two of the dogs, then flipped open a rear lid. Bottles and cans floated in ice-laden water, and the vendor grabbed an aluminum can and a plastic bottle.

What was most impressive was that he managed to do all this within about five seconds. Nate hadn't seen hands move that fast since he last witnessed his father playing three-card monte.

Not particularly wanting to dwell on that memory, he walked back to the stairs alongside Elizabeth. "It's funny, I was here for a class trip when I was a kid. The teacher let us get hot dogs for lunch, and the experience was almost exactly the same. Just three things different." As they sat on a stair, he took a bite of the hot dog and tried not to laugh as he chewed. "Tastes the same, too."

That got Elizabeth to raise an eyebrow. "Three things? All right, I can guess the gloves. We're the same age, so we can both remember a time when people were actually allowed to *touch* food."

Nate chuckled as he swallowed. "Yeah."

"That leaves—what?"

Shaking his head, Nate took another bite before answering, remembering again that Elizabeth was dogged, not observant. "Better mustard. When I was a kid, you were lucky if you got a brand-name yellow mustard. This is actual brown mustard with small seeds in it. That was the super-expensive stuff when we were kids. And the soda choices back then were just Coke, root beer, and Tab."

"Ah, yes." Elizabeth popped the last bite of her first dog into her mouth. Nate honestly couldn't recall if she'd chewed any of it, and he'd been sitting next to her this whole time. "You know," she said after swallowing, "they still make Tab? Nearly impossible to find it in L.A., but I've found several places in New England that carry it."

"You drink Tab?"

She shook her head. "No, saccharine gives me a headache, but Anton is addicted to the stuff."

"How's he doing, anyhow?"

"He's a junior in high school now."

Nate winced.

To her credit, Elizabeth noticed right away. "I'm so sorry, Nathan—Sam would've been in high school by now, wouldn't he?"

Waving it off, as he didn't particularly want to dwell on

the subject of his dead son, Nate said, "Don't worry about it—I was the one who asked."

"True, you did." She shook her head. "We'll be looking at colleges soon. And by 'we,' sadly, I mean just me and him, since his father has officially decided not to have anything to do with his life beyond the child support payments. He moved to Winnipeg, of all places, a year ago, and gave up his visitation rights." She sighed, looking at Nate. "I envy you your relationship with Maggie. At least you're on speaking terms."

Unbidden, the words Maggie had said to him, after the team brought down Blackpoole and again after Kiev, arose in his mind: that she didn't love him anymore, but that she liked the man he'd become. Somehow, it didn't surprise him that his ex-wife had come to be comfortable with the new Nate Ford before Nate himself could manage it.

"But enough of this," Elizabeth said, patting Nate on the knee. "You didn't summon me here for nostalgia, you summoned me to ask about the Brillinger Zoo policy."

"Yeah, about that—why are you working on that *and* on the museum? I thought you just handled the animal-related stuff."

"Ah, Nathan, you never were all that good at understanding consequences. With Ian's departure and the board, in their infinite shortsightedness, deciding to not hire anyone new anytime soon, resulting in a staff of eight where once there were a dozen, the company rearranged things a bit. We're now given assignments based on geographical regions, not on type of policy."

Nate blinked. "That's insane."

"Yes, but it makes travel arrangements considerably cheaper, which was the point."

Trying very hard not to think about what Elizabeth was saying about consequences, Nate barreled forward. "All right, what I'm wondering is why is it that the zoo's policy had a rider attached that requires the general manager to sign off on any insurance claim."

This prompted a derisive snort from Elizabeth as she bit off more hot dog. "Well, as little as I think of IYS's board of directors, they are paragons of virtue in comparison to those of the Brillinger Zoo. I've never seen so many frivolous claims in my life. We came within a hairsbreadth of canceling the policy, but then Marney stepped in and asked if she could fix it by having her approve all claims." She ate the last of dog number two and, after chewing and swallowing, said, "Honestly, Nathan, there are times when I believed that they were *trying* to get the zoo shut down."

Nate nodded while he sipped some water and wiped the sweat from his forehead. They were sitting right in the sun, and he was starting to seriously feel the heat. "Do you know who on the board made the claims?"

Shaking her head, Elizabeth said, "Couldn't say. They were all sent by the group as a unit. The official submission was by the chair, but it could've been anyone on the board who suggested it and pushed it through—or the board as a whole voting on it. Who knows?" She gulped down a great deal of her soda, then let out a truly impressive belch, its volume and resonance in direct contrast to the size of the person uttering it. "Excuse me," she said with a demure smile.

Chuckling, Nate said, "I'm not sure that's really excusable."

"Fair enough." She got to her feet. "I do need to get back inside. Did that answer your question?"

"It did, actually." Nate also rose.

"Good." She put a hand on his arm. "I meant what I said, Nathan. You are living the dream. You get to help people in ways that I can't even imagine. Hell, *you get to help people*. There are times . . ." She shook her head. "It's a dreadful job. I gravitated toward animal-related policies because I knew that, at the very least, I'd be helping creatures who are incapable of defending themselves. After all, the food chain never took paperwork into account."

Nate smiled.

"But now—" She let out a very long, very tired sigh. "I wish I could do what you're doing."

This brought Nate up short. Circumstances had conspired to put him into this situation, but he couldn't imagine *choosing* it. It had been chosen for him, by Sam's death, by Victor Dubenich, and then by the team members themselves.

Weakly, Nate said, "Well, good luck, Elizabeth—and thanks. In all seriousness, the next time you're in New England, call me. We'll have a proper lunch. I know a great pub."

"McRory's, right?" Elizabeth started jogging up the stairs, calling out behind her, "Let's try somewhere else, all right? I prefer not to have my food move. Take care of yourself!"

As she went up the rest of the stairs, Nate said, "Elizabeth?"

She stopped and turned around, an inquisitive look on her face.

"There's nothing glamorous about what I do. Powerful people have tried very hard to kill me, and almost succeeded. I've served time in jail. Hell, I've been shot several times—I can't even lift my arms over my head anymore. This isn't exactly what you'd call a great lifestyle choice."

Elizabeth walked back down the stairs until she was eye to eye with Nate. "Allow me to refute your points, Nathan. I'll give you jail—though I will add that it was medium security and your sentence was commuted. But you were shot on the job while you were working at IYS, too—by an art thief, if I recall the story correctly—and powerful people tried to kill you then, too. The difference is, now you're doing what you do to assist people in need rather than serving a corporation whose purpose is to try to avoid paying the very services that people specifically pay us to provide. I'd definitely say you've moved up in the world."

With that, she turned on her heel and went back up the rest of the stairs, eventually being swallowed by the museum's revolving door.

Nate turned and ambled slowly down them, heading toward the parking lot where he'd parked his car for an exorbitant rate, and muttered to himself, "The food doesn't move . . ."

|||||| FOURTEEN ||||||

NOW

Amalia Sanger walked into Michael Maimona's office, trying not to scream.

Unsurprisingly, as soon as he glanced upward and saw the look on her face, he hit control and S on the computer keyboard. The disk drive whirred as it saved whatever he was working on—next weekend's sermon, from what he'd said half an hour ago when he went into the office.

"What is the problem, Amalia?" he asked.

"That new doctor. I don't like her." Even as she said the words, she winced. In her head, when she'd rehearsed this, she'd sounded forceful, but when she actually spoke, she sounded—well, whiny.

Michael folded his arms and leaned back in his chair. "What, precisely, do you not like, Amalia? I don't know how much of a physician she might be, it's true, as we've been

fortunate enough not to need those services from her, but—"
He shook his head. "Have you seen what she's done with the
files? Amalia, for the first time since I opened this place, I
can *find* things in those bloody cabinets."

Amalia let out a small growl. "I *know* that, it's just—
Something about her feels *off* somehow."

"What, precisely? Her bedside manner is superb. Honestly, I've never seen the patients more at ease."

The words then burst out of her. "She's *too* good with
people! Nobody who's *that* good with people becomes a
doctor."

Michael couldn't help himself. He laughed, long and hard.
Removing his glasses in order to wipe the tears away, he
started to say something, but was consumed by more parox-
ysms of laughter.

All Amalia could do was stand there and take it, annoyed
that he was responding so cavalierly to her opinion, even
though his reaction was pretty well justified. Her accusation
was, on the face of it, ridiculous. Eventually, she had to say
something, which she did when his laughter started to die
down. "Are you finished?"

"Oh, thank you, Amalia. That was the best laugh I've had
all year."

That wasn't making her feel better. "I'm *serious.*"

"So am I." Michael's face finally lost the laugh and grew
more stern. "Amalia, in my life I have met dozens of people from Médecins Sans Frontières, and they have come in
quite the dazzling array of shapes and sizes. They all have
bizarre, ridiculous stories to tell that sadly I cannot share due
to the sanctity of the confessional. But believe me when
I tell you that I have seen women of far more appeal, aes-

thetic and otherwise, than Dr. Onslow who have gone into medicine—specifically of the type that we practice here, to wit, by the seat of our trousers." He smiled. "Besides which, why would anyone actually try to decipher our filing system, much less fix it, unless they were sincere in their desire to aid us, yes?"

Amalia admitted that he had a point. "But what about that Smith fellow?"

Michael nodded. "Now, he concerns me. I'm sure he believes his motives to be as pure as those of Dr. Onslow, but I doubt we will come through his visit unscathed."

"The Americans have *never* had our best interests at heart."

Before she could continue her tirade, Michael's phone buzzed. He picked it up. "Yes?"

Through the receiver, Amalia could hear the tinny voice of Catia at the front desk. "Reverend, two SUVs have just pulled up in front of the clinic. They have government plates."

Amalia winced. "Probably more medical shipments they want to 'confiscate.' You should *never* have taken those damned animals! This is going to bite us on the—"

Putting his glasses back on, Michael stood up and stared at Amalia, finishing her sentence. "—on the ass. So you keep saying. And yet, you have not been able to answer the question of how we would have paid for the adrenaline and penicillin."

Amalia fumed. Their need for those medicines was dire, and the money from the zoo had solved that problem, not just for the moment, but for the next half year at least.

The pair of them walked past the now well-organized

files to the front of the clinic. Amalia had to grudgingly admit that she liked seeing the wire-frame boxes atop the cabinets empty for a change.

Holding up her hand to block the midday sun from her eyes, she saw Aloysius Mbenga climb out of one of the two black Escalades that were now parked in front of the clinic.

Michael stepped forward. "Minister, I would like to thank you for the insulin—but there would be little point in doing so, so I will not. My gratitude was not your goal, yes?"

Mbenga regarded Michael, hands on hips. "The goal was achieved, in fact, but there were complications. Ones that trace back to this very clinic."

"What are you talking about?" Michael sounded as confused as Amalia felt.

"You recently added a doctor to your staff."

"No, I did not."

Amalia tensed. Lying to someone as powerful as Mbenga was not the wisest course of action.

But then, neither was engaging in a legally dodgy animal transaction while living under a corrupt regime that had a fondness for blackmail.

Then Michael kept talking. "I have, however, accepted the services of a volunteer, who will be here until the inoculations next week are completed."

"Yes, a Dr. Bernadine Onslow." Mbenga regarded Michael carefully, but Michael gave away no surprise that Mbenga knew the new doctor's name. "It's actually her handler who concerns us."

"What about him?" Michael asked.

"For starters, his name is not John Smith."

Feeling ridiculously vindicated, Amalia said, "I *knew* that wasn't his name! It just *had* to be fake!"

"How do you know this?" Michael asked, as if that mattered.

"Because I've met him before. Shortly after he stole our shipment, he started doing rather sloppy surveillance of my home, and my chief of security was able to get a picture of him—though he was, sadly, unable to capture him. His real name is Eliot Spencer, and he used to work for a—a former business associate of mine."

Amalia couldn't help but ask, "So he doesn't work for the CIA?"

Mbenga's gap-toothed smile chose that moment to show up, and Amalia involuntarily shuddered. "Oh, it's possible he's been in the American government's employ—the man is a rather talented thug—but he's not one of their agents, no."

Michael was nodding. "Which means that Dr. Onslow—"

"Is likely not who she appears to be. I'm afraid I must take her into custody—if for no other reason than to help locate Spencer. He and I have some unfinished business."

"That won't be necessary," said a familiar, yet not familiar voice.

Turning around, Amalia saw Dr. Onslow walking out of the clinic—but she was talking differently now.

"'Bout bloody time you wankers figured it out." Onslow now sounded like she came straight from the streets of north London. She walked right up to a rather shocked Mbenga and held out a hand. "My name's Annie Kroy. And I believe we've some business to discuss, you and I."

TWO AND A HALF HOURS AGO

"Excellent," Aloysius Mbenga said to the woman on the other end of the phone call. "Wear the red dress, please. I find that to be the most aesthetically pleasing one." He did not add that he also found it the easiest one to remove. Last time, she wore a blue dress undoing the clasps of which caused him to waste ten minutes; by the time he was done, he was barely still in the mood.

And since he was, in essence, performing for two, getting out of the mood would be problematic. Tereza got cranky when Mbenga didn't perform to her standards.

But the red dress just slid right off. Much easier.

Once he closed the connection, he walked over to the sideboard and poured himself a drink. Eventually, he would need to put in an appearance at the office—he tried to show up at least once a week so the commoners saw how incredibly hard he was working as minister of finance. Of course, that office included an empty desk with a computer that wasn't even plugged in, and a drinks cabinet very much like the one in here. He took the occasional meeting in the room, and allowed his picture to be taken while pretending to work at the nonfunctioning computer, but most of his actual business was done here at the house.

Just then, Ahmad, his chief of security, walked into the living room. That wasn't entirely accurate—Ahmad didn't "walk" anywhere. He always seemed to be marching, and you could tell that when he stopped marching, he had to force himself not to salute. But then, that military training was why Mbenga had hired him in the first place.

The security chief was wearing a black T-shirt and cargo

pants, and he pulled a smartphone out of one of the latter's many pockets.

"Minister, I believe I saw someone trespassing on the premises." He held the phone's display toward Mbenga, who leaned forward to see a picture of a vaguely familiar-looking person. "My men are tracking him down now. Neto says that it's the same one who took the shipment from the clinic."

Mbenga's eyes widened. "And he came here?"

Ahmad nodded.

"Very well. I would very much like to speak to him about why he stole our merchandise—and how he disabled the Escalade." He took a sip of his drink. Towing the Escalade had been expensive. Not that Mbenga couldn't afford it, but it was the principle of the thing.

Something about that man's face was bothering him, though.

"Is there something else, sir?"

That was why Mbenga paid Ahmad so well—he was observant, to the point where he could tell that something was annoying Mbenga. "I'm not sure. May I see that picture again?"

"Of course."

Again, Mbenga stared at the picture of a white man with long brown hair, and—

That was it! "Spencer!"

Ahmad frowned. "Who?"

"It was before your time." Mbenga put his drink down and pointed to the door. "Get out there—put *all* your men on this."

"Sir, five of our men are out there already. He surprised Neto and his men before. This time—"

181

"Just trust me, you will need *everyone*. I don't know what that bastard's doing here, but I want him alive and in front of me in five minutes."

Nodding, Ahmad said, "Yes, sir!"

As the security chief exited, Mbenga put his head in his hands. First Interpol shut down all his weapons pipelines, then the shipment got ambushed by none other than Eliot Spencer.

THREE HOURS AGO

"You want me to do *bad* surveillance?" Eliot asked incredulously.

"Yes. Otherwise, they won't be able to see you."

"I don't *want* them to—"

"Normally," Sophie explained patiently, "you don't, but this time you need to be identified. I'd rather do it in such a way that makes Mbenga think he has the upper hand. Make him think he's forcing me to change my timetable. Besides, the two of you have a history, and—"

"It's not just me and Mbenga who have a history."

Sophie was unable to stop the huge smile that broke out on her face. This was the other shoe she'd been waiting for.

Eliot frowned. "Why are you smiling?"

"Because I suspected from the moment you first told the story of what happened when you came here with Moreau that there was more to it than you were saying. You provided excessive detail right up until the end when you were talking about Mbenga's wife. And then you were gone last night for—"

Holding up a hand, Eliot said, "All right, all right, I did more than just put a finger to her head."

"That's what I thought." Sophie tried not to sound *too* self-satisfied. "And what happened when you visited her last night?"

"Doesn't matter," Eliot muttered.

Sophie was actually surprised at that answer. He wasn't usually so transparent. "Eliot, muttering 'doesn't matter' is as good as admitting that—"

"*Nothing* happened last night," Eliot snapped. "Yes, I visited Tereza, but—" He closed his eyes, then opened them.

LAST NIGHT

Eliot had very little trouble getting past Mbenga's security. It wasn't anywhere near as good as it had been nine years ago—but then, Mbenga's own life was more secure now. He was a member of the government, after all, and he was in good with the dictator.

Eliot spent about an hour observing the security routine, and determining the patrol patterns and how best to get past them without hurting anyone. He could've done it in a quarter of the time *with* hurting them, but that would just put Mbenga's people on alert. Plus, it would make it harder to get out.

Once he'd figured out the route of least resistance, he worked his way to the window that he expected was still Tereza's bedroom.

It was. She was just as beautiful.

She lay on her four-poster bed—the same one she'd had

eight years earlier—dressed in only a diaphanous nightgown, sipping a glass of an amber liquid that was probably brandy. Her long dark hair was short now, cut close to the scalp, but this served to accentuate her lovely, angular face, particularly the cheekbones. The nightgown also did a good job of showing off her athletic body, though Eliot noticed that she was less toned than she had been the last time he saw her. It seemed as if she no longer exercised, though she was still quite slender.

Opposite the bed was a wide-screen TV. Eight years ago, it had been a large television, not this high-def LCD. Given her taste for on-screen sexual acts, it didn't surprise Eliot that she'd upgraded.

Eliot couldn't see the screen from this vantage point—which he considered a blessing—but since he'd already seen that Mbenga was in a meeting in the living room, he knew that it had to be an old recording.

He tapped lightly on the window.

Tereza turned, looked up, frightened, but upon recognizing Eliot, she softened. Getting up from the bed, she walked to the window and opened it. The coolness of the mansion's central air-conditioning wafted across his face, drying the sweat that was a constant reminder that he was in Malani.

Then Tereza put a hand on her hip and said, "You know, when I heard that a single person took down Neto's team and disabled their car, I had a feeling you were back."

Eliot smiled warmly. "Nice to be recognized."

"Indeed. When Neto came back with the tow truck, he tried to convince Ahmad that it was a team of mercenaries that took them down, but he soon admitted the truth." She cupped his cheek with her right hand, the left one still holding the brandy. "It is very good to see you again, Eliot. I've missed those—those *evil* hands of yours."

Wincing, Eliot said, "Listen, Tereza—"

"You can't stay, though. In fact, I really need to get dressed—Aloysius and I are going to some manner of function as soon as his meeting ends. There'll be media present, so I must go as well, much as I loathe doing so."

Eliot frowned. "Since when?"

She shook her head. "Ah, Eliot, my sweet Eliot—do you imagine that I have hair this short for aesthetics? It is the result of chemotherapy."

"I'm sorry," Eliot said with genuine feeling. "I had no idea."

Tereza chuckled. "No reason why you should. Aloysius has gone to great lengths to keep my illness a secret. The cancer is currently in remission, but it has already come back twice. I'm afraid that if you wait another eight years to see me, it will likely be to visit my grave."

"Don't talk like that," Eliot said gently.

"You're kind to say so, but I've long since made peace with God. I will die with no regrets." Then she kissed her finger, and placed that finger on Eliot's lips. Her skin was smooth and warm. "Well, perhaps one or two regrets."

"Listen, I'm not workin' for Moreau anymore."

"Given that he's languishing in a San Lorenzo prison, I should think not. Yes, I *do* keep track of things, even now."

Eliot nodded, unsurprised. "Actually, it was my team that put Moreau there. We take down bad guys—and your husband may be next."

KEITH R. A. DeCANDIDO

"And you wish to know where my loyalty lies?"

"I just don't want you to get hurt."

"Ah, Eliot." Tereza shook her head and walked away from the window, sipping the brandy. "I'm afraid the time for such considerations is long past." She turned back around. "I will not help you in any attempt to harm my husband. But I won't hinder you either. I told you that I've made peace with God, and that includes my turning a blind eye to everything Aloysius has done. I will go to hell for that, but so shall he for committing those acts in the first place. But if you're here to hasten his punishment for that in this life rather than waiting for the next, who am I to stop you? Besides, I am not without resources of my own, should something happen to Aloysius. You need not worry overmuch about me."

"Okay," Eliot said neutrally. He'd been hoping that she'd help—be the inside person on whatever grift Sophie wound up pulling—but he'd been expecting the opposite. Her staying out of it would have to do. "I gotta go."

"I know." She walked back to the window, bent over, and leaned over the sill.

Her kiss was at once softer and more intense than it had been eight years ago.

"Good luck," she whispered, then closed the window, slicing away the precious air-conditioning, leaving him once again trapped in the sauna that was Malani.

Based on his observations, Eliot only had another two minutes before the patrol pattern would shift to one that would make it a lot harder for him to leave. So he spent a minute and a half just watching Tereza change into the formal wear for the event that evening.

She knew he was still there, too, which made Eliot feel a bit less guilty about watching her dress.

He was going to miss her.

THREE HOURS AGO

"And then I left to come pick you up on the docks. When I say it doesn't matter? That means it doesn't matter. Period."

Eliot stared at Sophie, almost daring her to respond.

He should have known better, because of course Sophie *did* respond. "But it does matter, Eliot—it matters to you."

"It doesn't matter *to the plan*, and that's what's important." He stood up pacing around the hotel room. "So you want me to watch Mbenga's house, but do it so they see me?"

"Exactly," Sophie said. "Mbenga needs to know you're back in order to make this work."

"Fine. I'll manage it, somehow." He sighed. "'s like asking Hardison to hack with one hand tied behind his back. Or Parker not to use her lock picks to pick a lock." He stared at Sophie. "Or you to do only half a grift."

Sophie raised her eyebrows. "I do it all the time. How do you think I convinced the reverend that I was a doctor with a secret agenda? Just do part of the job."

"Fine, I'll figure it out."

"Good." Sophie got to her feet and put a hand on his shoulder. "I'm sorry about Tereza. She's one you *really* care about, isn't she?"

Eliot shook his head. "How can you read other people so well, and completely misread me?"

187

Frowning, Sophie asked, "What do you mean?"

Looking right into her eyes, Eliot said, "I care about *all* of them."

TWO AND A HALF HOURS AGO

For the third time in the last twenty minutes, Eliot deliberately passed up an opportunity to hide from the patrols, keeping his face out for an extra half second.

Unlike the other two times, though, there was a specific reaction. The guard Eliot allowed to see him yelled, *"¡Aí está ele!"*

Two other guards responded to the call, and all three of them gave chase as Eliot ran past the hedges that stood alongside the mansion. The idea was to make them think he was heading for the driveway before he cut through the hedges and jumped the wall.

They were, Eliot noticed, armed with MP5s, but so far they were keeping them strapped to their shoulders, safeties on. Eliot wondered how long that would last.

Two more men ran out from around the corner, straight toward Eliot. One of them was the leader of the gang from the Escalade—Neto, according to Tereza. Neither of them was armed, and Neto cried out, *"¡Ao vivo! ¡Ao vivo!"*

For whatever reason, Mbenga wanted Eliot alive. He didn't stop running and went straight for Neto and his compatriot, spear-handing each man in the throat without breaking stride. Both men stumbled backward, their hands moving automatically to their necks. Eliot then elbowed one in the solar plexus while punching Neto in his. They both doubled over, and he kneed one in the head, then tossed him at Neto.

They were both down for the count long enough for Eliot to start running again, but now the other three were almost on him.

One was ahead of the other two, and he swung the barrel of his MP5 right at Eliot's head. Eliot blocked it with his left forearm, metal hitting bone with a jarring impact, which he ignored with the ease of long practice, though when he got back to the hotel, he was definitely going to need to ice the arm.

Twisting his wrist, he grabbed the barrel and yanked it out of the soldier's hand. The man's surprise at that gave Eliot enough time to palm-heel him in the temple, which sent him crumpling to the ground, insensate.

Unfortunately, that left Eliot open to the other two, who each punched him in the side. The one on the left, he was able to block with the MP5. But the one on the right hit a rib, due to Eliot's open stance. His arm was still up from the palm-heel strike, and he couldn't drop his elbow fast enough to block the punch.

The one on the left cried out in pain from punching a rifle, so Eliot ignored him long enough to hit the nose of the one on the right with a hammer fist. The soldier was completely unfazed by that, which was unusual, and he let loose with another punch at Eliot's stomach.

Eliot shifted the MP5 to block that one, then swung the rifle in an angled arc over his head so that the barrel slammed into both men's jaws along the way, sending them to the ground.

"Don't move," said a heavily accented but young-sounding voice behind him. He then felt the barrel of an MP5 in his back.

Eliot would have thought that General Polonia's troops would be better trained than that.

Counting to two and a half, he whirled around and grabbed the barrel of the weapon, pushing it aside to his left. The soldier looked shocked, and his finger squeezed the trigger. Eliot felt the vibration of the MP5 and the heat of the barrel as the bullets shot through it, but the rounds themselves went harmlessly off to his left, which was all that mattered.

Then Eliot pushed the MP5 barrel downward and toward the soldier, which twisted the man's trigger hand in such a way that Eliot could slide the weapon out of his grasp.

In response, the soldier head-butted Eliot—but he did it with his forehead against Eliot's crown, so the soldier himself was the one who stumbled backward, stunned, while Eliot just felt a mild ache.

"Three lessons," Eliot said as he removed the magazines from both MP5s, tossed them aside, and started walking toward the soldier. "One: When you headbutt someone, you hit with the crown onto the forehead, not the other way around. Two: *Never* put a gun right on someone's body like that. MP5's got an effective firing range of about three hundred feet, so you don't need the barrel to be right on your target where he can grab it and mess up your shot. And three?"

He sucker punched the kid, who went down in a heap.

"Don't get so distracted by your target talking to you that he gets too close."

Yet another cry of *"¡Aí está ele!"* signaled more soldiers. Last night, Eliot had determined that there were nine soldiers assigned to Mbenga's mansion. Hardison had confirmed this number, adding that there was also a chief of security, Ahmad Sierra; the nine Eliot had counted were part of a rotating group of soldiers assigned by Polonia to guard the mansion.

Based on what Eliot had seen so far, this was the crap duty Polonia gave to the new recruits and the screwups.

With these five down, there were still five to go, assuming that Sierra was also going to go after him. He needed to get out of there.

Unfortunately, they were cutting him off from the exits. Two soldiers were coming around from the back of the mansion, one was coming from the front, and the other two from the driveway. If he tried to go through the hedges and jump the wall, he'd be a sitting duck, especially since the two closest to him were armed with MP5s. Mbenga's desire to keep him alive wouldn't necessarily carry weight now that Eliot had taken down five of their comrades.

So he took the one route that wasn't cut off: the mansion itself. Mainly because there was no way anyone would be crazy enough to go there.

Which was, in this case, the best reason to do it.

He ran quickly toward the kitchen service entrance. There were windows that were much closer, but they were closed, locked, and made of ballistic glass, so there was no way he'd be getting through them.

But, as he recalled from his previous trips, the service entrance to the kitchen was always open during the day to facilitate food deliveries.

Throwing the door open, Eliot ran into the foyer and quickly recalled the layout of the house. He could either run toward the kitchen, which would be filled with the cooking staff, who might get hurt, or toward the dining room, which should be empty at this hour.

He chose the dining room, even as he heard the footfalls of the two soldiers who were closest behind him.

The room was long and narrow, with a huge table in the middle that seated ten. A white lace tablecloth covered it, with each place set with what appeared at first glance to be good china (and Eliot would expect no less from Mbenga's dining room, since opulence was very much his thing). Hanging over the table was a crystal chandelier, with a large, mirrored sideboard on the far wall and a window looking out on the front yard taking up the entirety of the rest of the near wall.

When Eliot was halfway through the room, running between the table and the window, the two soldiers came in. Reaching between two chairs, he grabbed the tablecloth and yanked it out, sending plates, glasses, napkins, and silverware flying with a massive clatter. That got both soldiers to skid to a halt, so Eliot grabbed a chair and swung it across the floor, sweeping out one soldier's legs, causing him to fall backward.

Even as the crashing china echoed throughout the room, the sound was overtaken by the rat-tat-tat of MP5 fire—the soldier's finger spasmed on the trigger finger. That meant the safeties were off, to Eliot's lack of surprise.

He then stood upright and threw the chair at the other soldier, which he knocked aside. Eliot followed up with a left jab to his face. The soldier took the punch and then hit with two jabs of his own, which sent Eliot back a bit.

But then the soldier took a second to raise his MP5, an

eternity that allowed Eliot to grab an overturned ceramic serving bowl that had tumbled near him. Just as the soldier was about to fire, Eliot flung the bowl, Frisbee-like, at the man's face.

Blood spurted from the man's nose as he fell backward, crashing to the floor in a mess of arms and legs. Eliot put the finishing touch on him by swinging a ladle at his head.

The fight had taken all of five seconds, but that was all the time the other three needed to arrive.

These three, though, weren't armed.

To Eliot's bitter amusement, one of the soldiers had a shock of curly blond hair—which stood out more than a little in this region of the world; Eliot figured he was a mercenary from Europe—another had a thick mustache, and a third had a long nose and dark hair. He found himself thinking of them as, respectively, Harpo, Groucho, and Chico.

Harpo was the first one in the room, and Eliot was still holding the ladle, so he swung it like a tennis racket, backhand, slamming Harpo in the jaw, dropping him to the floor.

Groucho then lunged for Eliot, who stepped back with his right leg to avoid being grabbed, hit the man in the jaw with his left elbow, then poked him in the throat with the ladle, finishing him off with a knee kick to his groin.

That put Groucho out of it for a bit, as he was now in the fetal position on the floor next to Harpo. Chico, however, was able to land a punch to Eliot's solar plexus.

Doubled over, trying to catch his breath like the proverbial monkey in the water, Eliot felt Chico kick him hard in the ribs. He fell to the floor, and Chico moved to stomp on his head. However, Eliot managed to throw his left leg up with a side thrust kick that Chico easily deflected, but that kept him from completing his stomp. While Chico steadied himself by planting both feet on the floor, Eliot thrust both his legs between Chico's feet, then spread them outward like a pair of scissors. His left thigh and right shin collided with Chico's Achilles' heels, and he fell backward to the floor.

Eliot then crab-walked forward while lifting his left leg, dropping his heel down onto Chico's face.

He'd never liked the Marx Brothers anyhow.

Clambering to his feet, Eliot hobbled toward the door to the dining room, leaving a pile of moaning soldiers on the floor. It would be less than a minute before at least one of them would get up and go after him, so he had to move.

The far door took him out into a foyer, which had a staircase leading to the second floor and a door to another staircase under it. Then Eliot remembered where that second staircase led.

He took the stairs three at a time, bounding down them and trying not to think about the pain that shot through his chest with each jump.

Mbenga's mansion was built on a small hill, so while the massive parking garage was beneath the ground at the front of the house, it was at ground level in the back.

When he got downstairs, he found himself confronted with a row of thirteen identical black Escalades. Idly, he wondered if Polonia got a bulk discount. On the end was a red Ferrari. Eliot considered then rejected the sports car—Mbenga's personal car would stand out like a sore thumb, whereas nobody would look twice at yet another government SUV. In fact, they'd most likely look away from one.

As he tried to remember how to hot-wire one of these

things, he noticed that the one on the far end, closest to the garage door, was a bit banged up—including several indentations roughly the same size as Eliot's foot in the driver's-side front door.

Tereza had said that they had towed the Escalade Eliot had sabotaged.

With a smile, Eliot went to that one, peering in to see that, yes, they had left the keys in the ignition. Why not? After all, the vehicle couldn't start.

First Eliot got under the Escalade, looking for the GPS tracker. Once he found it, he took his smartphone out of his pocket and used one of Hardison's programs to search for the GPS's frequency, and then block it.

Once the phone told him that was done, he opened the dented door and released the hood, then pulled the brown fuse out of his shirt pocket. People with new cars never thought about the fuses. Raising the hood, he reached once again for the box on the driver's side, popped the lid, and replaced the fuse.

Then he got into the Escalade. Sure enough, there was a garage door controller in it. He pushed the button and the door obligingly slid upward. Turning the key, he started up the engine and headed out of the garage and down the driveway.

He heard several angry cries in both Portuguese and English, and a few rounds shot from an MP5—one of which took out the back window, causing Eliot to flinch briefly.

But in seconds, he was out on the open road. By the time what was left of Mbenga's security got to the garage and gave chase, he'd be long gone—and untrackable thanks to his jamming the GPS. He considered and rejected the thought of thanking Hardison for the program on his phone. After all, he could just as easily have yanked the GPS out.

"Sophie," he said for the benefit of his earbud, "I shot up the flare. Mbenga should be coming to you within the hour."

NOW

"My name's Annie Kroy. And I believe we've some business to discuss, you and I."

Sophie stood in front of the Maimona Clinic, her hand out, waiting for Minister Mbenga to accept the handshake.

Instead, he simply stared at her. "I'm sorry, Ms. Kroy, but I have no idea who you are."

"I'm Mr. Spencer's employer, is what I am. He was doin' a recce on my orders."

Amalia stepped forward. "What is going—"

Mbenga interrupted her. "Why did you give him such orders? And are you aware of who he is?"

"He's a former lackey of Damien Moreau's. But you already know that, don't you?" Sophie finally dropped her hand and started pacing around Mbenga. His two goons tensed, but didn't take any action. "That's why I hired him. You see, what *I* need is a source of weapons to sell to some business associates in Belfast."

"You're English," Mbenga said.

Amalia muttered, "This morning, she was South African."

"What I am is a businesswoman," Sophie said quickly. "I could give a toss who I work with, long as their money's all right, all right? I had a deal with Tony Kadjic, but Interpol and the FBI captured him, so things've gone all tits up. I've got people in Belfast who need RPGs, and I heard you were someone I could buy from. I wanted to make you an offer. And I know you've got a supplier of RPGs 'cause Spencer snatched him one off you."

Mbenga's mouth widened into a gap-toothed smile. "I have yet to hear an offer, Ms. Kroy. All I have so far is someone injuring my security and stealing one of my vehicles and my property."

Sophie smiled. "Yeah, about that. See, Mr. Spencer knew you'd got Moreau's ways in. What neither of us knew were how good you were without havin' Moreau around, so I asked him to suss out your operation. As for an offer, how does a hundred thousand quid per grab you?"

Nodding, Mbenga said, "I believe we can discuss terms—"

"Somewhere else." The reverend stepped forward, and Sophie could hear the anger in his voice. "I do not think this conversation to be appropriate for the front of my clinic."

"I couldn't agree more," Mbenga said. "Ms. Kroy, if you wish to continue this negotiation, come to my mansion— along with Mr. Spencer, my Escalade, and my RPG—at seven P.M. tonight."

"Cheers, then. We'll see you at seven."

Mbenga nodded, and he and his goons got into the two Escalades and drove away.

"Eliot," Sophie whispered, "we're in."

FIFTEEN

One day soon, Nate hoped to enter his apartment and *not* find Alec Hardison already there.

Hardison *had* a place of his own. At least, Nate was fairly certain he did. He had to be showering and changing clothes *somewhere*, after all. And Nate had managed to achieve privacy on a few occasions. Some of those occasions even involved Sophie.

It was odd. He made an effort to keep track of the movements of several people he barely knew—Dean Chesny, dying in a private hospital bed; Jack Latimer, currently at one of his Chicago offices—but he had no idea where Hardison was when he wasn't with Nate. Same for the others—except Sophie. In fact, he hadn't even known where Parker lived until recently, and he wasn't entirely sure that she still lived in that warehouse.

He made a promise to himself to talk to Sophie about it when she got back from Malani, a promise he knew full well he would under no circumstances keep.

As Nate entered the duplex apartment, a glass half filled with Irish whiskey from downstairs in hand, he wondered if he could just ignore Hardison and go right up the spiral staircase to take a nap.

Then Hardison said, "Nate, I finally got through the encryption on McAllister's computer."

That brought Nate up short. "I thought you said that'd take at least a couple of days."

"Yeah, I *thought* it would, but—" He reached for something on the table, but couldn't find it. "Where the *hell* are my remotes?"

Then Nate saw the last thing he expected to see: a small monkey head sticking up from behind the couch.

Speaking very calmly, he said, "Hardison. Why is there a monkey in my apartment?"

"Parker!" Hardison cried out, looking toward the spiral staircase.

"Sorry!" Nate heard Parker's voice from upstairs. She came dashing down. "I thought Alec was up there with me."

The monkey—which was clutching one of Hardison's remotes—ran toward Parker and leaped up onto her shoulders, wrapping itself around her neck like a mink stole.

"Parker, I—" Nate hesitated, raising his hands and shaking his head briefly. "I don't know where to start. First of all, you were upstairs. Second of all, you brought a monkey into my home. Thirdly, you brought a monkey into my home and took him upstairs with you."

"What's the big deal about going upstairs?" Parker asked

with her usual ability to utterly miss the point. "I mean, I've *been* up there. I've even pretended to be dead up there."

"Parker, that's not the point."

Hardison held out a hand. "May I please have my remote back?"

Looking at the monkey, Parker said, "Alec, give him the remote."

Wincing, Hardison added, "And can we *please* name him something—*anything* else?"

The monkey—Alec—held out the remote, which Hardison snatched.

With a sigh, Nate tried again. "Parker, why did you bring a monkey here, into *my home*?"

"It's also our office," Parker said defensively.

"No," Nate said slowly. He pointed to his feet. "*This* is our office." He pointed at the staircase. "*That* is my home. I'm much more particular about who I let up there, and you can rest assured that that monkey is *not* on the list."

"But he followed me! In fact, he helped me find McAllister's office!"

Hardison put his head in his hands. "Parker, for like the nine-hundredth time, *I'm* the one who led you there."

"You verified the route, yeah, but Alec here—"

"Parker!" Nate barked. He'd had enough.

She frowned. "Fine. I have to go get all that stuff Hardison said I need, anyhow. C'mon, Alec."

As Parker moved to the door, Nate took a long gulp of his sipping whiskey. He was very proud of the person Parker had become in the years the team had been together. When they first were assembled by Victor Dubenich, Nate had balked at Parker's inclusion, deeming her to be insane. It was, of course, more complicated than that. The sociopathic thief he'd been hired to work with back then had been created by the foster care system, refined by Archie Leach, and unleashed on the world. Leach had once boasted to Nate of having created the "perfect thief" in Parker, but that left it to Nate, Sophie, Hardison, and Eliot to turn her into a *person*.

And she was making excellent progress. But sometimes . . .

Looking over at Hardison, he asked, "Stuff?"

Hardison held up both hands. "Look, man, there's no way we're gonna get her to lose the monkey. Hell, I ain't even holdin' out much hope for renaming. So if we're gonna be stuck with the thing—"

"*We* are not going to be stuck with it. At best, *she* is going to be stuck with it."

Nodding to concede the point, Hardison went on. "Either way, she needs to feed it, so I gave her a list of what the monkeys eat and how to take care of them. So she's off to get some fruits, nuts, vegetables, and eggs." A small smile, then. "I just hope she remembers about the box for—"

"Anyhow," Nate said quickly, since the one subject that interested him less than the feeding of Parker's new pet was the animal's elimination habits. "You said you broke the encryption?"

"Yeah. McAllister had a *nasty* encryption, but then I realized it was similar to the one the Bank of Iceland used when I—"

"Hardison!" Nate had already lost several minutes to useless digressions, and really just wanted to get on with it.

"Hey, this was a decryption worthy of the finest minds at Langley, and I think, especially after putting up with that damn monkey all morning, I deserve some accolades."

Nate just stared at Hardison, who dropped his gaze and shook his head ruefully.

"Which I obviously won't be gettin' right now. Okay, I got good news and I got bad news. Good news is—we finally know where our client's black rhinos wound up." He wiped the remote off with his palm before clicking on it. The big screen lit up with a black-and-white layout of the grounds of McAllister's estate, with boxed sections in purple. Each purple section was labeled with the names of animals: GIRAFFE (2), LION, EMU, and so on.

Hardison moved his finger on the track pad on his netbook, which moved a cursor around on the screen. One cursor went over the emu, and a date popped up next to the cursor.

And then Nate saw it. One of the purple boxes had the legend BLACK RHINOCEROS (2).

"Lookee here." Hardison put the cursor over the black rhino box.

Nate read the date that popped up. "That's the day after the *Black Star* arrived at Boston Harbor with no black rhinos."

"And the day another *Black Star* arrived in Portland with two black rhinos on it. Figure another day for transpo, and bingo. We now officially have a mark."

"Right. What's the bad news?"

Hardison clicked again, and the image changed to that of a map of the area around Brillinger Zoo. The zoo itself was in red, with the land around it in yellow. Pretty much the whole area north of Brillinger was either red or yellow. "Turns out that McAllister has been quietly buying up the land *around* the zoo. Ain't enough to do much with on its own, but you add the zoo to the equation, and *bam!*" He hit a button on the remote, and the red changed to yellow, providing a nice big yellow blob.

"So he wants to buy the zoo?"

"No, he wants to buy the land the zoo's on."

"And turn it into something else." Nate shook his head. "Marney will never sell, so—"

"So he's doing what he can to make the zoo collapse. Thing is? That was Plan B."

He clicked again, and the map was replaced by a screen-grab of an e-mail from a few years ago. Nate peered closely at it.

FROM: Declan McAllister <declan@decmcall.com>
TO: Norm Brillinger <manager@brillingerzoo.com>
SUBJECT: My Offer
ATTACHMENT: NorthBrillinger.ppt

I obviously heard about what happened with the bear the other day, and I have to say how sorry I am that you had to endure that. It's a terrible tragedy, and one that nicely points up what I said when we had lunch last week, to wit, you're not cut out for this. I know the zoo's been in your family since the 1800's, but it's not the 1800's anymore, it's the 2000's, and it's time to move on. Now, I showed you my proposal, and I've also attached it here as a powerpoint, and I think you should seriously consider it before somebody else gets hurt.

Besides, wouldn't a planned community like North Brillinger be the perfect legacy for you, instead of a zoo that everyone will remember as the place where a bear went crazy?

> Take another look at the powerpoint and give me a
> call.

Nate frowned. "All right, so he was trying to get Marney's father to sell after the bear attack. Makes sense. What's North Brillinger supposed to be?"

"Funny you should ask." Hardison clicked again, and a PowerPoint presentation began.

Images of luxury condos, tree-lined streets, playgrounds, schools, and parks all flashed by while Revolutionary War–style music—a flute and a drum—played. Then a deep voice started to speak: *"North Brillinger. A planned community for the twenty-first century. A place where people can live safely and happily in the beauty of central Massachusetts."* All the images were computer renderings, but then there was a photograph of a tree-filled area. *"The paperwork has already been started to create a state park, as well as the Brillinger Museum, dedicated to the historical legacy of the Brillinger family from the* Mayflower *all the way to today. Ground can break this year, resulting in a fully up-and-running community by 2015."*

Hardison stopped the PowerPoint, for which Nate was grateful, as the music was exacerbating the headache Parker and her monkey had given him.

"If he started the paperwork . . ." Nathan started.

"Yeah, not so much," Hardison finished. "I checked, and there's been no application by McAllister—or anyone else, for that matter—to make any land anywhere near Brillinger into a state park in the past ten years."

"He'd never be able to do this by 2015 either." Nate shook his head. "There's infrastructure, services, water, electricity, permits, not to mention the incorporation process. No, 2015 would be impossible, even if he'd started the day after he sent that e-mail. Wouldn't Brillinger have realized that?"

"He may not have cared." Hardison clicked again, this time bringing up another e-mail screen-grab. "Just to warn you, Marney's old man wasn't big on, y'know, grammar. Or punctuation. Or capitalization."

FROM: Norm Brillinger <manager@brillingerzoo.com>
TO: Declan McAllister <declan@decmcall.com>
SUBJECT: RE: My Offer

thank you for your email declan. I do appreciate what youre saying because my legacy has as you know become very important to me since the diagnosis. I will think about what you are saying though and get back to you as you suggest.

the main problem of course is marney she has had her heart set on taking over the zoo after im gone, and it will break her heart to sell it. but the zoo is also failing and theres nothing we can do about that.

I will be in touch soon my friend.

yrs
norm

"What diagnosis?" Nate asked. "He died of a heart attack."

"That's what he *died* of, yeah." Hardison clicked again, this time providing a medical chart for Norm Brillinger from a visit to a hospital in Northampton one month before this e-mail exchange.

Nate winced. "That's an oncology report." He took another sip of his drink.

Hardison nodded. "When Norm Brillinger died of a heart attack, it happened when he was a month or two from dying of colon cancer."

"Marney must not have known." Nate shook his head. "Okay, so McAllister cooks up a story about 'North Brillinger' in order to convince Norm to sell the land the zoo is on before he dies of cancer. But he obviously *isn't* putting together a planned community, so what's he really up to?"

Again, Hardison replied, "Funny you should ask." Another click brought up another e-mail screen-grab, dated a week before McAllister's e-mail to Norm Brillinger, and the day before the cancer diagnosis came in for the latter.

FROM: Declan McAllister <declan@decmcall.com>
TO: "Tartucci, Salvatore, COO" <startucci@elmcapital
.com>
SUBJECT: Dead Zoo

You were right, the bear was definitely the straw that broke Norm's back. What little interest he had in running a zoo is pretty much gone. I had lunch with him today, and I think I've sold him on the "North Brillinger" nonsense. Good call there, by the way, he didn't really show much interest until I started explaining about his legacy. It shouldn't take much to push him over the edge, and then we can get the preserve up and running.

Nate's eyes widened. "Preserve?"

Hardison nodded slowly. "McAllister applied for permits in Vermont to make his estate into a hunting preserve, but it was rejected by the state legislature because it's a residential area and the community got all up in arms because of safety issues. But the zoo's *already* a designated recreational area, so turning that into a hunting preserve is easy."

"And as an added bonus, you can hunt rare wildlife, including a few endangered species. Some people would pay a pretty penny for that."

"Yeah." Hardison clicked off the screen. "There's still a bunch of files I haven't gone through yet, but these are what I got from the key-word searches. I'll do more once I'm done updating Annie Kroy's online profile for Sophie and Eliot's meet-up with Mbenga."

"Good." Nate finished his drink and was thinking very enthusiastically about the next one. "Now I have to tell a daughter the truth about her father."

|||||| SIXTEEN ||||||

Sophie pulled up to the front door of Mbenga's mansion in their rental car, Eliot right behind in the Escalade, with its dented door and blown-out rear window. In the passenger seat next to Sophie was the large box from the clinic that Eliot had taken from Mbenga's thugs.

Two soldiers stood outside the front door, and Sophie wondered if they were the same ones Eliot had seen when he came here with Damien Moreau nine years earlier. Given that they were soldiers in a different army from the one that existed when Eliot was here before, she figured they probably weren't.

When they climbed out of their vehicles, Sophie handed Eliot the box.

She whispered to him, "I keep meaning to ask—were you the one who put that gap in Mbenga's grin?"

Eliot just smiled.

The soldiers silently opened the large wooden door. Mbenga was waiting in the foyer, holding a folder. "Welcome back, Ms. Kroy. Ah, and Mr. Spencer. What a chore it is to see you again." That last was said with a wide smile, showing off the gap between two teeth.

"I'm just here to do a job, Minister. Same as last time." Eliot was, at Sophie's instruction, using his best aw-shucks-just-doin'-my-job voice, the one where the version of his southern accent with the light consonants came through. It softened him, made him less intimidating. (When the southern accent with the heavy vowels came through, people tended to run away very fast.)

"Your job? That is laughable, Mr. Spencer. Please do not insult my intelligence by telling me that *everything* you did was your job."

"I worked for Damien Moreau," Eliot said softly. "You really think I did anything he didn't tell me to do?"

Sophie watched as Mbenga turned this over in his head. After a second, she said, "Gordon Bennett, can we get on with it? You two wanna chin-wag about the past, do it on your own time, all right? Let's get this done so I can get back to some real weather. Heat's makin' me barmy, it is."

"Of course, Ms. Kroy." He nodded at the soldier who'd opened the door, who took the box from Eliot. The four of them then went into the living room.

Sophie quickly took the room in. Brand-new leather couch facing the fireplace, an older easy chair, also leather, but not matching the couch. Between them was an end table containing an early Rodin sculpture that Sophie knew was a fake—she had the original in her storage unit in Los Angeles, having stolen it from the Rodin Museum in Philadelphia fifteen years ago—and hanging over the fireplace was a Rembrandt that Sophie knew *was* genuine. In fact, she'd thought that particular portrait to be lost. For a moment she was disappointed at the character she'd chosen for this grift, as Annie wasn't much of an art lover. She was still tempted to make Mbenga an offer for it.

The mantelpiece had several hideous figurines, as well as a wedding photo of Mbenga and a woman Sophie assumed to be Tereza. She was quite beautiful, and Sophie could see how Eliot would be taken with her.

She also knew that both Mbenga and Eliot were right. Moreau no doubt did instruct Eliot to seduce Tereza—Moreau was the type of man who would use *every* resource at his disposal, including that of his enforcer's charisma—but the affair ended up becoming far more than his boss's instructions.

There was also a sideboard behind the couch, and Mbenga walked up to it, placing the folder on the back of the couch. "May I offer you a drink, Ms. Kroy?"

"G and T, if you've got some." Sophie followed him to the sideboard. "Feel free to hold the T."

"Of course."

As Mbenga poured a glass of gin, the soldier put the box down and opened it. After inspecting the inside, he turned to Mbenga and nodded.

The minister handed Sophie the gin. "Thank you for returning my property to me. I assume the insulin has been sent back to the clinic?"

"What'm I gonna do with insulin?" Sophie asked. She and Eliot had in fact given the insulin to the Reverend Maimona (under the doleful gaze of Amalia) that afternoon.

After Mbenga poured himself some of what looked to Sophie like brandy, he picked up the folder. "I had my man in Interpol send me over their file on you."

Of course, Sophie did not respond in any way that betrayed her surprise or concern that Mbenga had a contact in Interpol. Possibilities flew about in her mind, though. Was Sterling the mole? No, that wasn't really possible. Sterling was the biggest bastard in the history of big bastards, but he would never be on the take. He took too much pride in being good at his job for that.

Did Sterling know about the mole? That was a tougher question. The team had worked with Sterling twice, once in Kiev, once in Dubai, and both times he withheld information. It stood to reason he'd do so now as well.

Was this why Sterling was in such a rush—and using her and Eliot in the first place? That was likely, and indeed fit perfectly. While Sophie agreed with Nate's hypothesis that Sterling was being given a timetable, it didn't make all that much sense that he'd have one. The very nature of Interpol was to build their cases slowly and meticulously, all the while dealing with multiple jurisdictions. So why would they rush Sterling to close this case quickly and move on? Unless, of course, there was someone above Sterling who was trying to quash his case—someone who just provided Mbenga with a file on Annie Kroy, recently updated by Hardison.

All this went through Sophie's mind in a second. Even as it did, she was responding to Mbenga with a small smile and an appreciative look. "You got my Interpol file? Nice job."

"Thank you." He opened the folder and stared down at it. Sophie could only make out a photo of her wearing the designer coat she usually favored as Annie (not that she would have dreamed of wearing it in this oven). "It seems you're a person of interest in several money-laundering cases, not to mention having Tony Kadjic listed among your known associates, just as you said."

" 'Associate's' a bit strong, yeah? Never even got the deal done, there." She nodded her head at the file. "Give us a butcher's, I'd love to see what else they got on me."

Mbenga closed the folder and tucked it under his arm. "Perhaps one day I shall. When our relationship has—deepened."

Holding up her gin in a mock toast, she said, "Well, let's get that deepening started, then."

"I notice you did not bring any money with you to pay for the RPGs."

Sophie regarded Mbenga with disdain. "You think I'm haulin' pictures of the Queen around? Wake up and enter the twenty-first century, old son. When I see the goods, you get a wire transfer from my account in the Caymans."

Mbenga winced. "That is—problematic. I prefer these transactions to be cash. Less of a trail that way."

"Thought you were the minister of finance. You *run* the bloody trail, don'tcha?"

"*Manage* the trail, yes."

Nodding in understanding, Sophie said, "General Polonia? He wants his cut?"

"If this is to be a wire transfer, I'm going to have to ask for a fifteen percent increase in the price."

Sophie snorted. " 's not a bad rate, that is. Most dictators take twenty-five percent, in my experience."

The gap-toothed smile came back. "Is that a yes?"

She clinked her gin against his brandy. "I'd say we've got us a deal, Minister."

Eliot then turned toward the door, his entire body tensing.

"What is it, Spencer?" Sophie asked.

"Someone's coming. A lot of someones."

Mbenga frowned. "I'm not expecting—"

The living room had two entrances: the one Sophie and Eliot had used, from the foyer, and a door opposite it. Sophie had no idea where it led, but that door flew open now, and three soldiers burst in holding up large rifles at the same time that four more came in through the front door and moved into the living room.

In Portuguese, one of the soldiers cried, "Do not move!"

Sophie did not move.

|||||| SEVENTEEN ||||||

Nate Ford found Marney Brillinger at the wolf enclosure.

He'd spent the ninety-minute drive out to the Brillinger Zoo hoping to come up with a good way to tell Marney that her father had been all set to ruin her dream when the heart attack hit.

Ninety minutes later, he still didn't have anything.

One of the many reasons why Nate had gone into insurance instead of, say, becoming a police officer was that he absolutely detested giving people bad news. When people received bad news, they became horribly emotional, and they became difficult, if not impossible, to read or to get information out of. Nate needed good information in order to figure out patterns and solve problems.

Insurance was perfect because by the time he got involved in a case, all the bad news had been delivered to all the parties. Grieving family members had already started to deal with the loss of their loved ones, victims of theft were already past the anger at the loss of their property, and so on.

Even now, by the time people came to him at John Mc-Rory's Pub, they were at their wit's end—not their wit's beginning. Nate was a last resort, not a first one, so his clients were far more likely to be emotionally drained than all psyched up and messy. It was why he immediately called for Sophie when Walt Whitman Wellesley IV had broken down in the bar.

So when he walked up to Marney, who was resting her elbows on the fence around the wolf enclosure, he decided to stall with the same opening Hardison had used. "I have good news and bad news."

"Y'know, it's funny," Marney said. "Everyone talks about how nasty wolves are. Wolves at the door, wolf in the fold, wolf in sheep's clothing. 'Let me in, it's cold, and the wolves are after me!' But have you ever actually *watched* wolves?"

Nate didn't have the heart to observe that all of the wolves in the enclosure were asleep. There were five of them, with a large female sleeping in the middle, three smaller ones sleeping near her stomach, and the large male on the periphery, close enough to protect them.

Marney kept going. "They protect each other. They look out for each other, and if anyone tries to interfere with the pack, heaven help them—but mostly, they all make sure the rest of the pack is safe. It's funny, in fiction, they always talk about these huge packs with alphas and omegas and big fights between packs—but that's mostly only in captivity. In the wild, most packs are closer to nuclear families." She shook her head and stood upright. "And yet they have this reputation for being evil. When the Kerrigans first talked about you, they were going on about how there are wolves in the world, but the more I think about it, the more I think you *are* the wolves. And you protect the pack. So do I get the good news first, or the bad news?"

Nate pulled a tablet out of his jacket pocket. "The good news is, we found your black rhinos."

Her eyes widening, Marney said, "That's amazing! God, you couldn't lead with that? Who cares what the bad news is after *that*? When do I get them back?"

Wincing, Nate said, "We're still working on that. And trust me, the bad news is pretty bad." He activated the tablet, tapped on an icon that Hardison had conveniently called *Marney*, and then handed it to her.

As she scrolled through the collected e-mails that Hardison had put into a single file, the expression on her face slowly modulated from giddy to confused to angry.

When she got to the last one, she turned away and stared off into space, holding out the tablet for Nate to take back without looking at him.

After an uncomfortably long pause, Marney stopped staring at some indeterminate point to Nate's right and looked at him. "I don't suppose you obtained any of this legally?"

"I'm afraid not. It's proof, but it's not proof that will hold up in court."

"Yeah." Marney blinked a couple of times, then stared right at Nate. "I could use a drink, Mr. Ford. Would you like to join me?"

"Sure," Nate said readily.

They walked in silence past an empty space that Nate suspected was where the black rhinos were supposed to go,

Little Madagascar, and the Pink Flamingo Café before arriving at the administration building.

Marney's office was a mess. Everywhere Nate turned, he saw piles of paper: on the floor, on her large metal desk, on the small bookcases, and stuffed in front of the books on the shelves. The two guest chairs had piles of papers and binders and such, and she lifted the pile from one and placed it on top of the pile on the other so Nate could sit. The walls were covered in posters from other zoos: the Bronx Zoo and Central Park Zoo in New York, the San Diego Zoo, the Dublin Zoo, the Taronga Zoo in Australia, and the Franklin Park Zoo in Boston. Staring at the latter, Nate said, "I remember going there when I was a kid."

"Your father take you?"

"No," he said emphatically. He took a seat in the cleaned-off desk chair as Marney sat opposite him. "It was a school trip. Right when Bird's World opened up in the mid-seventies."

Opening a desk drawer, Marney pulled out a bottle of Gentleman Jack, a premium version of Jack Daniel's, and two glasses, both of which had the Brillinger Zoo logo and an animal design. Marney gave Nate the tiger, keeping the lion for herself.

As she handed over Nate's drink, she said, "You know, they can't actually drink this stuff where it's made? The Jack distillery's in Lynchburg, Tennessee, and that's in a dry county."

"Here's to not living in a dry county, then." Nate held up his glass, and she clinked it.

"You know what the worst part is?" Marney asked after she'd sipped her drink. "I'm not even a little bit surprised. My father *hated* running the zoo, but he kept insisting he

218

loved it. He was always doing that—trying to protect me by not telling me things. I only found out about the bear attack because it was on the news and in the papers." She shook her head. "And of course, he didn't tell me about the cancer. Why tell your only daughter that you're dying?" She sipped more of her drink.

"We all protect what we care about in different ways," Nate said quietly. "Sometimes we help other people. Sometimes we lie to them because we think the truth will hurt more. And sometimes we lie down just outside the rest of the pack. Honestly, I might've been happier if my own father was a little *less* forthcoming about what was going on in his life." He took a sip of his drink. The whiskey burned in his throat. "My old man was a gangster. Worked out of that same pub you found me in. Jimmy Ford was a fixer—anybody needed anything done on the sly in Boston, you went to Jimmy Ford."

"And now you're the fixer?"

"I guess so, yeah. It's funny, a year ago—two—I would've denied it." Nate gave her a wry smile. "Might've even thought about throwing this drink in your face."

"Glad I didn't meet you a year ago, then," Marney said with a small smile that fell in short order. "Y'know what? I was wrong. The worst part *wasn't* that he didn't tell me. That was just him being him. No, it's that those bastards played him. McAllister, I can see, but Sal? I mean, I know they went to school together, but I can't believe that Sal would go for that."

Nate leaned forward. "What do you mean?"

"Well, McAllister's a collector. He could give a damn about the animals, he just likes having exotic things. He doesn't want to save anything, he just wants to *have* things so he can say he has them. He's also a greedy bastard, so I can see him selling out to hunters. You know how much people would pay so they could say they bagged a polar bear or a tiger?"

"Quite a bit, I'd imagine."

"Especially since it's so incredibly illegal. I'd love to get Fish and Wildlife up there, but there's no probable cause, is there? And he probably can fake up paperwork for all of it."

Nate needed her to get back on track. He already knew McAllister was a lowlife. "You said Sal wouldn't go for it?"

"He's a lifetime member of PETA. These posters? He got them for me as a member of each one of these zoos. He's a conservationist nut—the biggest one we have on the board, to be honest. I can't believe he's involved in trying to shut the zoo down."

"Maybe he is, and maybe he isn't. McAllister lied to your father. Maybe he lied to Tartucci also."

Marney frowned. "And if he did?"

"Well, the problem with working outside the law is that we can't just report things to the police—at least, not always. But when two people are doing something illegal together, the trick is to get them to turn on each other."

"How do you do that?"

Nate smiled. "Leave that to me." He sipped the rest of his drink, and then placed the glass on a teetering pile of papers. "Thanks for the drink. I'll be in touch." He got up and moved toward the door.

"Mr. Ford?"

He stopped and turned around. "Yes?"

"Thank you. You had no obligation to tell me any of that.

And some people would've considered it cruel to let a daughter know that her dead father had feet of clay. But—well, it was one more lie, so what difference does it make? I found out about all the others in the end, so it's only fitting that I found out about this one. And maybe now—" She sighed. "Maybe now I can finally feel sorry for him."

"Maybe."

"Is your father still alive?"

Nate didn't want to get into his convoluted history with his father. "He's back home in Ireland," he said neutrally. "I haven't seen him much lately."

Marney laughed, then. "Well, that tone of voice sounds familiar."

"What tone is that?" Nate tried and failed not to sound defensive.

Getting up from her chair and walking around to the other side of the desk, she said, "The tone of a child who loves his father—but doesn't like him very much. My father made me crazy, and I hated him more often than I liked him. But he was still my father, and after what you told me, I like him even less—but I love him even more. That doesn't make sense, does it?"

"Love never does," was all Nate found himself capable of saying. "Thanks again for the drink."

"Next time you see your father, tell him you love him. Even if you don't like him."

Nate just nodded, and then left the zoo office, heading toward the parking lot, suddenly desiring to get very far away from this place.

On some level, he knew that Marney was right. Jimmy Ford *was* his father.

But Jimmy Ford was also a criminal. Sure, Nate was, too, now, but there was a difference. Nate helped people who needed it. His dad would say he was helping people, too, facilitating deals, and loan-sharking and so on, but that was just a cover. Jimmy Ford only was in it to help himself. Nate's purpose was more noble than that.

There were days when he even believed that. Days when he could admit that he wasn't the same as his father, despite the fact that he used the same bar, despite the fact that he all but held court at McRory's the same way as Jimmy had, despite the fact that the last thing his father said to him before getting on the boat to Ireland was that he was proud of his son because Nate had become as ruthless as Jimmy . . .

Getting into his car, Nate pulled out his smartphone and searched for the nearest bar. He needed another drink. Or two.

|||||| EIGHTEEN ||||||

Eliot tensed. By himself, he probably could take out seven guys, especially in a room full of furniture that he could use as shields and weapons.

But with Sophie here, he couldn't risk it. She was standing right in the middle of the room, completely exposed. (As was Mbenga, but Eliot wasn't concerned about *his* safety.)

So he stood his ground. For now.

The four men who were closer to Eliot were keeping their distance. Each had his MP5 trained on a different part of the room. So Eliot started slowly inching his way closer to one of them, not moving more than a millimeter or so per second.

Sophie, of course, had her own methods of dealing with such a development, but where Eliot's were physical, hers were not. "Oi! What's all this, then?"

Then an eighth figure walked in. Eliot recognized him

right away, even though he'd never actually met the man on any of his visits to Malani. It was impossible not to know who he was, as his angular face, hawk nose, and red beret were pictured on every coin and mark note, portrayed in murals at the airport and throughout Malani City, and depicted in several portraits that hung throughout their hotel.

Though Eliot couldn't help but notice that he seemed mighty short for someone named after a god.

"General!" Mbenga cried. "I—I don't understand! What's the meaning of this—"

Olorun Polonia held up a hand and spoke in a surprisingly soft tenor. "I would not speak if I were you, Aloysius. It will only make your position worse." The general ambled slowly toward the center of the room. Eliot kept his eye on him at all times—the soldiers were going to take their cues from him—but continued to move ever so slowly closer to the nearest rifleman.

"General, please, I—"

Polonia shot Mbenga a look. "What did I just say?"

"Look, General," Sophie said. "I don't know what's goin' on, but—"

The general again held up a hand while regarding Sophie coolly. "Your name is Annie Kroy." Polonia didn't phrase it as a question. "You're a money launderer, an arms dealer, and a criminal. And you're trying to make a deal with my former minister of finance?"

Mbenga's eyebrows raised, his eyes widening. "Former?"

Though still looking at Sophie, Polonia said, "Aloysius, you seem to be having an issue with following simple instructions. If you speak again, Tereza becomes a widow two and a half seconds later. Am I clear?"

In reply, Mbenga nodded silently, then gulped down some of his brandy.

"You were attempting to make a deal with a member of my government, one that was not sanctioned by the head of that government, to wit, me."

Sophie held up both hands. "Look, I'm happy to give local politics a miss. I'm just tryin' to get my mitts on some RPGs. I've got blokes back in Belfast waitin' for these."

"I'm sorry, but they'll have to wait just a bit longer." Polonia leaned back, still staring at Sophie but raising his voice. "Thank you, Agent Sterling, it seems your information was quite correct."

Eliot balled his hands into fists, and the seven hundred and fourteen different methods of murdering James Sterling that he'd come up with over the last few years all went through his head even as the man himself walked into the living room—smirking, of course.

"My pleasure."

"Who's *this* geezer?" Sophie, naturally, stayed in character.

"Jim Sterling, Interpol." Sterling walked into the center of the room, standing as the third point on a triangle that included Sophie and Polonia. "And you're Annie Kroy. Quite a catch for me, this."

Eliot unballed his fists. If Sterling was calling Sophie by her assumed name, it meant he wasn't interested in exposing them.

Probably.

"Minister Mbenga, you have two choices right now. I can arrest you, or I can turn you over to General Polonia."

"I dearly hope you take option number two," Polonia said. "Captain Havrati has been so—so *bored* lately."

Eliot winced. Havrati had been King Lionel's chief torturer. Somehow, Eliot was not surprised to see that he had remained in his position with the new regime.

Mbenga started shaking. "I think I will submit myself to arrest, Agent Sterling."

Sterling tilted his head quizzically. "Now, why would I let you do that?"

"I—" Mbenga opened his mouth, and shut it. Then: "I—I can make it worth your while! I have a contact in Interpol! He's been providing me with files! I can give you everything."

Nodding, Sterling seemed to consider the notion, even though Eliot knew damn well that it was what he was hoping for the entire time. "That's actually a good answer. With your permission, General?"

Polonia held up both hands and moved toward the door. "I am grateful, Agent Sterling, for your exposure of this particular snake in my garden."

And then Polonia made the biggest mistake he'd probably ever made in his life: he walked close by Eliot.

Eliot kicked downward at the area just below Polonia's left knee, and the general stumbled. Reaching out with his right hand to grab at the 9mm Beretta holstered on Polonia's belt, Eliot grabbed Polonia with his left into a choke hold that arrested his downward motion.

"I'd put your weight on the right leg, there, General," he said as he thumbed off the safety and put the Beretta at Polonia's temple.

All seven MP5s were now pointing at Eliot, but his back was to the wall, so any shot would have to get through Polonia.

"Some a' you I know are sharpshooters," Eliot said, "but

I've got the safety off this weapon in my right hand. Even if you can shoot me and not the general, I guarantee my finger'll spasm."

"Do as he says," Polonia said to the soldiers through clenched teeth. To Eliot, he added: "You will not leave this country alive."

"Ain't the first time I been told that. Ain't even the first time I been told that in this house." Louder, he said, "Ms. Kroy, come *on*. Let's go."

Nodding, Sophie walked toward the door. "Sorry we couldn't do business."

Sterling said, "I don't think you'll be doing any kind of business in Malani again, Ms. Kroy."

When they got outside, the same two soldiers were on duty, and they raised their weapons at the sight of Eliot, Sophie, and the limping general, but the latter cried, "Stand down!" right away.

"Smart move, General."

There were four Escalades parked outside—the one Eliot had come in as well as three more—plus the Focus he and Sophie had rented.

"Bloody hell, you get a bulk deal on those?" Sophie asked.

Making sure he was standing in a position so that Polonia's body was still between him and any shot that the soldiers could take, Eliot took the Beretta off Polonia's temple and used it to shoot out one tire each on the four Escalades.

Sophie got into the driver's side of the Focus while Eliot maneuvered himself to the passenger side. He opened the door, and said, "Start it up."

Nodding, Sophie turned the ignition key and put the car in drive, her foot on the brake.

Then Eliot threw Polonia to the ground, cried, "Go, go, *go*!" Sophie hit the accelerator, and only then did Eliot close the door.

The soldiers immediately started firing their MP5s as Sophie drove down the winding driveway, but they lost their target in fairly short order, and wouldn't be able to pursue on wheels for a few more minutes.

While Eliot ejected the mag from the Beretta and tossed it out the window, Sophie said, "Hardison!"

"Already on it," came the hacker's voice in their ears. "Which passports you got with you?"

"They're back at the hotel, and we can't stop there," Eliot said.

Sophie shot him a look. "Yours, maybe. I've got Sarah Jane Baker and Katherine Clive."

"I thought Katherine was dead," Hardison said.

"Well, technically, but—"

"Let's go with Sarah, since she won't actually set off any warning bells. I gotta move, I gotta meet up with one of the zoo board here in Worcester. Eliot, you—"

Eliot shook his head. "I got my air marshal badge, so I can get on."

"All right, good." Eliot could hear Hardison tapping away at the keys on his little computer. "Okay, Soph, you're on Vista Atlantic Flight 22, a red-eye to New York, which leaves in an hour, then a commuter flight up to Boston out of JFK. And before you start pissin' and moanin', the next direct flight to Boston's not till tomorrow, and I'm bettin' General Polonia'll be shuttin' down the airports by then tryin' to find you two."

"Hardison, if he—"

"Don't worry, right now, there's no cell reception any-where in the vicinity of Mbenga's mansion. And he got rid of the landlines three years ago to save money. So you should be good for a while."

"He owns a Rembrandt, and he's pinching pennies over phone lines?" Sophie shook her head.

"You're welcome," Hardison said in his snotty, you-don't-appreciate-me voice. "Now I gotta go, you two a'ight?"

Eliot was about to give a very tart response, but Sophie cut him off. "We're fine, Hardison, thank you. We'll see you tomorrow."

After Hardison went offline, Sophie said, "So much for keeping an eye on Sterling."

"The son of a bitch just sold out a middle-management functionary in order to do a favor for a dictator."

"And he exposed a mole in Interpol. Likely the same higher-up who was trying to sink his case."

Eliot snarled. "Probably was after the mole the whole time. Now we're on the run from an entire army, and he gets his arrest *and* brings down a corrupt cop." He slammed the dashboard. "Dammit!"

They drove the rest of the way in annoyed silence. Eliot, however, did come up with a seven hundred and fifteenth way to kill Sterling.

NINETEEN

NOW

Sal Tartucci was actually having a good day, right up until Debbie said there was someone from the FBI to see him.

Luckily, Charlie was out to lunch when that happened, but Dorian was in her office, and the CFO was staring daggers at him as the federal agent—a lanky African American with facial hair and a toothpick out of the side of his mouth—came into the Elm Capital offices.

"How you doin'?" the agent asked, holding out a hand as he approached Sal's office door.

Sal pointedly didn't return the handshake and stood in the doorway. "What is this, Agent—"

"Oh, sorry, my bad." He reached into his jacket pocket and took out a leather case that opened to reveal a badge on one side and an FBI ID with the man's picture and his name.

"Special Agent Allen Thomas—just need to ask you a few questions, no big. Can I come in?"

"Okay, fine, so what *is* this about, Agent Thomas?" Sal didn't like this, the FBI just coming out of nowhere, especially after what happened to Andrechuk last week.

"Just some routine questions, Mr. Tartucci, about an associate of yours, Mr. Declan McAllister."

At that, Sal breathed a sigh of relief. Elm had been managing some of Andrechuk's funds, and the news that he'd been siphoning off pension money had made Sal very nervous. Dorian had assured him that everything was okay, that Elm hadn't done anything wrong, and that the feds would probably leave them alone, but when this guy showed up . . .

However, Dec had nothing to do with AA Investments, so Sal stepped aside and indicated the interior of his office. "C'mon in, Agent Thomas."

Thomas sat down and took the toothpick out of his mouth. "Thanks a lot, Mr. Tartucci."

As he sat down, Sal said, "I gotta tell you, though, Dec ain't an 'associate' of mine. I mean, we grew up together, but—"

"So you're denying a connection between Mr. McAllister and your work on the board of directors of Brillinger Zoo?" Thomas immediately took out a notebook and started jotting down notes.

Sal swallowed. "Uh, no, I ain't denying anything. I'm just sayin' that we ain't associates. We're *friends*."

"Right, so you and your *friend* haven't been associating with a person of interest in an international investigation of violations of the Endangered Species Act of 1973?"

"Um . . ." Sal swallowed again. He knew that Dec had

232

never been a hundred percent in compliance with that act, but he also knew that it was all in the service of *saving* endangered species. That was why he himself had agreed to help out. "Look, Dec wouldn't go breakin' the law."

"Never said he did. All I asked was if you were aware if he was associating with—"

"A person of interest, right." Sal shook his head. "Like I said, he's my friend. I don't know everybody he *associates* with, but I can tell you that the odds're pretty good that one of 'em might *happen* to be a person of interest in your case, 'cause he deals with wildlife and stuff. I mean, we're both involved with the zoo—though I gotta tell you, personally, I think that the zoo model's outdated."

"Right. So, to be clear, you don't know a *thing* about Mr. McAllister's meeting tomorrow with Armageddon Santiago?"

Sal blinked. "Who?"

"You don't know who Armageddon Santiago is?"

"Should I?" The name rang no bells with Sal at all. And he was pretty sure he'd remember somebody with the first name Armageddon.

"Guess not. Okay." Thomas put the notebook away and then got to his feet. "Thanks a lot, Mr. Tartucci. I'm sorry about this, I'm just tying up some loose ends."

Frowning, Sal asked, "Loose ends? Whaddaya mean?"

"I'm moving on to a different branch of the Bureau, so I gotta dot all my *t*'s and cross all my *i*'s, kna'mean?" He reached into his jacket pocket and pulled out a business card. "Listen, if you hear anything about Mr. McAllister meeting with Santiago, do yourself and him a favor and call this man."

Sal took the business card and looked at it. "Special Agent Taggert?"

"He's a good man. He'll hook you up. Thanks for your time, Mr. Tartucci."

"Yeah, sure. Don't mention it." Sal watched the federal agent walk through the bullpen and out the main door.

He stood staring at Agent Taggert's card for a few seconds. Then he sat down at his computer and did an Internet search on Armageddon Santiago.

The first hit he got was for the abstract of a magazine article about Armando Alejandro Díaz de Santiago, who took on the nickname "Armageddon" when he appeared on some cooking reality show or other. The Web site had only the first few paragraphs of the article, with the rest only available to the subscribers of *21st Century Chefs* magazine. Sal didn't buy those magazines, as they very rarely contained anything to do with food. His papa and his nonna were the best cooks he'd ever had the privilege of eating with, and they were a helluva lot better than these so-called gourmets.

The article also had a picture. Sal had never seen anyone with such scary-looking eyes. He wondered what a chef was doing as a person of interest in an Endangered Species Act case.

Before he could read further, his cell phone rang. Grabbing it out of his jacket pocket, he saw that the display said DEC MCALLISTER.

"Hey, Dec."

"Sal, I'm sorry, but I'm gonna have to cancel this weekend—or at least put it off till Saturday. That okay?"

Normally, Sal wouldn't think anything of this, but having this phone call come only a couple of minutes after the FBI was asking about him got his hackles up. "Uh, I guess. What's up?"

"I need to take a meeting with someone. It's a chef that's coming in from Malani. Might be a good new venture for me."

"What, restaurants?"

"Something like that, yeah. Gotta go—so you wanna just come up Saturday?"

Sal shook his head. "Uh, yeah, that's fine. I guess. Sure. Yeah."

"Okay. You all right, pal?"

"Yeah, yeah, I'm fine. See ya Saturday."

After ending the call, Sal stared off into space for a moment. Something was wrong. Very, very wrong.

He wasn't sure why he didn't tell Dec about the FBI. Then again, cell phones weren't exactly the most secure form of communication. He'd ask Dec about it on Saturday when he went up to Vermont.

Turning back to his computer, he clicked on the next article about Santiago, this one dated just yesterday: a case against Santiago was dropped due to lack of evidence. He was accused of killing animals that were endangered and serving them to private clients.

Suddenly Sal found himself nauseated. He couldn't imagine that Dec would get involved with somebody like *that*.

Then his eyes widened. The case against Santiago was in the African nation of Malani. And the article stated that Santiago was departing Malani for good after "this terrible ordeal" and "pursuing a business opportunity in New England."

The blood drained from Sal's face.

HALF AN HOUR AGO

Declan McAllister had just finished reading through the week's magazines and was now going through the news feeds online. He always did this to start out his day, wanting to know what was happening in the world.

The magazines had been interesting enough, particularly the latest issue of *21st Century Chef*—though he wondered why anyone would go by the nickname "Armageddon"—and *The New Yorker*—which he read mostly for the cartoons, which were hilarious as always.

Online, he mostly read up on how the Palmerston Beavers were doing—he'd lost interest in Major League Baseball back during the strike of 1994, but he loved following minor league ball. They'd managed to beat the Lehigh Valley Iron Pigs 4–3. There was also a nice "where are they now?" article on Roy Chappell, a former catcher for the Beavers who'd apparently left baseball altogether. McAllister had always thought him to be overrated, but still, the article was a fun read.

Then another article caught his eye. He wouldn't even have noticed it if he hadn't read the piece in *21CC*, but the name Armageddon Santiago jumped out at him. He read the piece about Santiago considering leaving Malani, where he'd lived for years, after being accused of killing animals that belonged to endangered species and preparing them for a "select clientele."

His phone rang then. Peering at the display, he didn't recognize the number, though it had a 617 area code, indicating Boston.

"Declan McAllister," he said, after pressing talk on the phone.

"Yes, Mr. McAllister, hello. My name is, uh, Theodore Williams. I wanted to talk to you about a, uh, a business opportunity."

McAllister was sorry he bothered taking the call, and wondered how this jackass got his number. "I'm sorry, Mr. Williams, but I—"

"I got your number, uh, from Mr. Salvatore Tartucci? He and I have had some, uh, associates in common."

"Okay." Now McAllister was interested. Sal wouldn't have given out his number to just anyone. "And what is this opportunity?"

"Well, Mr. McAllister, I happen to know that you applied for and, uh, were rejected for, also, a grant to make your estate a recreational hunting ground."

Sourly, McAllister said, "That's a matter of public record, Mr. Williams." And he didn't appreciate being reminded of it. If the damn busybodies in the community hadn't gotten their backs up and blocked him, he wouldn't have had to go through all that nonsense to put the Brillinger Zoo under so he could buy the land and the animals.

"Right, well, let me ask you, Mr. McAllister, would you, uh, be interested in an alternative revenue stream for dead animals on your land?"

"Excuse me?" McAllister was now about to hang up on this man.

"Hear me out, please, Mr. McAllister. I mean, look, you wanted to allow people to kill animals on your land for sport, right? They, uh, pay you a great deal of money, and they go onto your property with rifles and things, and they kill the animal."

McAllister said nothing, unwilling to confirm or deny.

Williams continued: "What I'm proposing is the same thing, except the, uh, dead animals are the *start* of the process. See, I represent one of the greatest chefs in the world, and he's, uh, he's between engagements right now. His specialty, however, is the preparation of rare dishes—the rarity being the game animals used in the preparation of same. You, uh, you see where I'm going with this, Mr. McAllister?"

"Who is your client, Mr. Williams?" McAllister asked.

"I'm sorry, but he'll need to remain anonymous for the time being—unless you're interested?"

McAllister blew out a breath. "I'm sorry, Mr. Williams, but I actually am going to have my hunting preserve. I appreciate your offer, but it's based on faulty intel."

"Oh!" Williams sounded crestfallen. "Well, that's great for you, at least, Mr. McAllister. I'm sorry I wasted your time. You take care, now, and good luck with your new preserve."

"Well, wait a second, Mr. Williams." The more McAllister thought about this, the more he liked it, especially after what he'd just read online. He called up the article on Santiago again. "As you said, your proposal has the animal's death be the start of the process—why not have it be the middle?"

"I'm, uh, I'm sorry, I'm not following you."

Smiling, McAllister said, "I'm proposing to have my cake and eat it, too, Mr. Williams. People can pay me to hunt on my land *and* have your client prepare a meal from it afterward. I assume your client is Armageddon Santiago?"

"I'm, uh, I—" Williams swallowed, and McAllister grinned, knowing he had him over a barrel. "I'm not at liberty to confirm that, Mr. McAllister."

"Of course not. But I can tell you that I *am* interested."

"Tell you what, Mr. McAllister," Williams said. "My client's flying into Logan Airport first thing tomorrow morning. If you're willing to meet us there, we can, uh, begin the negotiations."

McAllister held up a hand. "Hold on there, Mr. Williams—right now we're just talking, not negotiating." That was a lie, of course—this had been a negotiation from the moment he answered the phone—but he didn't want to commit that far just yet. "But sure, I'll meet you."

They exchanged information, as well as pictures of each other, and agreed to meet at the luggage claim area for Vista Atlantic Airways at Logan the next morning.

Before ending the call, McAllister said, "Just by the way, Mr. Williams—you didn't make this offer to Sal, did you?"

"Oh, goodness no, Mr. McAllister. I could tell right away that Mr. Tartucci was, uh, not the right person to approach with this particular proposal."

"Good." That meant that Williams wasn't an idiot and did his homework.

After ending the call, McAllister did a bit more online research into Santiago. The more he read, the more he liked this guy Williams's idea.

Unfortunately, driving into Boston first thing in the morning, and likely spending most of the day there, meant he was going to have to put off having Sal over for the weekend. So he called him on his cell.

"Hey, Dec."

"Sal, I'm sorry, but I'm gonna have to cancel this weekend—or at least put it off till Saturday. That okay?"

"Uh, I guess. What's up?" Sal sounded distracted.

"I need to take a meeting with someone," he said neutrally, then added: "It's a chef that's coming in from Malani. Might be a good new venture for me." He didn't make any reference to Williams, just in case Sal got wind of what his client did when they spoke.

"What, restaurants?" Now Sal sounded incredulous.

McAllister chuckled. "Something like that, yeah. Gotta go—so you wanna just come up Saturday?"

"Uh, yeah, that's fine," Sal said distractedly. "I guess. Sure. Yeah."

"Okay. You all right, pal?"

"Yeah, yeah, I'm fine. See ya Saturday."

McAllister stared at the phone for a second. Sal didn't usually sound so distracted—but then, he *was* in the office, so it could've had something to do with that.

LAST NIGHT

"Okay," Hardison said, "I been listenin' to the bugs we got in both McAllister's house and Tartucci's office. Also been readin' some more e-mails from McAllister's computer. You know how McAllister lied to Marney's dad? Well, his pants are on fire with Tartucci, too. Ain't a single mention of huntin' anywhere in the e-mails."

Nate nodded. He'd figured that McAllister's mendacity extended beyond that of Norm Brillinger.

Hardison clicked on his remote, calling up a Word file to the screen. "Tartucci's actually written a few memos to the board about how the 'modern zoo model' is no good, and they need to look into 'alternative animal care,' whatever that means. But he's also been a member'a PETA his whole life, and he donates to half a dozen zoos."

Again, Nate nodded. "Right, Marney told me that. What else can you tell me about Declan McAllister?"

"Well, get this—he subscribes to *magazines*." Hardison grinned. "Isn't that adorable? Kickin' it old-school."

"Some people *do* like magazines, Hardison."

"Yeah, people who *don't* like search functions, indexing, and easy access and who *do* like landfill."

Nate closed his eyes and sighed. "Hardison, what does he subscribe to?"

"Let's see—*The New Yorker, National Wildlife Magazine, Rolling Stone, 21st Century Chef, Potbellied Pigs*—"

"What!?" That was Parker, contributing to the conversation for the first time while sitting in the kitchen with that damned monkey around her neck.

Hardison held up both hands. "I swear I am not making that up. *Potbellied Pigs* is a quarterly journal dedicated to articles, photographs, and tips and timesavers regarding potbellied pigs. Not just any members of the genus *Sus scrofa domesticus*, but *specifically* the potbellied variety."

Nate just stared at Hardison.

"What?" he asked defensively.

"I'm sorry," Nate said, "I just don't think I've ever heard you use Latin before—at least, not properly," he added, remembering the time Hardison had posed as a lawyer.

"Really? This is what you say to me, after—"

Not really having the patience for another one of Hardison's rants about how underappreciated he was—and also wanting desperately for this conversation to be over with so Parker would take the monkey out of his apartment—Nate asked, "What was the one before the one about the pigs?"

"21st Century Chef." Hardison clicked his remote, and a JPEG of the cover of the latest issue appeared on the screen.

Nate leaned forward to look more closely at it. "That's our way in."

"I—" Hardison blinked. "Okay."

"Hardison, I want you to create a mock-up of the latest issue of that magazine tonight, and then Parker, you're going to substitute it for the one in McAllister's magazine rack."

"You want me to drive all the way to Vermont?"

"Yes." It was one way to get the monkey out of his hair.

"Tonight?"

"Yes."

She smiled. "Cool."

Pointing accusingly at her, Hardison said, "No speeding this time, a'ight?"

Parker pouted. "You're no fun."

Briefly, Hardison looked to the ceiling in supplication, then quickly saw that the ceiling was parsimonious about providing such, as Nate had learned long ago, and so he looked back at Nate. "What'm I puttin' in this new, improved copy of the mag?"

"An article about an exotic chef. Mostly a puff piece, but mention briefly a rumor that he's been known to prepare delicacies made from endangered animals. Then plant some on-line articles about how he was accused of that in Malani, but the charges were dropped."

"And what am I supposed to use for art?"

Nate shrugged. "I'm sure you can find appropriate photos online."

Hardison asked, "And the *subject*? What do I use for that?"

That got Nate to smile. "The only chef on the team."

LAST NIGHT (A LOT LATER)

When Parker had inserted the jump drive into McAllister's computer during her first break-in through the hiking trail behind the property, not only did it run a program that copied all the data from that computer onto the drive, it also installed another program that gave Hardison a back door into the system. So the second time Parker needed to break into the property, Hardison just needed to hit a few keys on his computer, and she was in without the security guard on duty being any the wiser.

She and Alec had gotten from Nate's place to McAllister's estate in ninety minutes—half the time Hardison's GPS said it would take, though it helped that the roads were mostly empty this late at night—and then when she got to the estate, she gave Alec the new copy of *21st Century Chef* and sent him inside.

With a huge grin on her face, she watched as the little capuchin monkey snuck through the house, dodging cameras and sneaking under furniture, until he got into the family room.

"I cannot *believe* you are using that monkey," Hardison said over the earbud.

"What?" Parker was subvocalizing, so neither the sleeping McAllister nor the awake security guard would hear her. "He's small, he knows his way around the house, and if he's caught, people will just assume he snuck in from outside."

Sure enough, Alec placed the magazine in the rack, took out the other one, and came back.

Parker frowned when he came back to her, though, as he had not only the real copy of *21st Century Chef,* but also a copy of *The New Yorker.* "No! Put that back!" she whisper-shouted at Alec.

He just stared at her, holding out both magazines.

She took the former, but left the latter between his paws. "Take that *back!*"

Alec just sat there, offering the magazine.

Hardison asked, "Parker, what's goi—"

"It's fine," she said quickly, then glowered at the monkey. "Back, or I don't take you with me."

After making a really unfortunate *ack!* noise, the monkey turned and ran back toward the family room.

For several uncomfortable seconds, Parker waited.

"I don't wanna *say* 'I told you so,' Parker, but—"

Parker interrupted Hardison. "He'll be back."

And then he was, empty-handed this time.

Grinning, Parker said, "Good work, Alec!"

As Alec climbed up onto her shoulders, Hardison said, "I'm just gonna assume you were talkin' to me, there."

Parker stuck her tongue out at Hardison, even though he couldn't see it.

"I heard that."

Now Parker frowned. "How?"

VERY EARLY THIS MORNING

Trooper Mike Mazzarano had just come on duty when the Aveo went zooming by.

Today, he'd gotten I-90, the Mass Pike itself, which was always a good spot for lots of tickets. He was cruising eastbound at about seventy-five, looking for a good spot to stop and watch the crazies go by.

Then the *same damn* Aveo zoomed by him on the left! After the last time, he'd run the plates, and learned that it was being rented by a woman named Alice White.

He was *not* letting her get away this time.

Hitting the siren, he stepped hard on the accelerator. But this time, she didn't pull over. No, she *went faster.*

Snarling, Mike straightened his leg, mashing his foot down on the accelerator. This wasn't happening to him again. Not even if she cried.

The sun started to peek up over the horizon, and Mike found himself temporarily blinded by the light.

Blinking the spots out of his eyes, he saw—

—nothing. The Aveo was gone.

He hit the accelerator even harder, pushing the cruiser to one thirty—and then it started to shake.

With a grumble, he eased up on the gas, slowing down to a mere eighty, then eventually decelerated until he was on the shoulder.

He shook his head. She was probably just going to cry on him again anyhow . . .

|||||| TWENTY ||||||

NOW

McAllister had no trouble picking out Theodore Williams, as he was wearing the same ridiculous hat in Logan Airport that he wore in the picture he'd texted so McAllister could identify him. McAllister was morally certain that Williams wore that silly chapeau all the time and it was covering a bald spot. He could pick out an aspiring toupee wearer a mile off.

"Santiago and his agent flew into New York this morning," Williams said, "and they're, uh, on a commuter flight up here."

Nodding, McAllister said, "Fine." He had a friend in TSA and had already confirmed all of this.

"They, uh, got to the gate about twenty minutes ago, so— Ah, there they are!"

Following Williams's gaze, McAllister saw a man in a

sleeveless shirt and jeans, with a scarf around his neck, talking with an exotically beautiful woman.

Although his face was partially obscured by the large sunglasses he wore, it matched the pictures in the articles McAllister had read.

"Mrs. Velásquez?" Williams was raising his hand. "Over here, Mrs. Velásquez!"

Speaking with a thick Spanish accent, the beautiful woman said, "Allo, Señor Williams. It is good to see you again."

FOUR HOURS AGO

"You have *got* to be kidding me!" Eliot muttered from his seat on the plane, which was flying over the Atlantic toward New York. "Nate, we left Malani with nothing but what we happened to have on us. How're we supposed to—"

In his earbud, Sophie, who was three rows away, interrupted. "It'll be fine. Eliot, I'll need you to tighten the belt on your jeans and rip the sleeves off your shirt. And I've got a scarf for you to wear around your neck. I'll change into heels and the miniskirt I've got in my bag."

Eliot opened his mouth, then closed it. He should no longer have been surprised that Sophie had a miniskirt in her purse. He was convinced that the purse was like that stupid phone booth thing on that TV show Hardison liked: bigger on the inside than the outside.

During the layover in New York, Eliot ripped the sleeves off his flannel shirt and Sophie gave him the scarf, which he wrapped around his neck like a bandanna, as well as the large sunglasses, which had protected her eyes from the Malani sun. She herself had unbuttoned the top three buttons of the blouse she'd worn as both Dr. Bernadine Onslow and Annie Kroy, and exchanged the capris and hiking boots for a miniskirt and heels. The latter two probably fit in her shoulder bag. Eliot decided he didn't want to know what she did with the pants and footwear she was no longer wearing.

"Now we're set," she said.

NOW

"Who is this?" Sophie asked in a Spanish accent.

Nate responded using his slow, deliberate voice that he usually reserved for bureaucrats. She would have thought he'd use the sleazy-lawyer voice for this one, but she respected the choice. "This is, uh, Declan McAllister. Mr. McAllister, this is Armageddon Santiago and his manager, Mrs. Esmeralda Velásquez."

McAllister held out a hand. Sophie shook it—his grip was solid, yet somehow feeble. Then he offered his hand to Eliot, who simply stared at him until he awkwardly lowered it again.

Nate tilted his head at the other man. "Mr. McAllister here's got a wildlife preserve up in Vermont, and he's going to be opening one soon here in, uh, Massachusetts, and he might have use for Mr. Santiago's, ah, special services."

Sophie, who had been assured by Hardison that McAllister had shown no facility for foreign languages—one of his security guards talked to his wife on the phone in Spanish, and McAllister yelled at him for talking in a language

McAllister himself couldn't understand—spoke Spanish to Eliot. "Let's stall for time, shall we? I'll pretend that I'm passing on a message about Mr. McAllister here from Mr. Williams." Sophie saw recognition in McAllister's eyes only at the two proper names.

Eliot looked at McAllister. In a deep, Clint Eastwood-esque whisper, he asked, "What manner of animal have you?"

McAllister said, "Well, I'm not sure we should be talking about this in the open, but—well, I've got emu, lion, tiger, black rhino—"

"Ah, yes," Eliot whispered. "Is good. I have special marinade for rhinoceros that will bring out glory in black rhino. Is good!"

Sophie said, "We would love to inspect your operation."

"All in one place," Eliot whispered, hands gesturing. "All together, they must be, so I can plan feast properly."

"Um," McAllister said slowly, "it won't be a feast. Each meal will be prepared separately, depending on the wishes of the individual clients. And soon I'll be getting a much wider variety, including aye-ayes and red pandas."

"Mmm, delicious," Eliot whispered. "And still, must be seen together."

McAllister nodded. "Very well. Why not come to my estate in Vermont tomorrow afternoon? I'll have all the animals placed in one enclosure, so you can inspect them directly."

Sophie nodded. "That sounds most excellent, señor. We will see you then, sí?"

"Uh, sí." McAllister squirmed. He really didn't like foreign languages, it seemed. "I mean, yes. See you then."

FIVE MINUTES AGO

Sal Tartucci was going over a bunch of reports when his cell phone rang. The display indicated that it was the private investigator he'd hired to find Dec McAllister in Logan Airport and report on his movements.

"Mr. Tartucci?" the PI said.

"Talk to me."

"I found him at the Vista Atlantic luggage claim. He met with some guy wearin' a hat I didn't reco'nize, and then he met two people comin' off a plane. One's a wicked hot lady, the other one looks just like the picture you sent me. 'Cept he was wearin' sunglasses, but it was definitely the same guy."

"Okay. Yeah." Sal sighed. Dec really was meeting with Armageddon Santiago. He ended the call with the PI. "That son of a *bitch*!"

Then he pulled the business card Agent Thomas had handed him out of his jacket.

|||||| TWENTY-ONE ||||||

NOW

Jack Randall watched as the keepers brought the tiger to the final enclosure. They had put all the animals in the largest clearing on the estate. Normally, the bears were there alone, but the e-fence used to enclose them had been enlarged, then all the other animals were brought in.

Jack thought this was a dreadful idea, putting them all so close together, but McAllister said it was only for this morning when the special visitor was coming. McAllister didn't say who the special visitor was, only that it was none of Jack's business. At this point, Jack was used to that attitude.

So when a bunch of cars pulled up, Jack assumed that they belonged to the special visitor, and that he or she had an entourage.

That, at least, was what he believed right up until they got out of the cars and were all wearing blue jackets with FBI emblazoned in yellow on the back.

Grabbing his cell phone, he called the boss, who was in the family room, reading his magazines. "Uh, sir? The FBI's here."

"Excuse me?"

"The FBI, sir," Jack repeated. "They're here."

McAllister cut off the call and hurried over to the front door. Jack went as well, out of curiosity as much as anything; plus he was, technically, supposed to protect McAllister and the estate.

Opening the door, McAllister was greeted by a large, bald man with a thick mustache. "Are you Declan McAllister?"

"Um—yes, I am. What's this—"

"I'm Special Agent Taggert." He pulled a folded piece of paper out of his jacket. "This is a warrant to search the entire premises—house and grounds."

Taggert handed the warrant to McAllister, but he didn't take it, just standing there and muttering, "Something's wrong. There's no way this could've happened. I don't believe it." McAllister took out his cell phone, probably to call his lawyer.

Figuring it was his job, and thanks to a lack of instructions from McAllister, busy as he was now on the phone, Jack followed Taggert, since he seemed to be in charge—though there were about twenty agents altogether going through everything in the house, as well as the grounds.

Eventually, the lead agent made his way outside. Jack followed him. Upon seeing the dozens of wild animals all bunched together on the lawn, Taggert turned to Jack. "Uh, Mr.—"

"Randall. I'm Mr. McAllister's shift supervisor for security." It was a fancy title that just meant he was the security guard for this shift.

"Mr. Randall, I assume there's paperwork for all these animals?"

Jack knew damn well there wasn't. "I'm afraid you'll have to take that up with Mr. McAllister, Agent Taggert. I just take care of them."

"Mhm." Taggert pulled a cell phone out of his pants pocket and hit a couple of keys before putting it to his ear. "Yeah, this is Taggert. We're gonna need FWS in here."

Jack winced. If the Fish & Wildlife Service was coming in, he was going to need a new job, and soon.

Somehow, he was going to find a way to blame this on his brother-in-law.

LAST NIGHT

It had taken him all day, but Taggert had finally gotten through all his e-mail backlog. He'd managed to keep up with the most important e-mails while he'd been laid up with the ferret bite, but he had let a bunch fall by the wayside.

Now, though, he was back on the job. The doctors had cleared him, and as an added bonus, the ferret that bit him had been put down. He was ready to get back in the saddle.

Unfortunately, that mostly meant responding to the outstanding e-mails and filling out a butt load of paperwork.

Then, just as he was done, a call came in from a blocked number.

"Agent Taggert."

"Taggert, my man, it's Agent Thomas."

Taggert smiled. "Thomas! It's good to hear from you! Hey, I wanted to thank you for the card and those balloons that you and Agent Hagen sent me in the hospital. They really brightened my day."

"My pleasure, man, my pleasure. Listen, I got a line on somethin' that may be a good way for you to get back into the swing."

And then Thomas told him about a guy in Vermont who was hoarding wild animals illegally, and who might also have been involved in a scheme to defraud the Brillinger Zoo, one that might've included sabotaging a bear exhibit.

Taggert didn't want to admit that he'd never heard of the Brillinger Zoo, but that was okay. This sounded like a good case.

"Hagen and me, we'd go after it ourselves, but we're neck-deep in a UC op. In fact, I need to get back to it."

Nodding, Taggert said, "All right, we'll get right on it."

"Oh," Thomas said, "McAllister was workin' with a dude name of Sal Tartucci. Works at Elm Capital in Worcester. He seems a'ight, but something about him's hinky. Elm was involved with AA Investments, and you heard about what happened to them, right?"

"Yeah, I did." Taggert remembered seeing a news story about that, not to mention one of the e-mails he'd gone through upon returning.

Thomas added, "You may wanna check his online calendar, too."

"You got it. Hey, thanks, man, I really appreciate this."

"What'd I tell you, Taggert? I'm the coffee, you're the cream."

Grinning, Taggert said, "You bet!"

He ended the call and leaned back with a satisfied smile. Thomas was a good man. Taggert wasn't so sure about his partner—Hagen, he thought, was stringing McSweeten along—but Thomas had done right by him and McSweeten. Even while he was laid up, Thomas and Hagen helped McSweeten out in finally taking down Greg Sherman. They'd been trying to nail his operation for *years*.

Speaking of his partner, McSweeten chose that moment to come over. "Hey, I'm about ready to head home. Ready to end your first day back, partner?"

"Not quite." Taggert filled McSweeten in.

"All right," McSweeten said with a big grin. "Let's do this!"

NOW

For the second time this week, federal agents entered Elm Capital, but instead of one agent looking to ask Sal questions, this time it was a team of agents who were there to arrest him.

"What!? I don't—"

The lead agent, a dark-haired, smiling man named McSweeten, stood him up and handcuffed him. "Salvatore Tartucci, you are under arrest for suspicion of conspiracy to commit assault, and of conspiracy to violate the Endangered Species Act of 1973. You're also wanted for questioning in relation to Elm Capital's relationship with AA Investments."

"This is crazy, I'm the one who called *you* guys!"

"Should've worked out a deal before you incriminated yourself, then," McSweeten said with a smile, "and before you got into bed with Arthur Andrechuk. Don't worry, though, you'll have plenty of time to work something out with the AUSA. I think you guys'll have plenty to talk about. For now, though? You have the right to remain silent."

Sal planned to exercise that right after he said one thing: "Debbie, call Rachel Sommer, tell her to meet me at the Boston Field Office!" He was an idiot for not talking to his lawyer before calling Taggert, but he'd been so *pissed* that Dec was making deals with someone like Santiago that he didn't think straight, and just called the feds. He fully intended to make that deal that McSweeten was talking about, but his lips were going to stay sealed until Rachel and her law degree were in the room with him.

Then McSweeten said to one of the other agents, "Don't forget to check his online schedule."

Snorting, Sal allowed McSweeten to haul him out of his office.

Then the other agent said, "Got it. Whole schedule's here, going back to 2004."

"What?" Sal blinked. "That ain't possible!"

"C'mon," McSweeten said as he led Sal out of his office.

FOUR HOURS AGO

Hardison hit enter. "Okay, it's done. Sal Tartucci now has an online calendar that matches his movements and appointments. I copied most of it from Debbie's computer—that's Tartucci's assistant, she has *got* to stop using her birthday for her password."

Nate poured himself a glass of Irish whiskey. "And it

has the meeting with O'Malley, and all his dealings with Andrechuk?"

"Oh, yeah," Hardison said with a smile. "Including a few dealings with Andrechuk that didn't actually happen, but since I have access to all of AA's files, all's I had to do was change a few headers, and now Elm Capital's on the SEC's radar. Age of the geek, baby!"

Wincing, Nate slugged down about half of the whiskey he'd poured. He'd been hoping to get through the whole job without having to hear Hardison say that.

TWO NIGHTS AGO

Hardison looked at Nate. "What'm I puttin' in this new, improved copy of the mag?"

"An article about an exotic chef. Mostly a puff piece, but mention briefly a rumor that he's been known to prepare delicacies made from endangered animals. Then plant some online articles about how he was accused of that in Malani, but the charges were dropped."

"And what am I supposed to use for art?"

Nate shrugged. "I'm sure you can find appropriate photos online."

Hardison asked, "And the *subject*? What do I use for that?"

That got Nate to smile. "The only chef on the team."

"Fine," Hardison said, "I can do that. Oh, but there's one other thing, somethin' I got from McAllister—not the bug, but the computer." He clicked his remote, and there was a record of payment to Seamus O'Malley.

Nate frowned. "Why do I know that name?"

"He's better known as 'Smiles' O'Malley. He's a leg breaker. Mostly worked for O'Hare before we got him to turn state's."

"Right." Nate nodded, recalling that O'Malley was part of Brandon O'Hare's crew. That was their first job in Boston, the job that introduced him to the Kerrigans, who brought them *this* job.

Sometimes the universe made connections that seriously made Nate's head hurt.

Hardison explained: "McAllister's calendar has a meeting with Tartucci and someone called Smiles, and then the next day we get this wire transfer, and then the *next* day, the mess at the bear enclosure happened. What's funny is, the sheriff's office lists O'Malley as one of the witnesses they questioned about the incident after it happened."

"Interesting," Nate muttered.

FOUR HOURS AGO

Hardison said, "Taggert and McSweeten should be able to put two and two together. Between McAllister's computer and what I put in Tartucci's online calendar, they should both go down for the bear attack—no matter who gives up who. And having AA involved will just mess things up for them more."

Nate nodded. "Good. It's possible they'll both lawyer up, so I want to make sure there's *something* that the FBI can use as leverage. But either way?" He took another slug of his whiskey. "Those two are going down."

NOW

McSweeten guided the handcuffed Sal Tartucci into the back of his sedan, holding his head in so he didn't bang it.

After calling for his lawyer, Tartucci had made good use of his right to remain silent, which suited McSweeten fine. Tartucci was the small fish here, and the best one to make a deal with—which meant he had to wait for his lawyer to be present so the deal would be kosher.

Taking his cell phone out of his pocket, he hit the autodial for Taggert.

He picked up on the first ring. "Hey there, partner!"

"I've read Tartucci his rights."

"Yeah, I just Mirandized McAllister. It's gonna take forever to figure out what to do with all these animals, though."

McSweeten was unable to keep the grin off his face. "Yeah, but think about what this is gonna look like on our evals. Especially yours! Second day back, and a major bust!"

"Yeah," Taggert said. "We owe 'em another one."

With a nod, McSweeten said, "Yup." They didn't have to say who they meant.

After closing his phone and putting it back in his pocket, he made a mental note to tell Dad about this bust. He also wondered if he should send Hagen flowers. Or maybe write her another haiku.

|||||| **EPILOGUE** ||||||

James Sterling sat in the apartment he kept in Lyon, near Interpol's headquarters. Olivia was in her bedroom, doing an online chat for some chess Web site or other. She'd been very much in demand since her dramatic win in Dubai, which was also the last chess tournament that her stepfather, Robert Livingston, would ever host. It was shortly after that tournament that she'd come to live with him.

Between Olivia's testimony and the fallout from a building explosion in Kazakhstan, Livingston would be limiting his chess playing to whatever he could drum up in Dubai Central Prison.

The footage of Livingston's arrest was the second-most played MPEG on Sterling's laptop. The most played was still the death of "Rebecca Ibañez" in San Lorenzo. It never failed to bring a smile to his face; that footage tickled him on so many levels.

As he sat sipping a glass of Scotch, he double-clicked on another MPEG, one that he suspected would be challenging those other two for popularity.

It was footage from BBC World News. "Agent Anatoly Mazursky of Interpol was arrested today on charges of accepting bribes from representatives of the Malani government. One of those representatives was former finance minster Aloysius Mbenga, who was arrested in his home in Malani by Interpol agents on the scene. Interpol's secretary-general, Ronald Noble, said that Agent Mazursky was working alone, and praised the Interpol agents under Mazursky for bringing his criminal activities to light. In particular, he singled out Agent Hrothgar Mikkelsen, who will be taking over Mazursky's position as a supervising agent."

Sterling thoughtfully sipped his Scotch. Of course Mikkelsen had gotten the promotion. Sterling wasn't even angry about that. Mikkelsen had been with Interpol for the better part of ten years, while Sterling hadn't even been there for two. Besides, it was more important to get Mazursky out of there. He was rapidly becoming a hindrance to Sterling's ability to do his job.

Mikkelsen could have the promotion. And one of the first memos he'd get would be from Sterling, outlining his proposal for a new art-theft division—which, naturally, would be headed by one Jim Sterling, the man responsible for getting Mikkelsen his current job . . .

He felt no guilt about once again using Nate and his crew. He knew that Spencer and "Jenny" would get out of Mbenga's mansion unscathed. If they were the type of people who'd get caught under those circumstances, they wouldn't have been worth using in the first place.

They were handy to have around, Nate's little gang. They were that wonderful combination of talented and noble. The former was useful, while the latter made it so incredibly easy to poke them with a metaphorical stick.

Plus, of course, the challenge. That went all the way back to Nate and Sterling's days at IYS. Nate was the only person who could even keep up with him, and he had to admit he missed the competition they'd had when they were working together. They made each other better.

Now, though, it was just a perpetual game of chess. They hadn't played a game in years that didn't end in stalemate, and Sterling suspected that this would continue. But it wasn't always the endgame that mattered so much as the way you got there.

"Until next time," he said, raising a glass in toast.

The Reverend Michael Maimona had just entered his office, dropping the mail onto his desk as he sat down behind it, when Amalia came storming in.

"Have you seen the news? Mbenga's been arrested, and there is an all-points bulletin out for 'Dr. Onslow' and 'John Smith,' except their names are apparently Annie Kroy and Eliot Spencer. I *knew* we shouldn't have trusted them! And now we don't have a doctor for the inoculations—not, I suppose, that we ever *did*—"

Michael steepled his fingers in front of his face and chuckled. "Her name's not Annie Kroy either. The name she gave me was Sophie Devereaux."

KEITH R. A. DeCANDIDO

"She—" Amalia stopped, blinked. "Wait, what?"

"Her name is Sophie Devereaux, and she came here at the behest of the Brillinger Zoo. She was trying to determine if we swindled them out of the black rhinos."

Amalia frowned. "Then what was she doing pretending to be an arms dealer with Mbenga?"

"Helping us."

"Helping us?" Amalia threw up her arms. "She has caused nothing but trouble!"

"On the contrary, she helped us immensely."

"Name one way she did!" Amalia put her hands on her hips.

"I will, in fact, name four, yes?" Michael started enumerating points on his fingers. "She and Smith—or, rather, Spencer—helped get Mbenga arrested, which means he is unlikely to be attempting to run arms through the clinic any longer. She verified that we didn't defraud the zoo, so we might have dealings with them again in the future."

"Because *that* worked out *so* well," Amalia muttered.

Pointedly ignoring her, Michael made his third point on his ring finger: "She put our filing system in order. I think for that alone, she deserves praise, if not a Nobel Prize."

Amalia said nothing in response to that, but Michael could see the emotions playing on her face. She'd been wanting to get the filing system in order for ages. But she also had taken a dislike to Onslow/Kroy/Devereaux from the start.

Her solution to this dilemma was to avoid it and ask, "What's the fourth point?"

With a wide smile, Michael pulled one envelope—the only one he'd opened—from the pile of mail and handed it to Amalia.

She pulled the cashier's check out of the envelope and her eyes went very wide.

"This is—a *lot* of money. Who is this Leverage Associates LLC that the money is from?"

"Well, the return address on the envelope is a PO box in the States—but it came from Ms. Devereaux."

"Excuse me?" somebody said.

Michael looked past Amalia and saw a familiar-looking woman. She had the gaunt look and short hair typical of someone who'd recently undergone chemotherapy. However, she also wore a dress that cost more than he paid Amalia in a year, and she was carrying what looked to be a very heavily laden purse. "May I help you?"

"Reverend Maimona? I'm sorry, but the woman up front told me to come see you directly. I've come to volunteer— and also to be admitted as a patient. I have cervical cancer. It's currently in remission, but I'd like a doctor to keep an eye on me. I'm afraid my usual health care providers are no longer an option."

Amalia's eyes somehow grew even wider. "You're Tereza Mbenga. The minister's wife."

The woman nodded. "He is no longer minister, but yes, I am Aloysius Mbenga's wife. With his arrest, I find myself at odds. An—an old friend suggested that I come here. Eliot spoke very highly of your clinic."

At the word *Eliot*, which was "John Smith's" real name, apparently, Amalia's face soured.

However, Michael rose to his feet. "We certainly do appreciate anyone volunteering to assist, Mrs. Mbenga. Amalia, please make an appointment for Mrs. Mbenga to see Dr. Dos Santos as soon as she is free." Ines Dos Santos was the only doctor in the clinic with an oncology background, though she wasn't an oncologist as such.

"I should add, Reverend, that I am not seeking charity." Tereza placed the purse on his desk, which landed with a surprisingly loud clunk. "This is for the clinic."

"We hardly need purses," Amalia muttered even as Michael opened the purse.

The diamonds inside temporarily dazzled him as they glinted off the overhead light.

"This will do nicely, yes?" Michael smiled. "Amalia, please help Mrs. Mbenga."

Amalia gave him her dirtiest look, and he knew he was going to be hearing about this later. But he didn't care, because in one day he'd received more funds to run this clinic than he'd accumulated in the past two years.

He wondered if he should screw up sales of animals to American zoos more often . . .

Sophie was the first to complain when Nate said that they should hop into Lucille and drive all the way to the Brillinger Zoo. Normally at the end of a job, the client came to McRory's and expressed their gratitude. It was easier on everyone.

However, Sophie was far from the last person to complain. Parker didn't want to take so long a drive. Hardison had no desire to be outdoors that long. And Eliot didn't want Parker to bring the damned monkey.

Well, neither did anyone else, but convincing Parker of that—or convincing the monkey to vacate Parker's shoulders—proved impossible.

But once they got to the zoo, saw children gaping at the

animals, saw wolves grooming each other, saw tigers swimming, saw penguins gadding about—Sophie felt at peace. And grateful that she'd been given an opportunity to save this place.

As they walked toward the red pandas, where Marney was waiting, Sophie put her arm in Nate's. "Thank you," she whispered.

Nate just smiled back. He could be an uncaring bastard at his worst, and Sophie had seen him that way more than once, but at moments like these, he was at his best.

Sophie could see the effect of the zoo on the rest of the team. Parker was practically squeeing at all the animals, while Eliot smiled indulgently at Parker and enjoyed watching the creatures frolic.

Only Hardison was out of sorts, waving his arm in front of his face. "What is that *smell*?"

Eliot shook his head. "I keep telling you, it's fresh air."

"Man, what I'm smellin' is *not* fresh. It's *nasty*. When can we go home?"

"Hush, Hardison," Nate said as Marney turned and saw the five of them—well, six, counting the monkey— approaching.

"Mr. Ford! Welcome back to the zoo."

"Glad to be here."

Hardison muttered, "Speak for yourself, man." But he then screwed on a smile for Marney. Anyone who didn't know Hardison might even believe it to be genuine.

"It's been quite a week," Marney said with a bright smile. "Sal Tartucci was unanimously removed from the board of directors after his arrest, Declan McAllister's estate was seized by the feds, and FWS contracted us to take over supervision of the animals until everything shakes out. Normally, they'd get local animal control to deal with it, but these are a little out of their range. Some of them will get returned to the wild, and the rest—well, we should be able to buy them for the zoo!"

"Really?" Nate smiled knowingly. "How can you do that, if you're on the brink of financial ruin?"

"Funny you should ask," Marney said with a smile right back. "When I heard on the news that both Sal and his buddy were implicated in the bear attack, I called IYS, and spoke to a very nice lady named Elizabeth Turre, who said we might be entitled to a larger payout, since we were sabotaged—*and* the increase in our premiums will be revisited, since it wasn't due to negligence."

Nate nodded. "Elizabeth is good people."

"Yes, she is—and she's not the only one. Just this morning, we received a cashier's check for a million dollars. Mr. Ford, you didn't have to—"

Sophie said, "It's a donation—by definition, it's voluntary, and therefore something one doesn't have to do."

"But we did it anyhow," Nate said.

"Well, thank you. The only downside is that we'll probably have to pay for the black rhinos *again*—but the government will probably give us a good deal on them, and besides, with all these new exhibits opening up, we should be getting lots of new revenue, and not only that . . . but is that a capuchin monkey?" This last was added as she seemed to notice Parker for the first time.

"This is Alec!" Parker said gleefully. "And, uh, I brought him along because I wanted to donate him to the zoo."

Everyone turned to look at Parker. Sophie was especially

surprised, considering how Parker had obviously grown very attached to the monkey. Indeed, she spent the entire ride over ignoring the rest of the group and bonding with the animal. At one point, Sophie could have sworn she heard Parker mention building a little harness for him.

Marney blinked. "Really?"

Parker nodded and walked up to her. "C'mon, Alec. Time for you to go to your new home."

Surprisingly, the monkey ran straight onto Marney's shoulder. "Well, hello there—Alec? Is that your name?"

Hardison had his head in his hands.

"Yeah," Parker said. "I named him after someone I've always been able to rely on to be there for me."

Now Hardison looked up.

"He's a good monkey, and I'm sure he'll be happy here. Plus, this is a place that has people who are willing to clean up his poop."

Sophie put her hand in front of her mouth to stifle a laugh.

Hardison walked up to Parker and put an arm around her shoulder, right where the monkey had been. "Thank you," he whispered.

Parker smiled.

"Well, the good news," Marney said, "is that you can visit him anytime you want. I don't know how you did what you did—or why, if you had a million bucks lying around, you gave it to us—but you *did* do it, and you saved something my father and two assholes did everything in their power to piss away. The least I can do is make all five of you Lifetime Zoo Boosters. You get free admission anytime, and a discount on any merchandise."

Parker's eyes widened. "I can see him anytime?"

While Alec draped himself around Marney's shoulders, she said, "Absolutely. You people didn't just get me my black rhinos back, you uncovered a conspiracy that would've resulted in a lot of dead animals, ours among them. Might've even helped wipe out a couple of endangered species. You people did a good thing."

"That's what we do," Nate said quietly.

Eliot stepped aside after his phone beeped, but the rest of the team decided to take in the zoo. Parker and Hardison followed Marney to find a spot for Alec. Nate and Sophie wandered over to look at the red panda, which was asleep, and looking, Sophie thought, rather adorable.

"She's right, Nate," Sophie said. "This was a good thing we did."

"And to think, if Norm Brillinger hadn't died of a heart attack, this would probably be Declan McAllister's little hunting preserve by now, with endangered species becoming ever more endangered."

Sophie looked at Nate. "Do you want to talk about it?"

"About what?"

Rolling her eyes, Sophie said, "Don't try that on me, Nate. You can play detached mastermind with the others, but not with me. Marney had to clean up her father's mess—only it turned out to be a much bigger mess than she thought. You're telling me that didn't affect you?"

Nate turned away from the sleeping red panda. "What answer do you want, Sophie? Everything affects me, because everything affects everyone. It's just a question of degree. *Yes*, I'm trying to make up for what my father did, and I'm doing it by being far too much like him than I'm entirely comfortable with."

"But that's just it, Nate. You *are* comfortable with it. It took you bloody well long enough to admit it . . ."

Looking back at the red panda, he said, "It's funny, Marney was talking about how she loves her father, but didn't like him much. And when Maggie helped us take down Blackpoole, she said that she didn't love me, but liked me a lot more than before. It'd be nice to have both in one person, y'know?"

Sophie had nothing she could bring herself to say out loud to that. And even as she tried to compose the words, she found herself distracted by the sight of the red panda starting to wake up. It slowly opened its eyes and yawned, and then started to bat listlessly at a tree branch.

She put her arm in Nate's, and they just watched the red panda play with the branch in companionable silence.

Keep reading for a special excerpt from

THE BESTSELLER JOB

Coming May 2013 from Berkley Boulevard!

" 'Overblown'? 'Self-indulgent'? 'Sublimely awful'?" Sophie Deveraux stared indignantly at the screen of the laptop, which rested atop their usual table at McRory's bar and grill. A posh English accent added class to her outrage. She turned toward Nate Ford, who was sitting next to her, nursing his second Scotch, even though it was barely lunchtime. "Can you believe these reviews?"

He tried to pivot the laptop away from her. "Just some random opinions on the Internet," he said, dismissing them. "You shouldn't even bother with them. What do they know?"

"But it's not fair, Nate. I put my heart and soul into that show, you know that. How many actresses can play Cleopatra, Joan of Arc, Madame Curie, *and* Mata Hari in one night?" A classically beautiful brunette, stylishly attired in a striped jersey-knit sweater and slacks, she spun the screen back toward her. "And yet some snarky hack at *Boston Theater Buzz* says that my one-woman show had, quote, 'one so-called actress too many.' " She sighed theatrically. "Small wonder the show closed after only a single night, after hatchet jobs like that!"

"It's a crime," he agreed, none too convincingly. Unruly hair and a rumpled sports jacket belied his razor-sharp mind. A careworn face hinted at his tragic past, which included a dead child and a failed marriage—in that order. Shrewd brown eyes glanced at his watch. "So what's keeping our prospective new client?"

Sophie ignored his transparent attempt to change the subject. She turned toward the third member of their party. "What do you think, Eliot? Tell me the truth. Was my performance truly 'more cheesy than aged Harvati'?"

Damn, Eliot Spencer thought. His perpetual scowl deepened. A mane of long brown hair framed his surly expression. A scruffy goatee carpeted his chin. He was dressed more casually than either Nate or Sophie, in a flannel shirt and jeans. A weathered windbreaker was draped over the back of his chair. *I was hoping to stay out of this.*

Post-traumatic flashbacks of being trapped in a stuffy hole-in-the-wall theater while Sophie emoted for the ages surfaced from the darkest recesses of his memory, where he had done his best to bury them. That had been a long night; Afghanistan and North Korea had been breezes by comparison. No way was he telling her the truth about her acting. *I'm a hitter, not a sadist.*

"You have a very . . . distinctive . . . style," he said diplomatically. "Not everybody gets it."

"You see!" she said, vindicated. "That's just what I'm

saying. So which of my portrayals did you find most convincing? Cleopatra? Saint Joan?"

"Er, I honestly couldn't choose." He concentrated on his calamari, avoiding her eyes. Truth to tell, he hadn't been able to tell the characters apart. "They were all very . . . you."

"But you must have some preference," she pressed. "Please. I'm certainly open to *constructive* criticism."

He looked to Nate for assistance. *Help me out here, man*, he thought, but their ringleader stared pensively into the amber depths of his Scotch, apparently content to let Eliot take the heat. *Sorry,* Eliot thought. *That's not how we're playing this.*

"I don't know," he said. "What do you think, Nate?"

Nate shot him a dirty look.

Tough, Eliot thought. *You're the one who's sleeping with her. Sometimes. Maybe.*

He had given up trying to figure out Nate and Sophie's relationship, whatever it was. He figured it was none of his business, as long as it didn't cause trouble on the job. Bad enough that Parker and Hardison were kinda, sorta a couple these days. The last thing this crew needed was boyfriend/girlfriend crap getting in the way of staying in one piece. In his experience, emotions and missions didn't mix. That's why he kept his private life private.

"Yes," she said. "What about you, Nate? You know my work better than anyone."

Nate squirmed uncomfortably in his seat. "Well, I'm biased, of course, but—"

The door to the bar swung open, letting in a gust of cold air and an attractive redhead who looked to be in her mid-thirties. A scuffed leather jacket, turtleneck sweater, and jeans flattered her slim, athletic figure. A canvas tote bag hung from her grip. Henna tinted her long red hair. Emerald eyes were rimmed with red, as though she had been crying recently. Dark shadows under her eyes suggested that she hadn't been sleeping well. A small brass compass dangled on a chain around her neck.

"Ah, here's our client," Nate announced, sounding more than a little relieved by the timely interruption. "Only a few minutes late."

And none too soon, Eliot thought.

The woman glanced around the bar uncertainly before her gaze lighted on Eliot and the others. She headed toward them. Eliot sat up straighter. He didn't usually do the initial meeting with the client, but this time was different. He should've met this particular woman years ago.

"You must be Eliot," Denise Gallo said. "I recognize you from Gavin's photos."

"Likewise." He stood up and pulled out a chair for her, then introduced her to Nate and Sophie. "I'm sorry I couldn't make the funeral."

They had been running a con in Rajasthan when he'd gotten word that Gavin Lee had died in a hit-and-run accident in Manhattan. With Nate busy fixing a camel race, and the water rights to a crucial oasis at stake, hopping a plane back to the States for the memorial services simply hadn't been an option.

Not even for an old friend.

SEVERAL YEARS AGO

The terrorist camp was hidden deep in the Sumatran rain forest. A lush green canopy shielded the compound from

aerial surveillance. Hanging roots and vines, slowly chok-
ing the life from the trees that hosted them, added to the
dense foliage sheltering the camouflaged base, which con-
sisted of a large command center surrounded by several
smaller outbuildings, including weapons depots and muni-
tions dumps. As was common in Indonesia, the wooden
structures were supported by stilts that lifted them ten to
twelve feet above the jungle floor. Ladders, which could be
withdrawn to deter intruders, provided the only means of
access. Spiky vines covered the rooftops. Sentries, armed
with black-market AK-47s, patrolled the perimeter.

Bamboo, palms, ferns, and creepers encroached on the
camp from all sides. The abundant flora surrounding the
camp was a two-edged sword. While it effectively insulated
the compound from the outside world, it also made it easier
to approach the camp undetected. A moonless night filled the
gaps between the trees and underbrush with impenetrable
black shadows. Monkeys capered through the overhanging
branches, squeaking in the night. Nocturnal predators rus-
tled through the jungle.

Some of them were human.

Eliot Spencer, a fresh-faced young American soldier, lay
belly down in the ferns and vines abutting the compound.
Cradling a Heckler & Koch MP5 submachine gun, he spied
on the terrorist base. His hair was short, his face clean-cut.
Green camouflage paint, masking his features, matched his
jungle gear, which bore no identifying insignia. Only re-
cently inducted into Special Forces from the regular army,
he was primed for action.

His recon team had located the base a few hours ago.
After a terse, hushed huddle, it had been decided to clean

out the compound now before the terrorists could use it to stage more attacks and bombings on civilian targets and foreign nationals. At this very moment, the rest of the six-man team was taking up positions in preparation for an all-out assault on the central command center. The plan was to go in hard and fast before the rebels even knew what hit them. With any luck, the team would take out the whole nest in a matter of minutes, and maybe even capture vital intel on the guerillas' plans and support systems. Eliot judged the potential rewards well worth the risk.

Too bad he was stuck babysitting.

Gavin Lee crouched beside Eliot, armed only with a machete and his favorite camera. The young photojournalist had been embedded with the special forces team for a couple of weeks now, much to Eliot's annoyance. Sure, Gavin seemed like a stand-up guy who had endured the rigors of a jungle tour without complaint, but who in their right mind thought sticking a civilian into a military operation was a good idea? Eliot could only imagine what kind of strings had been pulled to get Gavin assigned to their unit in the first place.

"What's happening?" Gavin whispered. He wore an olive-green safari jacket with plenty of pouches for his film. His alert eyes scanned the camp as though already taking pictures with his mind. The moist tropical heat bathed his face in sweat. "When do the fireworks start?"

Eliot shot him a dirty look. He placed a finger before his lips.

Damn it, *he thought*, scowling at the photographer's loose lips. Remind me never to work with civilians again.

To his credit, Gavin got the message and shut up. He hun-

kered down into the greenery, keeping his head low. Eliot gestured for him to stay down.

That's more like it, *he thought.* I've got work to do.

A weapons depot rose up on stilts a few yards away. A bored-looking sentry, his rifle slung over his shoulder, stood guard over the tower. The guard munched on a durian, the spiky, foul-smelling fruit that was a staple of the local diet. Eliot could smell the pungent odor from where he was hiding. It made his gorge rise.

The guard finished up his snack and tossed the rind into the bushes, barely missing Eliot. Hefting his gun, he sighed wearily as he resumed his rounds.

Right on schedule, *Eliot thought.*

He waited until the guard had trudged past him before rising up from the brush like a ghost. Slipping out of the jungle, he crept up on the sentry from behind. He had left his own rifle behind with Gavin; this exercise required speed and stealth, not firepower. Noise was the enemy.

The sentry didn't hear him coming. Eliot grabbed on to the guard's gun arm to keep it pointed away from him, then clasped his other hand over the guard's mouth to stifle any cries. Yanking the man's head back exposed his throat to a forearm strike that silenced him long enough for Eliot to drag him backward onto the ground, where his head hit the earth with a muffled thud. The impact stunned the guard, allowing Eliot to wrench the AK-47 from his grasp. He slammed the butt of the weapon into the man's skull. The sentry went limp.

The whole takedown had taken less than a minute.

So much for that, *Eliot thought.*

Confident that the sentry had been neutralized, Eliot

sprinted over to his main objective: the elevated weapons depot. Moving with practiced skill and efficiency, he attached a wad of C4 explosive to the nearest stilt. The timer was set to go off in a matter of minutes, right before his fellow commandoes stormed the compound. The result would be one heck of a distraction, not to mention maximum shock and awe.

Least I'm doing something useful, he thought. Besides babysitting.

"Eliot! Behind you!"

He spun around to see that a second guard had arrived unexpectedly, possibly to relieve the first. Rifle in hand, he was creeping up on Eliot. It was unclear if he intended to kill or capture the intruder, but he already had the drop on Eliot. The young soldier found himself looking down the barrel of the man's AK-47, even as the timer on the C4 counted down behind him.

This was not good.

A flashbulb went off in the jungle, distracting the sentry. Startled, he swung his gun toward the flash, away from Eliot.

Eliot saw his chance. Snatching his combat knife from its sheath, he hurled it at the sentry's exposed back. The six-inch stainless-steel blade lodged deep between the man's shoulder blades. He fell forward, his rifle firing wildly into the jungle.

Gavin!

Shouts arose from the command center. Eliot didn't need to check his watch to know that the C4 was going off any second now. He scrambled away from the elevated platform, *diving for cover. The weapons depot exploded with a deafening boom, lighting up the rebel base and the surrounding rain forest with billowing red flames. Smoking debris rained on the ground. The shock wave buffeted Eliot. His ears were ringing.*

"Gavin!" he shouted over the din. "Gavin?"

All hell broke loose. Explosive charges blew away the stilts supporting the command center, which toppled over onto the ground. Special Forces, almost invisible in their camo gear and night-vision goggles, charged the ruins of the center, opening fire on the disoriented survivors, who scrambled from the wreckage only to be met by grenades, smoke bombs, and automatic weapon's fire. Caught by surprise, and battered by the crash and explosions, the disorganized guerillas were no match for the highly-trained soldiers. Lifting his head from the ground, Eliot was glad to see that the good guys already had the terrorists on the ropes.

Mission accomplished.

But what about Gavin? Scrambling to his feet, Eliot plunged into the jungle in search of the reckless photog, who had definitely not kept his head down as instructed. Eliot braced himself for the sight of Gavin's bullet-riddled body.

Some babysitter I am, he thought.

To his relief, he found Gavin alive and well among the bamboo and ferns, frantically snapping photo after photo of the chaos engulfing the terrorist base. Eliot felt like punching him.

"What the hell were you thinking?" he shouted. "I told you to stay put!"

Gavin grinned at him. "You're welcome."

"That's not the point," Eliot said, even though he knew the other man had probably just saved his life. "You trying to get yourself killed?"

"Not going to happen."

Gavin lowered his camera and reached beneath his shirt. He drew out a small metallic object, about the size of a Cracker Jack prize, dangling from a chain around his neck. Looking closer, Eliot saw that it was a miniature compass.

"My lucky charm," Gavin explained. He tucked the compass back beneath his shirt. "Makes sure things always go in the right direction."

Eliot had to admit it. He liked the guy's attitude.

And he owed him one.

"Better hang on to it," he said.

"It's fine," Denise assured him. Her slender fingers toyed with the compass on its chain. "Gavin would've understood. He knew what your life was like." She took off her coat and sat down at the table. "He always spoke highly of you."

"You, too." Guilt stabbed Eliot in the gut. Gavin and Denise had been together for a couple of years now; it wasn't right that he was only just now meeting her for the first time, and under these circumstances. "I always meant to visit you folks. Lord knows Gavin kept inviting me, but . . ."

"I know." Sorrow tinged her voice. "You think you have all the time in the world and then . . . ." She choked back a sob. Her eyes welled with tears. "I'm sorry. It's just that, it's still so . . ."

Eliot instinctively placed his hand over hers. "It sucks what happened—and what's still happening."

"Why don't you tell us about that?" Nate suggested. He handed her a tissue. "Eliot told me something about your situation, but I'd like to hear it in your own words."

"Yes," Sophie said. "We all would."

"All right." Denise dabbed at her eyes. She took a moment to compose herself. "It's all about the book. *Assassins Never Forget.* Have you heard of it?"

"Hard to miss," Nate said. "It's a big bestseller, isn't it?"

"More than we ever imagined." She reached into her tote bag and took out a thick hardcover with Gavin's photo on the back. "Months on the *New York Times* list. Book clubs. Audio deals. Foreign translations. Major studios bidding for the movie rights. It would be a dream come true, if not for . . ."

Her voice trailed off.

"Gavin's accident," Nate prompted. "And his brother."

"His no-good, *estranged* brother," she said angrily. "It's ridiculous. Brad bullied Gavin when they were kids, then ditched him after their parents died. They'd hardly spoken for years. But now Brad has swooped in as next-of-kin to claim Gavin's literary estate."

"Cutting you out of the picture," Nate said.

She displayed her bare left hand. "No ring, no will, no power of attorney." She shook her head. "I suppose that must sound incredibly foolish and irresponsible now, but we had no kids and, before *Assassins* hit it big, not much in the way of assets to worry about. We always meant to get our legal house in order, one of these days, but, like I said, we thought we had all the time in the world . . ."

Nate handed her another tissue.

"So now I'm just the girlfriend," she added bitterly. "And Brad, of all people, gets to profit from Gavin's success."

"Even though you had plenty to do with the book as well," Nate said.

"You could say that, I guess."

"Don't be modest," Sophie said. "Eliot told us all about it. You were Gavin's unofficial collaborator, researcher, and editor. You read every draft, offered your input, encouraged him to keep writing . . ."

Denise nodded. "We slaved over that book, together. It was our whole lives."

"And now you're getting screwed by Gavin's loser brother," Eliot snarled. He had never met Brad Lee, but he'd heard about him from Gavin. Brad was an ex-con and small-time criminal who was nothing but an embarrassment to his more righteous younger brother. "That's not right. I know how much Gavin loved you. He would have wanted you taken care of."

"It's not just about the money," Denise insisted. "It's about Gavin's legacy, and everything we hoped to accomplish. *Assassins* isn't just a page-turner; it's an exposé, a fictionalized account of true events, meant to shine a light on the shadowy world of covert black-ops activities: arms smuggling, money laundering, illegal assassinations, wiretappings, break-ins, and renditions, etcetera." Her voice grew more heated; she was clearly passionate on the subject. "Gavin and I intended to use the book to raise public awareness of such abuses. We wanted to donate a majority of the proceeds to human-rights groups, but, knowing Brad, he's just going to milk the book for all its worth—and maybe even hire some hack to churn out formulaic, action-packed sequels with no real substance or content."

More tears leaked from her eyes. She placed a loving hand on Gavin's author photo. "We were going to make a difference, Mr. Ford. *Gavin* wanted to make a difference. You can't let Brad take that away."

"I get it," Nate said. "I have to wonder about that hit-and-run accident, though. Is it possible Brad was behind it?"

"His own brother?" Denise winced at the idea. "I don't want to think so, but . . ."

"We can't rule out that possibility," Eliot said, half hoping that Brad was responsible for his brother's death. Every time Eliot thought about Gavin being run down at some lonely street corner, he felt like hitting something. Hard and more than once.

Brad Lee might do.

"What about Gavin's agent?" Sophie asked. "Can't he do something?"

Denise shook her head. "He's sympathetic, but Gavin's name is on all the contracts. Legally at least, I'm nobody."

"Not to Gavin you weren't," Eliot said. He might not have seen Gavin in the flesh recently, but they had stayed in touch over the years. He knew how much Denise had meant to his friend. He glared fiercely at his partners. "C'mon, Nate, Sophie. We've got to do this. For Gavin."

"All right," Nate said, convinced. "Let's steal back a book."

Sophie's heart went out to Denise. As an artist herself, she could only imagine what it must feel like to lose a loved one, then see his artistic legacy squandered and corrupted.

She wondered what sort of scam Nate had in mind to set things right. The Gypsy Blanket? The Donkey Roundabout? Maybe even a variation on the Deaf-Mute Duchess?

That could be fun, she thought. *I haven't run that one in years.*

Sophie was a grifter, one of the best. "Sophie Deveraux" wasn't even her real name, but it suited her for now. Sometimes she almost forgot she had ever been anyone else.

Almost.

While Nate and Eliot picked Denise's brain a bit more, Sophie flipped through the hardcover copy of *Assassins Never Forget.* Not a bad title, she reflected, and sadly accurate in her experience. She'd survived her share of assassination attempts, both before and after she joined Nate's crew, and knew only too well how old enemies had a tendency to come sneaking out of the past when you least expected it. A healthy degree of paranoia was essential in their line of work.

In fact, was it just her imagination or did she suddenly feel as though she was being watched?

Tiny hairs prickled at the back of her neck as she lifted her eyes from the book to discreetly scan the familiar bar. At first, all she saw were the usual regulars and a smattering of new customers caught up in their own affairs, but then her eyes made contact with those of a solitary stranger spying on her from a table by the front entrance. The man was thin and gangly, with pale skin sorely in need of a little sun. Horn-rimmed glasses, with lenses thick enough to serve as magnifying glasses, perched upon his nose. An olive-green hoodie partially concealed his face. A full glass of ale sat neglected before him. He looked away furtively, as though embarrassed at being caught peering at her. He thrust a smartphone into his pocket.

Sophie frowned. Granted, she was hardly unaccustomed to male attention, but was this fellow just another random admirer or something rather more ominous? Not wanting to alarm Denise, she kept her concerns to herself as she fished through her own bag for her phone. If she could snap a photo of the peeper, Hardison could always run it through one of his comprehensive facial-recognition programs and see if this was anybody they needed to watch out for.

Better safe than sorry, she thought. *Now where the devil is that phone?*

"It was nice to meet you, Ms. Deveraux," Denise said, distracting her. "And thank you all so much for hearing me out."

"Our pleasure," Sophie said, taking her hand. She tried to keep one eye on the peeper, but then Eliot got up and helped Denise on with her coat, momentarily blocking Sophie's view. "And, please, call me Sophie."

"All right." Denise looked anxiously at Nate. "Keep me posted, okay?"

"Don't worry about it," he said. "We'll be in touch."

Eliot escorted her toward the door. Sophie scooted out from behind the table to peek around him, but a gust of cold air hinted that she was already too late.

Sure enough, the peeper was gone, leaving a nearly full glass of ale behind.

Nate noticed her staring at the empty table. "Something wrong?"

"I don't know," she said. "Perhaps."